SYLVAN DREAD

Sylvan Dread

TALES OF PASTORAL DARKNESS

BY

Richard Gavin

THREE HANDS PRESS
2016

OTHER BOOKS BY RICHARD GAVIN

FICTION COLLECTIONS:
Charnel Wine
Omens
The Darkly Splendid Realm
At Fear's Altar

ESOTERICISM:
The Benighted Path: Primeval Gnosis and the Monstrous Soul

AS EDITOR:
Penumbrae: An Occult Fiction Anthology
(co-edited with Patricia Cram & Daniel A. Schulke)

First Three Hands Press edition, May 2016.

Hardcover: ISBN 978-1-945147-02-9
Trade Paper edition: ISBN 978-1-945147-00-5

Jacket design by Jim Dunk and Daniel A. Schulke.
Interior book design by Joseph Uccello.

Printed in Canada.

www.threehandspress.com

TABLE OF CONTENTS

Thistle Latch

NOONTIME IN AUTUMN often sparks in me memories of Lattice Rayburn. I knew him in boyhood and even today I can still list many details about him: the strange coat of green corduroy which he wore even on the warmest days, the lyrics to the crazy songs he would improvise and the trilling sound of his voice when he sung them. These and other aspects I remember. But I cannot remotely recollect his face, though I am certain that he had one.

Rayburn (I used his given name only once, the first time I encountered him in the great ravine behind my house. Rayburn threatened to force-feed me mud if I called him that again) lived in a large wooden house a few doors down from the narrow maisonette I shared with my widower father. I had been dimly aware that a boy about my age dwelt in the house whose condition and design plainly evidenced that it was haunted, but I had rarely seen him on the opposite side of the mullioned window through which he seemed to study me every morning while I waited for the school bus. For a while I assumed that Rayburn attended a different school, or perhaps was mentally deficient. One October day he confessed that he was homeschooled but said no more about it.

Though he was often at his bedroom window, Rayburn's more common habitat was the crooked wilds of the ravine. He was forever building things in those woods. In fact, our first proper meeting occurred inside one of his creations. It was a Sunday afternoon and my father had encouraged me to amuse myself outside so that he could nap in peace. I gathered up whatever toys happened to be my favourite at the time and set out for the ravine. I roamed listlessly, half searching for a place to play, and then I found the patterns.

To my childish eyes they were merely circles. The passage of time has allowed me to appreciate them as something more complex, lemniscates perhaps, or the DNA helix. Most importantly was the fact that it was a living design, composed of writhing grubs. Their plump bodies pulsed but never broke their composed formation.

What impressed me then and now is how organic this creation appeared. Were it not for the unnatural geometry and the incongruity of so many grubs pressed firmly into the soil, I would have believed that nature had produced it.

Along with his considerable skill, I also respected the fact that Rayburn never destroyed or even truly disturbed the habitats he adorned. They seemed to be tweaked from the woods rather than forged from them. How Rayburn achieved this I never came to know, though I have my theories.

It is only fitting that the way Rayburn first introduced himself was by frightening me.

I had been surveying the grub-studded earth, following the curves with my eyes. I should have been looking behind me, for the sound of rustling leaves panicked me. I lunged forward to flee, fearing an animal attack.

But the shape that emerged from the copse was human. Its face was hidden behind a section of tree bark into which jagged holes had been punched, creating the crudest of masks. Tangles of weeds, which had been knotted along the mask's jagged edge, hung like filthy locks. The stout figure had its arms outstretched in order to flaunt what I guessed was intended to be a cape. In truth it was more of a shawl made from thick coarse-looking vines which had been loosely woven together.

A muffled voice asked me what it was I sought.

My answer was, "Who are you?"

"I am the ghost in the vines! I guard the woods while they sleep! Who gave you permission to wander through the forest's dream?" shouted the hidden mouth.

He brandished a stick and jutted it toward me like a sword. That was the moment I realized there was something special about Rayburn, for it was not a tree branch he held at my throat, but a snake. The creature was rigid yet visibly alive, for its eyes blinked and its tongue darted in and out of its mouth. It was Rayburn's playmate, one utterly committed to his game. How he had trained the serpent to do this was the first of many mysteries where Rayburn and the wilderness were concerned.

Finally, Rayburn lowered the snake and raised his mask.

Thus began my fascination with him. I say fascination because Rayburn and I were never friends in any real sense of the term. He confounded and often frightened me. Hindsight has led me to suspect that the real reason I would wander down the ravine and spend the occasional Saturday afternoon with him is because his life somehow made mine seem richer, more balanced. He was the first child I'd encountered who clearly occupied a lower rung on the ladder than me, and as ruthless as that sounds, that fact actually bolstered my faith in myself.

The ways in which his inferiority manifested were never blatant. He was always relatively clean (as much as can be expected from a boy who practically lived in the ravine) and actually appeared better fed than I did. But there were other signs, little flashes that occurred whenever Rayburn seemed to let too much of his true self shine through during our time together. For example, his speech often slipped into a queer kind of baby-talk, the sort of babble one hears from someone who mumbles in their sleep. But (and this I think is important) it was not gibberish. There was a *consistency* to it. Were my memory better I would list some of the alternate words Rayburn used to describe specific things in the ravine, but the only one I recollect clearly was *caw-gri-gaw*, which was what Rayburn called the talons of blackbirds, which somehow he and I would discover in the most unlikely of places (woven into a spider's web, dangling from a bug cocoon, standing like a petrified tree between two stones...) *Caw-gri-graw*. We used to collect them all the time.

Aside from this almost autistic verbal tic, Rayburn also used to demonstrate *too much* of an affinity for nature. Bird watching or pressing flowers are one thing, but Rayburn never engaged in anything so detached or civilized. He would spend hours laying amongst lichen or attempting to imitate the exact sound of the wind as it tossed the trees about.

The last two autumn afternoons I spent with him were such because Rayburn proved to be too much for me. During our penultimate encounter I found him squatting under a fallen yew. His cheeks were puffed up and he was humming a strange tune to himself while he rocked back and forth. When I asked him what he was doing, Rayburn replied by simply opening his mouth, which was seething with live cicadas. Their stinging song was awful to hear, amplified as it was by Rayburn's skull.

He behaved himself during our final time together, but Rayburn unnerved me nonetheless. That afternoon passed innocently enough; we hiked the trails, pretending we were discoverers of a new and distant planet. It was late in the fall, so dusk rode in fast on the tails of the afternoon.

"I should be getting home for supper," I'd told him, buttoning my coat to the growing chill.

Rayburn silenced me by pressing his finger to his lips. He pushed me down behind one of the mounds. My fear was thick and cold and glassy. The idea of peering about the top of the mound to see what Rayburn had hidden us from was unbearable to me.

After a few moments passed I waited until Rayburn was facing me, then I mouthed the word 'What?'

He leaned in and whispered, "They sometimes show themselves if they think there's no one else around..."

I ran home that evening, blindly and wildly. Rayburn had shouted something to me but I could not decipher it. The shadows had begun to thicken and I came to appreciate my fear of the dark, which lingers to this day.

That was the last time I ever spoke to Rayburn. Although he remained in the neighbourhood I noticed that he eventually stopped watching me from his window.

A few months later he disappeared.

Rayburn's was not the first disappearance in my hometown. They had actually begun a full year before he vanished. At the time the natural assumption was that Rayburn had fallen prey to the Iron Hans Killer, but recently I received evidence to the contrary. His fate, it seems, was something far darker.

By chance of birth I happened to have grown up in an era when the concept of abduction, of danger lurking behind the doors of one's neighbourhood, was simply not discussed. I will not go so far as to say that such things did not occur. They were simply not spoken of and therefore I came of age blissfully ignorant of all the ugliness I had somehow managed to avoid. It was a conspiracy of silence; I use that phrase specifically because in manhood I discovered that the schools had held meetings with parents and police, that notices had been discreetly mailed home which gave detailed instructions on how to covertly enforce the town curfew and ensure that children never played alone, etcetera. My father never again sent me out to play when he napped in the afternoon.

Children intuit. Children find a way to suss out problems and negotiate the ways that they can understand these problems.

All through that autumn when the Iron Hans Killer first struck it was obvious to all the children that there was some new presence in the town, some mounting but elusive threat. But it was an unidentifiable presence, one that we inflated and gave context through playground rumours. However much our elders chose to shelter us, we were all too aware of the fact that some of our peers were missing.

The alleged perpetrator of this string of disappearances earned the nickname the Iron Hans Killer long after the whole ugly ordeal was over and done with. Roughly fifteen years after the case was closed a writer of sensationalist crime books endowed the man who suffered these crimes' consequences with the title the Iron Hans Killer. Like the character in the Grimm's folktale, this man was a misfit, a tramp who left the wilderness only to end up in a cage.

I shall spare you having to endure the lurid book and will provide you only with the relevant details: Iron Hans was innocent but was needlessly killed by another inmate in the prison cafeteria line. The real child murderer was caught many years and several victims later in another part of the country.

The ravine behind my father's home was raked over by forensic teams. The bodies of the missing children were disinterred and eventually given proper burials in ground less savage than the ravine.

Rayburn's corpse was not among those found.

I have provided this history for a purpose. It is important that you understand these ancient details in order to appreciate the shock and disbelief I experienced when Rayburn re-entered my life, some three decades since his vanishing.

Two months ago my father passed away after a protracted illness that chewed up his body, but not before it tore apart his mind. I confess I did not visit him often while he lay adrift in medicated limbo, but those few occasions where I did fill the vinyl chair beside his hospital bed were filled with shouts, mutterings and nonsense talk as my father drifted in and out of consciousness. His words were hauntingly similar to the babblings Rayburn used to mutter to the flora and fauna of the ravine.

This was the first mnemonic twitch that related to Rayburn.

The next came just days before my father succumbed. He had been sleeping deeply and when he finally opened his eyes they shone with a clarity I had not seen since before he fell ill. His head rolled to one side. He smiled when he saw me. With a dolorous voice he said, "I've been meaning to tell you that I received your letter. I haven't read it yet, I apologize. I promise I'll respond to it soon..."

His eyelids fluttered like frantic moth wings. They closed and sealed off that clear and lucid gaze permanently.

As I hadn't written my father a letter since I was away at summer camp when I was twelve, I took his message to be meaningless but still cherished the direct way he had managed to deliver it. In the weeks following the funeral I finally began the daunting task of clearing out the old house and preparing to put it on the market.

I found the letter by chance. How I knew it was the epistle my father had spoken of is something I cannot explain, at least not in any convincing way. I can only say that the minute I pulled that brown paper envelope that was anything but crisp I sensed its significance, not to my father but to me, for I was the addressee. The pencilled script was loopy and faint and very crude.

My father had the letter secreted in a plastic bag along with a stack of old bills and supermarket flyers. The envelope bore neither stamp nor postmark, making its delivery a mystery. I sat down on the wooden bench of the front hallway, holding the letter in my hands. I was both building up and delaying the opening. I was genuinely unsure whether or not I wanted to see what was inside.

The strips of amber-coloured tape had almost no adhesive left. One tug and the flap gave.

Inside was a single sheet of thick construction paper, Halloween-orange. I removed and unfolded it.

It was not a letter, but a map. Childishly cartoon-like, the illustration consisted of a variety of green arrowheads, which I presumed were meant to indicate trees, and a crooked path that snaked between them. Roughly in the centre, the very heart, of the page was a teardrop of vivid purple, standing out like the proverbial X on a juvenile treasure map.

There are, I believe, certain forms of knowledge that run deeper than our intellect, possibly even deeper than our intuition. There are things we simply Know. Absolutely nothing in that cartoon map suggested a connection to Rayburn or the ravine that housed our 'friendship.' For all I knew that envelope could have been part of some forgotten game I'd played in childhood. It could have easily been rotting along with other clutter in my father's junk room.

But this rationale did nothing to stop me from slipping on my shoes and making my way toward the gate at the far end of my childhood backyard.

The wooden fence was bowed and flimsy. My attempts to scale it were a harsh reminder that I was no longer a young man. Scraped, achy, and breathless, I made it to the other side.

Nostalgia tends the garden of memory, fecundating the authentic until it blooms and bloats into some gorgeous distortion. Naturally I expected the ravine to look and feel much smaller than the sprawling Arcadia it had become in my mind, much the way the rooms of my father's old house had shrunken and grown paler during my many years of absence. Sadly, my suspicion was confirmed.

I managed to walk the ravine from end to end with a swiftness that made me heartsick. Standing at the edge of a rustic path that once felt boundless and immortal was a cold shot that wrung the finest aspects of my boyhood into tiny husks, so brittle and bloodless. I allowed myself a somewhat forced shudder then gave the ravine one last loving survey. I stood on the shallow lump that had once been a magic mountain for Rayburn and me. The ghost in the vines had long ascended. What stood before me now was nature's Golgotha; the sad little interstice of forest that sat between past glory and a kingdom that was still eons away from manifestation.

To this day I cannot say whether the uniform, almost industrial greyness of those woods was authentic or merely the taint of my melancholia, but the ravine appeared to be as sculpted ash, a landscape painted by an artist with only one drab colour on his palette. I drew in a deep, patient breath then set about to go to my father's house and resume my chore.

Somewhere between the rim of the forest and my back fence a flash of colour tugged at my periphery. It was so vivid, so startling that I stopped in my tracks and peered into the thickets. Evening always falls swifter in autumn, but it seemed as though the darkness came upon me instantly, as though a light switch had been flipped. These conditions made the dab of vivid colour all the more noticeable. It was the violet-and-white bloom of a thistle.

I did not think of the map right away, even though it was clear that the teardrop of lavender was likely supposed to represent a thistle. I moved toward it as though I were a moth and it a radiant and captivating flame. The ash trees grew very close together there, forcing me to squeeze sidelong between their swollen trunks. The thickets were a hopeless entanglement of piercing thorns. I wondered what type of wood they were, for the bark was a swirling of light and dark, as though the thickets had been chiseled from fine marble.

The thistle was growing sideways. It sprouted vertically from the cold mud, then bent in a runic angle and jutted west; a glyph of some higher geometry. The fine stem was threaded through a tangle of branches that were smooth and bright, as though they had been lacquered. This too had geometry: it was an arched door of woven wood and was of meticulous construction. The door was set into a small mound, the very one that Rayburn had first appeared upon as the ghost in the vines all those years ago.

I reached to the thistle and touched it, noting that it had been knotted upon the door's boughs and thus acted as a latch.

I pulled the latch free and eased the door back.

Beyond the door the mound appeared to have been bored out. It was a claustrophobic indentation that smelled cloyingly damp. In my confusion I did not hear whatever had approached me from behind. I only realized someone or something was there when I felt the forceful shove against my back.

Winded, I fell forward into the damp enclave. Then I saw the woven door swing shut.

The space was so tiny I couldn't stretch out of the foetal position I found myself in. The darkness created by the door was absolute. I pressed against it. The weave was astonishingly firm, almost immovable.

High-pitched cacophonic laughter taunted me from the other side. I shouted threats and elbowed the door with all the momentum my predicament allowed.

Only when I stopped resisting (though just to collect my thoughts and find a better means of escape) did the door open, apparently of its own accord. I tumbled out into the tangled thickets. The night was almost as lightless as the inside of the mound, yet even this blackness could not prevent me from Seeing.

The ravine was...reveling. The woods were protean, the fauna corrupted and corrupting. It was a gaudy carnival, a non-human freak tent. The only way I can describe what I saw, or believed I saw, before me that night was to imagine that all the observable laws of nature, from animal behaviour to phototropism, were merely the result of nature performing the various functions they felt we needed it to perform in order to keep us placated. What I was witnessing was a nature that was not as it seemed, a nature filled with things that should not be.

Though most of what I witnessed was obscured by both impossible distance and a murky averse light, like glowing pollen that coated all things and made them appear as a photographic negative.

I can only describe the scene as orgiastic, but an orgy from which humans are forbidden. It was flamingly erotic and coldly violent at once. Nearest to me, I saw a tree being autopsied by a flock of whitish birds whose beaks and talons moved with surgical precision. The splayed trunk of that towering tree sat open like a great wooden book. Its insides were lasciviously pink. Great air sacs ballooned up and shrivelled, again and again. Bit by bit the birds were extracting this living pulp and administering it to the various attendants, like plant meal, like the Eucharist.

I experienced this scene briefly before falling face-first into the thickets. Miles above me I heard the distinct gibberish of Rayburn.

I awoke much later in the night, shivering and groggy. I managed to make my way back to my father's house. Though exhausted, I could not sleep at all.

I could leap to the obvious theory, that Rayburn possessed some form of godlike ability to impress his will upon the clay of living nature. There are reams of occult 'evidence' to support this, from alchemical lore to the modern mind-over-matter pop gurus. For a great while this was my theory and I lamented Rayburn's squandered potential. In the proper hands his ability could have led to environmental healing, to the discovery of new cures for any number of diseases. But instead this gift was packaged inside the twisted imagination of a lost boy.

However my perspective on this has since changed. I now believe that Rayburn's gift was pure. Those aberrations in the ravine were not of his choosing but were the desire of nature itself. This realization came after a dream, one in which Rayburn was perched upon one of the ravine's mounds. He was delivering a sermon. His message was conveyed in pantomime and ululations. I looked about me and realized that I was the only person there. And yet I knew that Rayburn had a large audience. I stared closely at the old growth trees and the hedgerows and the myriad woodland creatures. All of them were listening raptly. Rayburn then removed his face. It slipped off as facilely was a plastic mask. When the ravine entire followed his example my dream self covered his eyes and began to shriek in hopes of drowning out the mad laughter of the forest in secret revel. I woke up screaming.

I now believe that all those abominations of which Rayburn was so deeply fond and was so adept at creating were in fact nature's way of violating its own laws, of savouring that which is not good for it, that which should not be. The soul behind the human organism does this constantly upon itself; sinning against its own morality, pouring endless toxins into its vessel, acting recklessly in the face of life-threatening danger. Why should the soul behind the rest of the living world be any different? Perhaps all it needed was a willing conduit, someone who was only too happy to give form to the horrors the wilderness kept tucked in its own hoary Id.

The ghost in the vines? Some form of tutelary spirit, one who brought sorcery to the green things and the dumb beasts, just as the Fallen Ones are said to have brought magic to humanity.

Rayburn had come to this world bearing Play. I did not understand the rules of the game but I knew something of its scope, for I am now immersed in it.

My father was buried in the little family plot he'd purchased the year I was born. He rests alongside my mother. After the funeral I returned to my apartment and attempted to reinsert myself into my life. Wild dreams much like the one I just described were almost nightly occurrences. Other afflictions from my experience in the ravine are an unnerving habit of muttering to myself and a chronic nervous cough. Or rather what I believed to be a nervous cough. When I began bringing up blood I went to see my doctor, who immediately ordered a chest X-ray. He explained the results to me with a superb bedside manner. He even circled the lesion on the X-ray sheet with a bright red felt pen to distinguish it from the rest of my lung. It was, he said gravely, an aggressive form of cancer and then went on to explain our best course of action. None of his instructions registered. I was far too engrossed in scrying what the next phase of Rayburn's game might be. As I sat there studying the tumour as though it was a tea leaf pattern at the bottom of a fortune teller's cup, I wondered if this was Rayburn's way of initiating me, of letting me in on the secret.

This morning I drove back to my hometown. I spent the entire day in the ravine, studying, listening, ineptly deciphering every nest, all the stones, each quilt of fallen leaves. The ghost in the vines was no longer there.

Much later I found him, sprouting up defiantly from the narrow patch of grass next to my father's recent grave, the plot that is reserved for me. Standing there, staring at that colourful thistle latch that jutted from the soil like a mocking tongue, I was crushed under the weight of my diagnosis. I came to realize just how soon I would be occupying that plot that had been waiting here for me since I was an infant. In no time at all I will be part of this landscape, this wilderness. The last thread, the only thread, of hope that I cling to is my belief that when my coffin lid is pressed shut, Rayburn will unlatch the final gate.

Primeval Wood

*The dæmonic-divine object may appear to the mind an object of
horror and dread, but at the same time it is no less something that
allures with a potent charm, and the creature, who trembles before
it, utterly cowed and cast down, has always at the same time the
impulse to turn to it, nay even to make it somehow his own.*

—Rudolf Otto, The Idea of the Holy

CERTAIN MIRACLES ARE reserved for the wayward and
the damned. For just as every paradise has its nether-
world and each metropolis its slum, the miraculous has
its averse kin. Most people pass through this world
wholly oblivious to the aberrant blessings that haunt its
borders. But there are individuals among us who, by karmic debt or
some other cold twist of fate, lead lives that are hopelessly inter-
twined with this adumbrated reality, this misshapen plane of existence that thrums beneath the skin of the physical.

This crooked plane, this otherealm, leaves evidence of itself all
around us: the cold light gleaming through the smashed windows
of a derelict house, the child's toy bobbing listlessly upon the brackish water that sluices through a sewer grate, the claw-like digits of a
mannequin hand reaching up from a back alley dumpster.

Most view these clues as nothing more than freak-chance wed-
dings between the terrifyingly ineffable and the tediously banal;
mere heaps of happenstance and trickery. The more superstitiously
minded might take them to be ill portents, indicators of ideas that
are best left un-thought. But the wayward and the damned accept
these mutations as a Calling.

Although Neil Keller never really considered himself to be wayward in spirit—let alone damned—he was painfully aware of the fact that his soul had always felt attuned to spheres that were stranger and more distant than the sound and fury of the terra firma. Neil's greatest pleasure was dreaming, both during slumber and when wandering through his daytime routine. And whenever his imagination was unable to conjure visions swiftly enough for his voracious need, Neil would steal the dreams of others by reading weird fictions.

On this particular night, however, Neil did not have to look to the yellowing pages of his novels for an exotic experience. Sleep did this for him by sending him a dream; one that began with the image of a rotted pram in a storm drain.

Neil became aware that he was dreaming when he found himself traipsing across a trash-laden field toward a strange network of cement tunnels. He first mistook this grey construct for an underpass, but his dream-self soon identified it as a group of impossibly vast storm drains. Neil moved nearer to the labyrinth of stone throats, which seemed to gape wider in order to admit him. A soft hiss, some pseudo white noise, washed over all. Neil assumed that the sound was merely a surplus of rainwater gushing through the pipes. Yet even armed with this theory, he was hesitant to enter.

The faint squeak of metal that was screaming for oil cut through the static-hiss of the water. The sound was mechanical, but as Neil stood listening he couldn't help but note how similar the noise was to the whimper of a maimed animal.

The tunnels instantly became a fount of mournful feelings. Neil experienced a sense of loss for something he had never known. It was a grief with no centre. There was no tragic event to focus on, only a rush of sorrow that moved as forcefully as the unseen water in the drains. Neil feared that he would be dragged in by the undertow.

The squeaking thing wobbled slowly into view. It was a baby's pram, battered and filthy. The royal blue tarp of its canopy was slashed and muddy. One of its wheels was missing. The frame was bashed and bent; an ugly skeleton of dull grey metal scabbed with rust. The unmanned carriage halted, but the pealing sounds continued. No longer so metallic, the noises assumed the unmistakable shrill squawk of an infant fresh from the womb. A raw, burning fear draped over Neil.

The child's cries melded with the hissing of the storm drains. This sound also began to heighten its pitch until the tunnel was filled with a chorus of agonies.

Neil tried to back away but his dream-body seemed intent on doing just the opposite.

He shuffled around the pram until he came near enough to see the luridly bright blanket that padded the inside of its carriage. Whatever lay swaddled in this blanket was bouncing and twitching. The crying had grown less frantic now, and Neil wondered if it was his presence that had soothed the infant. He reached out to tug the blanket from the baby's face, when a sharp searing pain shot through his legs. A harsh crashing noise erupted in front of him. He must've tripped on the debris-laden ground.

Neil was mortified to discover that he had fallen forward, and in doing so had toppled the pram.

The coloured blanket had vomited out from the carriage and was sprawled on the base of the drain; a Technicolor puddle contrasting the drabness of the chute.

He was relieved to see the child still twitched, yet he was also amazed that it was not crying from the shock of the fall. Instead the bright lump seemed to be whispering. Then it moved.

Like a fibrous manta ray, the blanket and the living thing it concealed slid across the uneven terrain. It slithered toward Neil and then went still at his feet.

Before he was even fully aware of what he was doing, Neil was crouching down to part the reeking cloth to ensure that whatever was wrapped in it was unharmed.

A strategically placed band of shadow obscured the hump in the blanket, but he could feel that the stout chest of the child was without a heartbeat. Neil's insides chilled. He leaned over to offer the kiss of life.

The heartless thing took this opportunity to fling the blanket upward and wrap it taut around Neil's face. The reeking fabric stretched across his mouth and nose, mummifying him, snatching his every panicked breath. Neil tried to scream but was gagged by the blanket, which now seemed to be inching its way down his throat. A pair of tiny hands (far too strong and firm for their size) clamped onto either side of his head. Neil felt his life draining away...

The shriek that Neil released as he bolted up in his bed was hoarse and girlish. He gulped at the stale air of the darkened bedroom. The sheet was twisted over his left shoulder, tight as a tourniquet. Neil yanked it off as though it had been soiled. Bewildered, his senses still murky from slumber, he reached blindly to Kate's side of the bed in search of solace.

The mattress was vacant, cool. Kate had probably risen several hours ago and moved to the living room sofa. It was one of the little head-tricks she employed whenever the two of them had gone to bed with an unresolved argument still simmering between them. If she was too drained to make the journey back to her own apartment across the city, Kate would simply creep off to make a bed for herself on the overstuffed couch in Neil's living room. It was distance enough for her to make her point, yet near enough for her to enjoy her lover's morning apologies.

Neil pulled himself out of bed and shuffled down the hall, muttering Kate's name. He found the sofa unoccupied.

His concern swelled when he discovered that she was not soaking in a warm bath, nor preparing breakfast in the kitchen. Brief investigations of the backyard and study proved equally fruitless.

In his troubled state, Neil did not notice the missing items for some time. It was only when he began scouring the house for an explanatory note that he realized he'd been robbed. Panic gripped him. He was suddenly brimming with loathsome visions of what could have happened to Kate while he'd been sleeping in blissful ignorance. These ghosts of guilt mingled with the deep-rooted horror Neil was still experiencing from his ill-imaged dream.

He made his way to the bathroom, and that's where he saw it: a tiny post-it note affixed to the medicine chest mirror. The square of goldenrod bore two black-inked words:

We're Done

Neil recognized the handwriting, of course. He plucked the paper from the looking glass, crumpled it and tossed it into the toilet. Storming back through the living room, Neil shouted expletives with all the maturity of a spoiled child. He entered the study and his eyes immediately went back to the gap-riddled bookcases. It was Kate who had pilfered the books from their collective library before she'd left; more casualties of Neil's 'robbery.' In fact, now that he thought about it, everything that had gone missing in the house had belonged to her. Little things; her books, her toiletries, the few changes of clothes she stored in his closet. Of all of these, the books bothered Neil the most. The sight of his volumes leaning against one another to fill the gaps between them was depressing. Though he hadn't been ready to have Kate move in with him quite yet, he did think that their mutual amassing of books was a genuine bonding experience, a sign of stability. He sank down into his reading chair.

As much as it shamed him to admit, the disarrayed state of his book collection angered him. Kate had purposely disrupted the symmetry of his library, he was certain. Her actions had undoubtedly been designed to irk him.

For as long as they'd been together Kate had resented Neil's penchant for escapism. One of Neil's favourite rituals, one he performed more often than he should have, was what he called 'Proust Weekends.' Neil had developed the idea for this during his inaugural year of university, after he'd been forced to read *Swann's Way*. In the course of writing his paper on the novel's decadent author, Neil learned that Marcel Proust had composed most of the sprawling *In Search of Lost Time* novels while lying in bed, within the shuttered bedroom of his hermetically sealed apartment. The notion of cloistering oneself from the physical world in order to cultivate the terrain of reverie had struck a chord in Neil. From that day onwards he would regularly indulge himself in Proust Weekends; two days during which Neil would scarcely leave the comfort of his bed. In perfect health, he would spend the weekend sprawled beneath the sheets; reading, eating rich foods, smoking hash in his mahogany pipe, sleeping, and reading more. He'd tried initiating Kate into his lost weekends, but she found the whole process claustrophobic and pointless. She enjoyed literature, but only as a source of inspiration to go out and truly immerse herself in the world. She would usually only last until Saturday afternoon before flinging the bed sheets back in frustration and announcing that she was going for a long walk.

A fleeting glimmer of hope blossomed in Neil when he thought of Kate out on a long walk this morning. Perhaps she'd left the note in haste and was on her way back to reconcile with him right now, in time for them to make peace and begin their holiday together.

A small pile of paperbacks sat on a table in the centre of the study; his reading material for their weeklong vacation. Surely Kate wouldn't hold a grudge against him now, not after he'd spent what he thought was an exorbitant amount on a five-day lease of a cottage up north. Of course she'll phone, or come by. The Kate he knew would never leave things like this.

Neil rose to prepare breakfast for two.

By noon his confidence in her imminent return had twisted into a simmering rage. He was now convinced that what Kate was doing was nothing short of blatant disrespect, an act of malice. Neil stared at his luggage (which stood by the front door as a monument of their ruined trip) for longer than he should have. He nibbled at a piece of toast and drank the dregs from the bottom of the coffee pot. He tidied his bookcases, he showered, he shaved – all of these things were accomplished before Neil finally succumbed to the nagging desire to phone her.

He got the answering machine and reluctantly followed Kate's instructions to leave a message.

"Hulloh, Kate? It's me. Just wondering where you are. Please give me a call. It's now past noon and I need to know what's going on with the cottage this week. If you'd be so kind as to phone me and bring me up to speed, I'd appreciate it. Bye."

All four subsequent attempts to reach her ended with Kate's tinny-sounding voicemail greeting. Neil pictured her perched over her phone, growing giddier with each desperate call she received.

Believing that spite was the order of the day, Neil decided to scrabble down from the high road of courtesy he felt he'd been treading up until that very moment. He hurriedly secured the house, tossed his bags into the trunk of his car, and drove off.

It took nearly the entire three-hour journey before Neil began to feel somewhat level-headed. The bulk of the drive had passed by in a grey haze of guilt, fury and woeful disappointment. He was surprised to find himself feeling wistfully nostalgic for a vacation that had yet to take place, and in all likelihood never would, at least not the way he'd wanted it to; with Kate.

He pulled into a truck stop along the side of the rural two-lane highway he'd been tearing across all afternoon. He refilled his gas tank and then went inside to chew on a gristly hamburger in the station's cafe. After his 'meal' Neil took the opportunity to stock up on food and toiletries at the MiniMart that was adjacent to the rest stop.

On his way back to the car he fished out his cellular and dialled. The long-distance call was expensive, but it was worth it just to hear the computerized voice announce that Neil had three new voicemails. He held his breath while the machine ran through each one in sequence. The first was from Geoff Leeds, a newly appointed supervisor at Neil's office, who was calling in a panic over a missing client file. The second message was also from Geoff, this time he was gushing with relief as he informed Neil that the missing file had been located. He closed by wishing Neil a wonderful holiday. The third and final message was an automated announcement from a local carpet cleaning company about their newly reduced prices. Neil re-pocketed his phone. He was feeling crumpled and incredibly small.

Dusk had begun to blur the surrounding hills and tree-spiked valleys. The sprawl of woodlands on either side of the highway looked as though they'd been draped in a thin layer of gauze as a fog rolled in from the nearby tarns and tiny lakes. Neil piled into his car and began the final leg of his long, lonesome trip.

The village of Hawthorn Hill was even smaller than Neil had anticipated. The cottages merely peppered either side of the single main road, which wove through the leafy hamlet in a loop pattern. The other byways and side roads were unpaved; rustic and seemingly unpopulated. Hawthorn Hill's layout reminded Neil of an oversized cul-de-sac; an ouroboros village that wound back upon itself.

Each cottage dwelling was cozy, if a little sickly-sweet, with traditional colour schemes and cheerful adornments, such as wooden birds that nodded when the breeze hit them, or floral wreaths that pleaded for God's blessings on their pad. The lots that the homes stood upon were of average size, but Neil had grown so accustomed to the claustrophobic concentration of the city that he looked upon these properties with envy.

An utter lack of streetlights made reading the house numbers difficult, but Neil eventually located cottage seventeen at the top of a hill.

Number seventeen was virtually identical to all the other rentable cottages that hemmed the main road. The only distinguishing feature (to Neil's eye, at least) was that his temporary abode was adorned with white vinyl siding, whereas the others bore more lurid shades of pink, blue, and yellow. Neil followed the instructions the landlord had given him over the phone a few weeks ago. He found the key and his copy of the rental agreement (to be signed and returned ASAP to the landlord's cottage around the bend) in an envelope inside the cottage's mailbox. Neil found this level of rustic trust a little unnerving. He slid the key into the wobbly doorknob and unlocked the front door.

The shuttered windows transformed the interior of the cottage into a cube-shaped abyss, but Neil was too tired to feign timidity. He stepped over the foot-worn welcome mat, that's text had been transformed into a somewhat stranger tiding: WE___ME.

We.

Me.

Neil reached his hand along the living room wall, groping for a light switch. He found one, but the breaker must have needed to be flipped. The air inside the living room was cloyingly musty, like the smell of wet fur.

The blackness made Neil think of a sealed vault or fortress. He was almost disappointed to discover that the darkness was not total: the rear bedroom that ran the length of the cottage was partitioned from the main sitting room by large windows, and it was through one of these that the blue-grey moon shone.

Like a moth to a flame, Neil made his way across the living room, cracking his shin against the edge of an obscured coffee table for his efforts. Sputtering a spiel of curses through his gnashed teeth, he flung the pair of French doors open and hobbled into the bedroom.

A gust of damp night air gushed over him, and he immediately looked in the breeze's direction. One of the bedroom windows had not only been de-boarded, but also opened. Neil immediately felt violated, as well as mortified at the thought of a second abode being plundered in one day. But of course he wouldn't know if anything had been stolen from the cottage. Much like the 'robbery' he'd experienced this morning; the signs of intrusion here were far too neat and orderly to be the wake of an actual burglary.

The Queen-size bed sat perfectly centred in the pool of moonbeams, as though it was being spotlighted. Even more confusing than the open window with its fluttering lace curtains was the ring of objects that had been laid upon the floral-patterned duvet with great care.

Dog-eared photographs, stout bottles of perfume, a latchkey, a stack of letters bound together with butcher's twine, a bouquet of dried lilies; these random items formed an oval frame, large enough, Neil realized, for an adult to lie inside of. He lowered his hand and touched the duvet inside the circle. It felt warm. Neil backed away.

Unsure of what else to do, he moved through the rest of the cottage, de-shuttering and opening every window he could. The breaker box was located next to the antiquated fridge in the kitchen. Neil flipped the lever and the righted ivory coffin began to buzz. He switched on all the ceiling lights and surveyed his accommodations.

The rooms were narrower than Neil had expected. All the furniture appeared to be upholstered in the same gaudy flowers-and-vines-entwined pattern as the duvet in the bedroom, but on the whole Neil knew he could make do here. He was reasonably calm now, convinced that he had not been robbed and that the objects in the bedroom were either the property of the previous tenant or belonged to the cottage. They might have been set on the bed to clean a hutch or shelving unit and simply hadn't been put back. The warmth of the mattress was due of course to Neil's own hand.

Neil stepped into the bathroom, and when he saw the note that had been taped to the medicine chest, his head swam just a little. Had Kate driven all the way up here just to taunt him further?

The note contained the landlord's instructions on where and how to turn on the electricity and water. Neil followed the latter directions and brushed the remnants of hamburger from his teeth.

By the time he finished unpacking and clearing off the Queen-sized bed (which he now felt foolish for having specifically requested), a weighty exhaustion pressed down upon him. He felt as though he'd not slept in days, and was scarcely able to muster enough energy to undress and slide between the covers. The inside of his skull began to tingle with the prelude of sleep. Neil followed the white highway lines that soared past his closed eyelids until everything went dark.

The chirping of swallows woke Neil much earlier than he would have preferred. His cellphone read 6:19, and although the bed was comfortable, Neil knew that further sleep was impossible. He placed his phone back on the nightstand, noting for the first time that another trinket had been left for him in the house, along with the photos and perfume bottles. It was a slim paperback. Neil's bibliophile nature led him to tilt the volume to eye-level. Fully expecting a *Reader's Digest*-excision of *Gideon's Bible*, Neil was amused to discover that the book's title was *A Hiker's Guide to Hawthorn Hill*. A crude pencil illustration of a mud-brown wooded path was splayed across the cover. He set the book down in disinterest.

He tried to resist, but he couldn't help but replay yesterday's events in his mind. Only this time he found himself compounding them with neurotic fantasies about how Kate might have spent last night back in the city.

Neil rose and dressed. His minor enthusiasm toward a cup of Arabian blend on the porch was quashed when he discovered that the kitchen hosted no coffee maker. He sulked for a little while, but conquered this state of mind by pledging an oath that he would not allow this week to degenerate into a marathon of self-pity and woe.

He could think of no better way to begin the turning of this new leaf than by taking a hike in the bountiful woods of Hawthorn Hill. Walking always managed to clear his mind and re-centre him, which is why he often enjoyed a long walk after a prolonged period of reading. Fiction disjointed him slightly, so it always felt good to become re-grounded in open territory.

Neil donned his hiking boots, grabbed a sweatshirt and a bottle of water, and stepped out into the idyllic June morning.

One of the many paths leading into the woods actually snaked its way right to the edge of Neil's backyard. Its appearance was a kind of invitation, or so Neil told himself as he traipsed along the ascending trail.

The natural incline was not perceptibly steep, but Neil gradually began to find the climb to be more arduous than he'd desired. His lungs felt raw from breathing too heavily for too long and the coat of perspiration was beginning to cool his body far too much. Deciding that he'd had enough, Neil stopped to rest briefly before moving homeward.

A group of boulders sat at the edge of the path. Neil reclined himself down onto one, straining to catch his breath. The air felt oddly thin, as though he were on a mountain peak.

It was obvious how this village had earned its name, for the dark twisting hawthorn bushes seemed to sprout up in every crevice and patch of soil throughout the misshapen slopes. The woodland fumed the air with the rich scent of old, old soil. It was not the kind of clean, revitalizing fragrance one customarily finds in rural sprawls, but was rather close, like the stink of an old sofa festering in some neglected attic.

Feeling peckish and oddly vulnerable, Neil pushed himself off the boulder in order to start his homeward trek.

When he spotted the pair of vibrant white eyes staring out at him from the shaded tangles of a hawthorn bush, Neil experienced what he thought was a wholly new emotion, one that crackled and thrummed well beyond the human spectrum.

Gazing at the small set of watchful eyes that were set in an only slightly less-small visage, Neil came to know the ineffable Almighty, which showered over him in thin spears of light. Neil also tasted the sour toxins of Hell, which swallowed him in wellsprings of the most terrible beauty.

The pale eyes blinked, or so Neil thought. But he realized that these were not eyes at all...but flowers—tiny white blossoms. The 'blinking' occurred whenever the morning breeze ruffled their delicate petals. Neil exhaled something that was a mixture of a sigh and a laugh. He was quietly amused by the ways in which one's mind—regardless of how prone or immune it is to fancy—can instantaneously mould common flora into leering trolls.

But common flora does not grin.

Hawthorn branches cannot autonomously sprout the graven image of a feral child.

For that was what Neil was seeing, truly seeing. It was a small fetish, no more than four-inches-tall. The hawthorn wood it had been carved from held many shades and tints; some a smoky pale grey, some as dark as tombstone marble. The figure was of a child, or something like a child. Its body was small and although it certainly conveyed an infant's delicateness, the torso was scrawny and sickly, more akin to the body of a dying geriatric than a cheerful toddler.

But then, as Neil came to see, the grin of the idol was not an expression of happiness, at least not as far as he was concerned. Happiness implied lightness of being, airiness, joy. This face was not that, rather it was...ecstatic. A tiny thorn jutted out from between the child's bent lips—a piercing black tongue, an expression of playfulness, of mockery.

The child's arms were too plump for its ill-fed, bone-ridged torso, and the fact that its hands (whose fingers were tapered into claw-like points) were pressed together in a gesture of prayer made the piece even uglier. Worse still was the sight that met Neil's eyes when he could no longer resist the all-too-human temptation to examine the space between the idol's crossed legs. What Neil found was something he forced himself to believe was a mere knot in the wood, for the idea of a self-sodomizing withered child-thing was too obscene to fathom.

Neil's mind seemed to lower a drape in order to protect him from pondering the reasons why a thing like this would have ever been brought into being.

But he did see the thing, and continued to do so. In fact he was content to do nothing more than simply sit, his eyes locked with those of the carved creature in the bush.

He remained that way until a sound finally managed to break his meditation: the sound of crickets chirping in concert to welcome back the night.

Neil whipped around and saw that the woods were becoming smudged with shadow. He thought briefly that the morning sun had not yet fully risen, and that was why the woods were still so dim and damp. But the gloom did not lift, it thickened.

When he felt the aching rumbles of his empty stomach, Neil came to realize just how weak he felt, how drained, how disoriented.

At this time of the year dusk usually fell sometime around nine. Could he really have spent over twelve hours in mute contemplation? Surely someone must have traipsed past or at least near to him during the course of the day. Even the tapping of animal claws scurrying across wood and brush would have fractured his trance.

Neil began to tremble, and a moment later he was doubled-over, spitting up bile from his hollow stomach. He touched his forehead. It felt horribly hot, yet his insides were as cold as the granite slab that braced him.

'Sunstroke,' Neil thought as he feebly righted himself.

The length of the path ahead caused him to whimper, but hiking back was his only option. He had to seek shelter, perhaps even medical attention. Neil decided that if he encountered anyone along the way he would seek assistance, but for now he was on his own.

Before he took his first step Neil felt his hand reach—almost on instinct—into the razor-wire tendrils of the hawthorn bush. His fingers found the squatted idol. The figure came free with a sharp snap. It grinned up at Neil from inside his trembling palm. The frayed vestige of a stalk hung at the base of the idol's back; showing that it had sprouted organically from the boughs of hawthorn.

Neil held onto the figure as he walked, but did not think about it. His mind was too attached to visions of a hot bath, a soft bed and other creature comforts. Oxygen seemed to be evading him with every panicked breath he sucked in. He neither heard nor saw anyone else in the woods. At one point he even screamed for help, but the only response was the rustling of a flock of birds that flew startled from the summit of nearby trees.

When the back of his cottage finally became visible in the distance, Neil was quietly sobbing. He was burning up, and shaking almost uncontrollably.

Stumbling through the front doorway, Neil tossed his keys and the hawthorn figure onto the kitchen table and reached for the fresh fruit he'd set out that morning. The smell of food made him feel even queasier, but he tore into an orange nonetheless. He then retrieved two bottles of water from the refrigerator and guzzled both.

He stripped away his sweat-drenched clothing and soaked in a steaming bath until his fingers pruned. After this came two more bottles of water. Having no aspirin in his luggage, Neil opted for nature's balm: he crawled into bed and passed out; sleeping deeply and dreamlessly into the following afternoon.

Despite the fact that she'd spent most of the night tossing and turning in a bed that still felt alien to her, Kate was nonetheless embarrassed about having slept in until one in the afternoon. Even after her shower she still felt groggy, which made the sight of the tea Darren had prepared for her all the more welcome. Kate sweetened hers to the point of it being a liquid dessert before she joined Darren in the living room.

He was seated upon the sofa, staring at the section of newspaper that was splayed on the coffee table before him. Kate caught a glimpse of one of the photos; a casualty of a suicide bomber somewhere in the Middle East. The picture showed someone – male or female, Kate could not discern – whose scorched, bubbled skin was the red of crushed ochre. The few remaining tufts of hair billowed about the shrieking face; teeth, like a limestone ring, framed the well-like gape of the screaming mouth. Kate shuddered, tugged her robe more tightly around herself.

"Seems like the whole world's falling into hell," Darren mumbled into the hand supporting his chin.

"Now I remember why I never read the papers," Kate replied. She settled down in the cushioned window seat and gazed out at the group of children who were playing on the sidewalk beyond the glass. After a time Kate said, "I feel guilty about being here."

Darren folded the paper closed. "You're doing nothing wrong, Kate," he said without even looking at her.

"I shouldn't have left Neil that way. I should've just stayed and worked it out with him. He'd been planning this vacation for months, and then I had to go and ruin it."

"You didn't ruin a damn thing. Look, right now you're feeling guilty and maybe even a little scared, so you're probably giving yourself temporary amnesia about just how miserable you were with him. Fortunately I don't have that problem. You obviously came here because some part of you wanted to. Maybe that's a fact you'd rather not admit to yourself right now, but it's the truth. Trust me, Kate. Please. What you're going through happens to almost anyone who makes a major change in their life. It'll pass, believe me."

Kate stared into her steaming mug, half hoping that its soggy leaves would yield some oracular guidance.

Darren rose and joined her on the window seat. "Kate, if there's one thing I've learned about you it's that sometimes you think too much. I know that that's one of your main complaints about Neil, but maybe his over-thinking annoys you because it reminds you of yourself. You obsess over things and that's just not healthy. Please don't take this as an attack, because it's not meant to be."

"Really?"

"Really. Look, all I'm saying is that whenever people dwell on one aspect of their lives, that aspect becomes their life. They make mountains out of molehills. I'm really proud of you for driving all the way out here last night. It proves that you're not willing to let yourself obsess over Neil. Besides, you can't do anything to change things now anyway. He's probably gone up to that cottage, so why don't you just relax and we'll have some fun kicking around the city for a few days?"

Kate tried to resist smiling but was unable.

"Thanks, love," she said.

When he awoke, Neil felt somewhat rejuvenated. The temptation to while the day away in bed was great, but there were things that required his attention. He thought of driving out to a medical clinic to have a doctor look him over, just to be safe. Also, the lease had to be signed and delivered to the landlord, and he would require more food and sundries if he was to last the week.

Entering the living room, Neil was confronted by a perplexing sight. At first he thought the reddish lump upon the throw rug was a child's rubber ball. He stepped closer and saw that it was in fact a withered apple, left to rot before the stone fireplace. It occurred to Neil that he really should have given the cottage a decent cleaning before settling in.

He stepped into the kitchen and immediately concluded that he must have been so distracted by yesterday's drama that he'd unwittingly purchased half-spoiled fruit at the Mini Mart, for the other apples, as well as the bananas he'd bought were shrivelled and reeking. Neil tossed them into the trashcan.

He glanced over at the idol. It was lying sideways just as he had left it. He was mildly relieved by this, until he realized that this sense of relief must mean that some small part of him was expecting the idol to have moved on its own during the night. Neil picked up the figure, bounced it in his hand to remind himself of its heft, then set it back down on the small oak end table in the living room.

After a makeshift breakfast of a peanut butter sandwich and a mug of lukewarm bottled water, Neil located the lease and began a frustrating search for the engraved silver pen Kate had given him for his 35th birthday; a search that ended when Neil discovered that he had already signed the lease, probably during that initial groggy night.

He went to his car and drove around to the landlord's address.

The amount of labour that the landlord had invested into his own home must've been substantial, for his property looked as though it served as an ageless monument to Currier & Ives idealism. A manicured lawn sloped down until it met the gravel road. Twin rods of bowed wrought-iron held wooden pails, and the psychedelically coloured flowers that frothed over the pails' rims.

The house beyond was blue-grey. Its windows gleamed, and its paved porch appeared as freshly chiselled ivory. It was an immaculate abode, one that showed the potential inherent in the other cottages in Hawthorn Hill. The sight of it made Neil feel oddly comforted, and a little sorrowful. His sadness was not born out of loss, but from the revelation that he'd spent his life locked in a cocoon of other men's words, that he'd moved through this world purposely blind to all its natural beauty. This house seemed to be owned and cared for by people who were rooted in earthly life, people who had an enviable sense of place here, a feeling Neil himself had never really enjoyed.

The appearance of a woman on the lawn gave Neil a start. At first he was jolted by the suddenness of her arrival. (Later Neil would ponder if the woman had in fact been standing on the property for as long as he had, but these threads of thought – ones that proved how little notice he actually took of the world around him – were unsettling and a little depressing.) She stood on the muddy patch of grass that stretched between the side of the cottage and the well-trimmed hedge. An older woman, in her sixties at least, she was dressed in a pair of baggy slacks and, in spite of the mounting humidity, a cable-knit sweater. Her apple-doll face broadened with a smile so genuine it made Neil offer one in return.

She gestured for him to come nearer. Neil obeyed.

Once he was standing next to her Neil realized that the woman had shoed her feet in tattered slippers. The air at that side of the house smelled as earthy as the wooded trails that haunted Neil's memory; a deep, rich scent. Neil said hello to the woman.

"There's water," came the woman's reply. She turned and started toward the backyard, stopping at a metal table that sat atop a small stone patio. An umbrella shaded the tabletop and the lone chair beneath it. Neil could see an open book tented on the table, next to a plate and a half full plastic tumbler of water. The woman stood with her arms at her sides. Was she really offering him a sip from the cup she'd been enjoying? Neil thanked her and said he wasn't thirsty just now.

There was a rustling as a soot-grey cat, well fed and lynx-eyed, emerged from the nearby hedge. It scanned the yard, mewled and hissed, then slinked back into the brush.

"So how do you like our little corner of the world, mister...?" The woman's voice was soothing, as grandmotherly as her appearance.

"Keller," Neil replied. "Please call me Neil; Mr. Keller was my father. Hawthorn Hill is quite pretty, though to be perfectly honest, I haven't really had a chance to see much of it."

"Just arrived did you?"

"Yesterday."

"That's long enough to see." Neil wasn't sure if his hostess had intended the pair of words to be so ominous. Her face was still and unreadable. Even the wet, doe-like eyes that stared through the woman's spectacles revealed nothing as to the nature of her thoughts.

"H-have you lived here long? I'm sorry, I just realized I never got your name," Neil said with a chuckle that was too feigned to be taken as good-natured.

"Gwendolyn Freemont. And I was born here, Neil. I met my husband when he was employed as a village farmhand. That was back when we were both still in our teens. He was originally from the east coast. He comes from a family of fishermen, of course. My family were inland types."

"So you've lived here all your life?"

"Never even *been* anywhere else 'cept to town every now and again. I'm proud of that fact, actually. There's something to this village, I think. It's easy to settle in here. Maybe a little too easy, who knows? Are you a hiker, Neil?"

"A little bit. I actually did take a bit of one...a walk...last night... no, yesterday..." The words seemed to be eluding him. As the seconds passed, Neil felt as though his environment was dissolving into the pale. The details of the yard were, like soaked sugar, dissolving until only the faintest trace lingered.

"Did you find this book handy?" Gwendolyn asked. Neil's puzzled expression led her to lift the copy of *A Hiker's Guide to Hawthorn Hill* that was squatted on the metal table.

"Oh, that," Neil said. "No, I saw it in my cottage but I didn't use it. Do you recommend it?"

"I am a little biased," Mrs. Freemont said with a crooked grin. Her thin finger pointed to her name, which was printed on the cover.

"Oh, wow. I can't believe I didn't put that together," Neil felt a tinge of embarrassment.

"Mr. Keller, are you feeling all right?"

"I think I might be coming down with something. Ever since I arrived I've felt totally exhausted."

"That happens to a lot of city-dwellers when they come out here. There's a different pace in the country, a different pattern of life. Some folks feel the change more than others."

"Well, then I guess I'm one of the sensitive ones," Neil said with a half-smirk.

"That's right." Mrs. Freemont's words were iron-cast, final. "Came up to the Hill alone, did you?" she asked. Neil nodded.

"It wasn't planned that way, but..." His voice trailed off.

"Your life in pieces back in the city, is it?" Mrs. Freemont asked. She then retracted by saying, "Never mind, that's none of my business. I apologize."

"It's okay," Neil said, though he didn't mean it. "I think it's fair to say that I'm going through a bit of a rough patch, yeah."

"Good thing you're here then. This is a good place to pare down your life, start over again."

Neil tried to hand Mrs. Freemont the signed lease and the cheque. When she made no move to accept them, he set them on the table, weighting them under the guidebook. He was weary. He thanked Gwendolyn (for what, Neil was not exactly sure) and started back to his car. He could feel Mrs. Freemont's gaze upon him, even as he drove down the gravel road back to his cottage.

Neil felt better after he indulged in the shrimp pasta and Bordeaux that he'd purchased in town, but his mood wilted after he made the mistake of checking his voicemail again; still no messages from

Kate. Neil grabbed one of the paperbacks he'd bought at the drug-store and retired to the living room to read.

The sight of the idol on the end table stabbed his insides with hot panic. It was the first time he'd looked at it since returning from his errands. The figure was sitting in a small puddle of what Neil assumed to be water, until he touched it and found that the fluid clung to his fingertips like thick oil. Wincing at the mucous texture, Neil sniffed his fingers. They reeked sweetly of flowers.

This perfumed fluid, whatever it was, had ruined the hawthorn child. The figure's once-sleek finish had withered into a membrane of white mould. He was almost afraid to touch it, but he needed to see if the bleached spots could be wiped off.

The idol came apart in his hand. Soggy pulp sluiced through Neil's fingers, plopping down onto the carpet where they laid like globules of semen.

"Fuck!" Neil cried. For some reason the sound of his own voice terrified him.

He gathered up the shredded idol and tossed the remnants into the trash. Once this was done, Neil felt relieved. His head was clearer than it had been in days. His fever seemed to be ebbing.

A conveniently logical explanation of the fetish leapt into his mind: of course the hawthorn grotesque had not formed naturally; someone must have taken the time to carve and whittle the fetish without removing the branch from the bush. Once Neil snapped this appendage free, the figure was deprived of the nutrients and calories upon which it was dependent. Like any piece of flora, it shrivelled and died. One need not be a botanist to comprehend these basic laws of Nature. Neil wondered why he hadn't thought of this explanation until now. No matter. He took his paperback to bed and decided to distract himself with a tale of espionage. He dozed off around midnight.

At some point during his sleep there was thunder, then a great darkness that fell over his restless form.

Neil's squinting eyes were suddenly assailed; first by bright mid-day sunbeams, and then by the shocking sight of a stranger standing at the foot of his bed.

Even though the man's stature was slight and he listed with age, Neil was so startled that he flung the twisted bed sheets back and prepared to defend himself.

The old man's eyes widened with panic. He held his rough-skinned hands before him as if to hold back Neil's panic.

"Easy, son, easy," he said. "I'm the landlord. Calm down." Neil lowered his trembling fists. He felt extremely light-headed. "Now, I'm sorry if I scared you," the old man began, "but when I came by and saw that your car was still here I was worried that something might've happened to you."

"Happened?" Neil asked, huffing.

"Yeah, you were supposed to return the key to me yesterday morning."

"I rented this place for the whole week," replied Neil.

"I know; from last Sunday up to and including Friday. I'm behind now, thanks to you. I've got another renter that's due here in about two hours and I need to get this place cleaned up before they arrive. You're lucky I don't charge you for an extra week!"

"What's today?" Neil asked as he lowered himself onto the edge of the mattress.

"It's Sunday, damn it. Now, I'm not going to ask you again, Mr. Keller. Get up and get going."

"What?" Neil shook his head. "This is crazy. Yesterday was Monday, that's the last day I can remember. I went out to your house and gave your wife the cheque and the lease and then I came back here and went to sleep."

"You talked to my wife, did you?" Mr. Freemont's tone was no longer irate; it was now one of resignation. His expression had softened from one of tight rage to a slack mask of empathy.

"You all right, Mr. Keller?"

"Fine," Neil mumbled. "I'm...I'm fine."

"Look, I don't know what kind of games you've been playing up here, son. But if you're not sick, I really do need you out of here."

The old man left the cottage, but not the property. Neil rose shakily and saw through the open front door that the landlord was unloading cleaning supplies from the back of his van. Neil attempted to double-check the date on his cellular but its battery was dead.

Somehow Neil knew that the old man was right. Five days had vanished.

Neil entered the kitchen and the sour aroma of spoiled food crowded his nostrils. Barely able to think, he moved robotically through the cottage, tossing whatever he did not need into a trash bag, and wadding up his possessions into his luggage. He needed to leave and leave quickly, not because of the landlord's threats, but because the thought of spending another moment in Hawthorn Hill was unbearable.

Neil placed the key into the landlord's hand and drove homeward.

The cityscape that came into view several hours later made Neil
smile weakly with relief. He veered into his driveway and stumbled
into his house. Every sight that had a few days earlier depressed him
due to Kate's absence was now delightfully reassuring.

Neil spent that evening resting on the sofa, trying desperately
to conjure a reasonable explanation for all that had happened—or,
more accurately, what hadn't happened—over the past week. Perhaps the hawthorn had infected him with some type of mononucle-
osis which had caused him to sleep for so long? But the notion that
he'd lost so much time in that cottage still terrified Neil. Anything
could have happened to him, anything might have been done by
him during all those veiled hours.

If it had been the hawthorn that made him ill, Neil was eager to
find any remedies he could. His initial thought was to find a walk-in
medical clinic, but in the end he decided that he would like to keep
the incidents of the past week secret unless it was absolutely essential to reveal his symptoms to someone.

He consulted the internet to see what he could learn on his own.

Botany websites offered precious little information that was
applicable to his dilemma. In fact, the only resource that offered
anything even remotely helpful (if such a term could be used) was
a public message board about witchcraft and herbal alchemy. Neil
skimmed a few of the posts that composed the 'Ill-Powers of Hawthorn' thread:

WiseWytch6: Can't say I recommend using hawthron boughs—a lot of
negative spirits can flow through them, sonofthestar.

NightSun: The Wise Ones of Olde often used hagthorn (which later became known as hawthorn) as a means of hiding from their persecutors.
Transmuting flesh into wood would assure immortality a lot more than
trying to become fully disembodied. Our spirits need "clay" (or matter)
to shape and toy with. If you think I'm making all this up, I'll give you a
little experiment to prove the validity of my stance: Light a candle in a
dark room and set it between yourself and a mirror or a bowl of water
or any other reflective surface. Stare until you are able to see your face
reflected in sharp clarity (this will take time, believe me). Then, using one

facial feature at a time, begin pronouncing "I am not this flesh," "These are not my eyes," "This is not my skull…" When your reflection vanishes completely (which, trust me, if you perform this exercise sincerely, it will) you can think of any image—a hawthorn bush, for example—and you will BECOME that thing. You may not be able to hold that state for long at first but, to use mundane parlance, practice makes perfect.

Hekate99: NightSun—You seem to be suggesting that a sorcerer/witch/ Wise One can ACTUALLY alter their bodies from flesh into wood. I think you're forgetting about the power of metaphor. SYMBOLICALLY we can do and become things that are PHYSICALLY impossible. There's a difference. To confuse psychodrama with physical reality will lead to a total break with reality.

NightSun: You say "total break with reality," Hekate99, but I say "find the heart of reality." Our bodies are nothing more than meditations, matter that is trained to take the shape and function that it does because it is the most beneficial and useful form possible. The key to the transformation of matter is very simple: ABSOLUTE FOCUS. One must train oneself to hold one thought and one thought alone. By doing this, we become in one sense more than human, and in another, LESS than human. Humans are microcosms; lazy composites of a thousand different meditations all going on simultaneously. If we whittle ourselves down to one single impulse, one lone meditation, we become Pure Entities. A woodwitch will be able to know and experience things that a fleshwitch can only dream of. I understand and appreciate your concern, Hekate99, because transmutation is rooted in dominion, and dominion is a very terrifying concept indeed.

Neil switched off his laptop and flung himself onto the sofa, exhaling harshly. His mind actually felt wobbly, as though the tether that normally kept his thoughts reined in had snapped. Visions were spilling out all around him, rendering his prostrate body weightless and seemingly formless. Neil opened his eyes and saw not a bone-pale stucco ceiling, but sky—luminescent grey sky. He then spotted what he initially mistook for black lightning; jagged spears of darkness that fractured the idyllic veneer. But this web of night was in fact branches; thin and gnarled, like arthritic fingers.

He felt his own fingers bending as if in sympathy with the misshapen flora. But when his eyes tried to look down, they could not. He could only see the twisting limbs that curled all around him. He felt rigid, yet also strangely content with his new immobility.

Through the wooden mesh Neil was able to perceive the silhouette of a man seated upon a stone slab just a few feet away. The
man's face was obscured by a strange haze, akin to heat waves rising off sun-beaten asphalt. For many minutes the man on the rock
remained as motionless as Neil, but then there was movement, a
slight one. Neil watched as the man stirred upon the stone, clasped
his blurry hands together and bowed his faceless head.

A bodily spasm erased the vision. Neil sat up, praying that his
heart would temper its now manic rhythm. The thought that he
was going to die there alone pounced on him like a beast. Neil was
finding it impossible to breathe. He needed open space and air. He
needed to be comforted by someone.

Neil staggered out onto his front lawn and the night air helped
crack the thickening panic. By now social conduct wasn't even a
consideration for him.

When he felt well enough to drive, he ventured out to Kate's
apartment. He needed to speak to her, to confess all that had been
happening. He was not seeking answers, merely solace.

He entered the vestibule of her building and buzzed her suite.
There was no answer. Neil went to the building's courtyard and
gazed up at her windows, which were curtained and dark. Not
knowing what else to do, Neil went home.

He phoned in sick for work the next day, during which he ate a great
deal and went for a long walk in an attempt to shake the fatigue that
now seemed to constantly plague him.

He returned to the office on Tuesday morning and found his
desk impeccably clean and organized. Neil's supervisor approached
him during lunch in the building cafeteria to welcome him back.
He praised the job done by the temp that had covered Neil's position during his vacation and an ensuing sick day. Unsure of how to
respond to this, Neil simply smiled and said "yeah." His attention
was elsewhere.

The ability to focus eluded Neil all afternoon. His thoughts
roamed through realms of knotted wood and beads of sunlight. He
wanted nothing more than to rest for a spell.

Shortly before five, Neil realized that the few attempts he'd made
at inputting some information into the company's database were
rife with errors. It was obvious that he was better off doing no work
at all.

Neil then bent company policy by using his computer to log on to the internet. The fact that these kinds of explorations were taboo thrilled Neil and made him feel as though he was plundering some secret vault where forbidden texts festered.

He found the same message board on witch lore that he'd discovered a few days earlier. The thread dealing with hawthorn offered no new postings. Neil's eyes fell upon the invitation to Join This Thread Now. Grateful for the relative anonymity that the 'net provided, Neil created a user account under the name A.SEEKER. He quickly tapped out a new message to the thread on hawthorn lore:

A.SEEKER: Hello to all of you. I am new to this msg. board. I would like to know if any of you have had any experience with hawthorn growing into strange shapes, such as things that look like people? Do any of you know of a spell that can cause plants to grow in unnatural ways? Thank you in advance for any guidance.

A thrill ran through Neil as he saw his message added to the thread. He drummed his fingers on his desk, hoping to receive an instant response. A roaming supervisor forced him to escape out of the internet and perform a pantomime of tasking until the end of his shift.

Traffic was uncharacteristically light for the homebound drive, but Neil still found the trek gruelling. His empty house no longer bothered him. He'd even managed to forget about Kate for most of the afternoon. Going straight to his PC, Neil went online and straight to the witchcraft message board. Seeing that his was still the most recent post in the hawthorn thread and that no one had responded caused him to sulk for a moment, until he noticed that one of the other members of the board had sent him a private message. Neil clicked on the Messages icon and read:

Dear A.Seeker, Welcome to the msg. board. I thought it best to contact you off-board/privately to respond to your initial posting.

I have had some experience with hagthorn Evolving into seemingly impossible forms. Do I know of "a spell" that can do such things, as you asked? No. That's not to say that such spells do not exist, just that I myself don't know of any. In my experience the unusual Evolution of flora is a symptom of something far grander than human sorcery. It is proof that all of Nature (by which I mean everything in the physical universe) is really a cipher. Every pattern of tree branches, every cloud formation, every single petal on every single flower; these things grow EXACTLY how they are meant to. How? By the will of the timeless and nameless Spirits of Place. Why? Because the Spirits are trying to spell the secrets of life out to YOU. What you see in Nature will not be what I see and vice-versa. All our lives the Spirits try to reach us through the medium of Nature. Most people are too ignorant to ever pick up on this, so the Spirits eventually abandon them. For the average person, being in the woods means nothing, and that's because it's the equivalent of an illiterate standing in one of the world's great libraries. An illiterate would see only coloured rectangles of paper and the occasional pretty picture. But to someone who knows how to read and loves knowledge, a library is a gift. For you, it's time to really READ Nature. Don't be fooled into thinking that trees and shrubs grow at random. They are forming an ancient dialogue between the Spirits of Place and the Chosen among humanity. If They have gone through the trouble of mutating a hagthorn into something fantastic so that you can discover Them, then it seems clear that you have been Chosen. You've been handed a Rosetta Stone, so to speak. Now it's your job to figure out what the Spirits want of you.

Do you have any pics of your hagthorn that you'd be willing to email me?

I hope this message gave you some clarity and insight.

Regards,
NightSun

Neil leaned back in his chair. He read the message twice more before moving back to the sofa. The gloaming filled the living room with meek shadows. The sound of his own breathing seemed disruptive to the perfect silence all around him. The idea of sleeping for centuries seemed not only plausible, but downright pleasant. Neil could feel his eyes fluttering shut, as if fleshy moth's wings draped them.

The flashback of the panic he'd felt, the hot jarring terror, when Mr. Freemont explained how all those vacation days suddenly dissolved. This memory of dread wrenched him awake. The cold white sleep that had been luring him from the world shrivelled and shrank like salt-doused slugs.

The living room had grown unbearably stuffy. His throat felt dusty, his lungs tight. Neil rose, then struggled to don a pair of battered runners.

The night air snapped at him as he made his way down the driveway to the sidewalk. The streetlamps flickered to life, but Neil found the dry lustre of the waxing moon a far more appealing light for his walk.

He was not exactly surprised when he found his rudderless journey had led him to Milestone Park, but he was bemused by how pleasing the sight of manicured green was, along with the tidy piles of boulders and the scattering of antique benches. Ordinarily he paid the city's parklands no mind. They were simply humanity's unspoken atonement for raping the land; a means of still having the illusion of rustic harmony in the midst of the cold, dry embrace of urban sprawl. But tonight's crossing of Milestone Park's threshold felt entirely new; a markedly unique experience. The flowerbeds were guarded by ultraviolet lamps with bug-spattered bulbs that reminded Neil of the eerie luminescence he experienced in dreams.

Neil wished he could have enjoyed the atmosphere longer, but a feeling of familiar dizziness welled up inside him. The strength ran out of his legs, alternating blotches of light and darkness began to splatter in his periphery. He was profoundly grateful to find one of the benches was both near and vacant. Neil felt his body slump down onto the wood, but some other part of him felt as though he was still hovering, as though his soul had somehow been knocked loose. He imagined this floating self looking down at the suit of meat it had once inhabited. How puny his body looked, so impermanent and crude.

There were better hosts to be found in nature, ones far less constricting than the drone called Homo Sapiens. Neil's floating self attuned its remote vision to the cluster of trees to its left and to its right.

Now Neil was no longer on the bench at all. He was in the trees, deeply rooted in the shaded boughs. There was a stranger seated on the bench. Somewhere in his wood-thoughts Neil suffered vague recollections of what it had been like to be human.

Something touched him. Neil snapped back. He was on the bench. A woman with a regal demeanour had her hand on his shoulder.

"You feeling okay?" she asked. "You need me to get a doctor?"

Neil shook his head.

"Too much to drink?"

"More like not enough to eat," Neil mumbled. "I'll be all right. I think I'd better just go home."

"You should get yourself some food first, but, yes, going home would be a good idea."

As he traipsed slowly out of Milestone, Neil struggled to avoid giving even a passing glance to the trees that stood as silent sentinels. The woods, it seemed, had faith enough in him to allow his escape.

Peals of shrill laughter (a woman's) rang out from somewhere behind him. The voice seemed directionless, its source impossible to pinpoint. But Neil was certain that this woman, whoever she was, was laughing at him. This bothered him, but not nearly as much as the fact that the laugh was so familiar to him. Kate was in the shadows, mocking him for his weakness, mocking him for actually believing that NightSun's crazy words were truthful ones.

Even as the distance between Neil and the park increased, Kate's ridiculing cackle did not fade.

Neil lifted his head from the pillow and looked upon the sun-stained interior of his bedroom. He had no idea what day it was. A common enough fear, but he had lost a clutch of days as it was, so the possibility that another chunk of his life had been shorn away was almost unbearable.

The clock radio provided a hint of balm when it revealed the time to be only a little after seven a.m. Reaching over to usher in the voice of a local station's newscaster actually required a great deal of willed effort, so immense was Neil's fear. Finally, after running down the current sports scores and the planet's financial woes, the man gave the date as Wednesday.

He still had time to clean himself up and make it to the office before nine. His molars ached, and he wondered if it was yet another symptom of supernatural intrusion. But as his tongue poked at the peanut that was lodged between his teeth, he remembered how he'd tried to remedy last night's dizzy spell by gobbling two candy bars he'd bought at the corner store. The sugar rush had given him energy enough to stagger back home, but now he was paying the price. (Kate had been the one with the sweet tooth. Neil hadn't been able to stomach confections since his teens.)

At ten minutes to nine Neil entered the office and immediately the sickness came over him. The fibrous grey walls of the cubicle labyrinth that surrounded him seemed to swell, to shrink.

Neil bolted for the men's room, and was relieved to find it vacant. He stood before the multiple sinks, resting his hands upon the counter, not daring to look up at his reflection in the looking glass wall. He splashed cold water on his face and tried to will his heart to beat in a less frantic rhythm.

The mirror had a painful entanglement of wavy lines and blotches. Neil sucked in deeply and hoped that the psychedelia would correct itself. But Neil's reflection failed to materialize. In its stead was a mask, darkly vague yet familiar somehow too.

The words of NightSun echoed through Neil's mind, like a soft scrap of dream that waking did not fully dissolve. "This is not my head..." The words sounded obscene when Neil uttered them aloud. He regretted speaking them, particularly when he saw the petal-eyed reflection grinning back at him.

Part of him wanted to hold onto the image, to know it, to be it.

But another memory leapt to the fore. The laughter. Kate's mocking cackle that he'd heard in Milestone Park.

The hagthorn was gone. Neil's familiar chalky black-eyed face threw back an expression that was one of either pity or disdain.

When he felt well enough, Neil reported to the receptionist that he had obviously suffered a relapse and that he was taking another sick day.

He took a cab back to his sanctuary. He locked the door, stripped, and crawled into bed.

He was unsure as to how NightSun's words had managed to tilt his world askew, but Neil knew that something had awakened inside his consciousness. Something that had been hunched in a long-neglected attic of memory had just stirred. Like an amnesiac who suddenly recalls and pronounces their own name after an age of living in the dark, a force was stirring inside Neil. He felt more alive than he had in years, perhaps more than he ever had before. The swell of unbridled being seemed too vast to contain inside one body. He fidgeted upon the bed. No position offered comfort, no thought would linger in his brain long enough to be fully yoked of its meaning.

He closed his eyes and breathed deeply. NightSun's request for pictures led Neil to the realization that he no longer had his idol. He had no evidence of its existence, nor any hope of ever seeing it again. Perhaps the key the Spirits had given him, assuming that's what the leering child-thing actually was, was forever lost, and along with it had gone all the secrets intended for Neil. His mind reached back to Hawthorn Hill. He struggled to remember what the fetish looked like. The thoughts were flowing much more leisurely now, parading past Neil's mind's eye with near-erotic slowness.

Part of him was back there now, enthroned upon a granite slab and domed by a cloudless sky. The boughs of the elms and the oaks meshed together, forming bent runes.

And the child was in his hands.

Neil was determined to study every contour, to etch its minutiae into his memory, to carve this sight into his soul as thoroughly as it had originally been carved in hawthorn. For memory was all that was left of the child-thing; vaporous, intangible thought.

But something was obscuring the wooden face. Neil squinted and strained. A small cloud of fog veiled the head's features, rendering them frustratingly vague.

A scent then filled Neil's nostrils, one that he first thought to be the natural perfumes of nearby flowers, but it wasn't. It was Kate's scent. Her hair and flesh come to him as olfactory ghosts.

Neil realized that it was Kate who was obscuring the idol. She was keeping him from remembering. She was preventing the Spirits from reaching him. She had always resented his dreamer's constitution.

Unwilling to let this be snatched from him, Neil rose and began ever-so-slowly to walk.

Darren took the corner more sharply than Kate would have liked. His tires stirred the rainwater that had been pooling along the gutters, casting a wave over a man walking his drenched basset hound. Kate was about scold him when she saw her townhouse complex swerving into view. Her irksome feelings were immediately replaced by a great sense of relief.

She was actually excited when she entered her own townhouse after having spent the better part of a week living out of a suitcase and sleeping on a pull-out sofa. She was home. She was also relieved to be home in the early evening, for it meant she could spend the next few hours gradually slipping back into her workaday routine.

More importantly, she would finally have the opportunity to speak to Neil, to present him with the speech she'd rehearsed to near-perfection over the last several days. She'd had to select her words with great care; it was a delicate situation after all, and if Neil understood anything, it was words. The lines she'd practiced to herself were well-crafted. They were diamond-clear, yet softly-wrapped: there would be no reconciliation between them, but despite what Neil had been led to believe, he was not entirely to blame for their estrangement. He was not wholly innocent either, but Kate now realized that her partner deserved more in way of an explanation than just a two-word note on a medicine chest mirror.

She'd fallen out of love with him. It was a painful thing to realize, but it was also secretly luminous, exhilarating. Neil's aloofness, his icy detachment from everything but his own ideas had for years made her feel inadequate, ill-suited to a meaningful relationship. It took a great deal of introspection before she was able to realize that the problem lay mostly with Neil and not her. In the days since Kate came to realize the well-buried secret of her loss of feelings for Neil, the world seemed renewed—a seeded garden of infinite possibilities.

A terse roll of thunder sounded in the hallway behind her. Kate let out an involuntary squeal and immediately blushed for having done so.

"Sorry, sorry!" Darren muttered as he picked up one of Kate's three suitcases. "I had to lug these things up from the car. First I'm your chauffeur, now I'm your pack mule?" He unzipped his coat and shook off the droplets. "The rain's finally letting up at least."

There was a lull as Darren attempted to interpret Kate's state of mind by her body language. What he did see troubled him. "Are you sure you don't want to stay at mom's place for another few days?"

"I've already used up some sick days at work," Kate began, "and that was after a full week's vacation. No, I need to get back to my old life. Or my new one as the case may be."

Darren shrugged. "Suit yourself. If you're sure you don't need anything else, I'm going to start back now."

Kate's mouth bent into something mildly akin to a smile. "Thank you, Darren. I really appreciate it. And be sure to thank mom again for me too. Being able to spend a few days back home was just what I needed. But as I said, it's time to put the pieces back together again. Anyway, it's not like I've been through any great tragedy, right? It's only a break-up."

"That's right," replied Darren. For some reason Kate was hoping that he would crack a smile when he'd said it. The two of them hugged briefly and Darren turned to depart.

"Are you sure you're all right?" he asked. His face, still soaked with rain, looked as though it were melting in the substandard lighting of the living room.

"I'll be fine." Kate's voice was weak with distraction. She eyed the telephone, glanced back at her brother, smiled. "Would you like me to make you a cup of tea or something?"

"No, I should start back. I have to work at eight a.m." He fished the keys out of his trouser pocket. "Call home if you need anything."

"This is home, remember?"

"Right. Well, I guess I'll be off then."

Once the sound of her brother's steps shrank into silence Kate moved to the phone. She was nervous and had to stop dialling Neil's number several times before she was finally able to complete the sequence. It rang until his answering machine responded. Kate hung up. She could not deny the worry that was awakening in the pit of her stomach.

Outside, the rain had been reduced to a directionless mist, a wet swarm. Fog obscured much of the hedge that lined the walkway leading from Kate's building to the parking lot before it. Darren zippered his windbreaker up to his neck, surprised at just how chilly and damp a June night could be. The sodium lamp cast a cone of orange illumination upon his parked car. The vehicle looked positively spectral.

'Strange how the elements can play tricks,' Darren thought as he unlocked the driver's side door. He was inside the cab with the engine running before it dawned on him that something felt wrong, very wrong indeed.

Had he really seen a figure staggering across the road? Darren switched on his headlights. Fog swirled around and through the beams like tadpoles. He squinted and peered out into the sea of grey wetness that had once been Kate's neighbourhood.

A black form emerged from the dull fog. Its movements were awkward, twitchy. The figure froze just long enough to cast a glance in Darren's direction. Darren refused to accept what stood before him in the night.

The figure stumbled forward, its arms outstretched and groping. Darren saw the thing trip when it reached the curb. It fell flat, righted itself and lumbered onward without pausing. The courtyard of Kate's building was its destination.

Panic seized Darren. He flung the car door open, struggled with his seatbelt until it finally gave, and then ran in the path of the shape.

He could hear the soft slaps of its apparently bare feet upon the interlocking brick of the courtyard.

"Hey!" Darren shouted. He felt embarrassed for doing so. His voice was loud and abrasive. In a much softer tone, he muttered, "Don't."

It was his parting word, for soon after speaking it Darren felt a pair of wood-firm hands pressing around the soft meat of his throat.

Kate gave up trying to reach Neil after her sixth attempt was met with the same recorded greeting. She was exhausted but too anxious to sleep. She drew herself a hot bath.

Her muscles went slack, grateful for the steaming water that now pooled around her body. She was so relaxed that the abrupt cracking sound actually caused her to scream.

She sat up, sloshing water over the tub's rim. The apartment had grown quiet once more. The noise sounded as though it had come from the living room; or perhaps the bedroom...where the sliding glass doors led onto her small patio. Someone, perhaps a thief who had cased her apartment and assumed that she was still out of town, had just broken in.

Kate reached for a towel and tried to rise as silently as possible.

Something shattered on the living room floor; a flowerpot perhaps. Switching off the bathroom light, Kate stood trembling against the tiled wall. She strained to hear, but only quiet greeted her. Creeping a step or two forward, Kate pressed her ear against the thin wood of the bathroom door.

The blow from the other side blasted the door from its hinges and sent Kate reeling backwards. She smacked the side of her head on something hard and fell back into the now-tepid bathwater. Light spilled in from the hall, showing the shape that moved into the bathroom and loomed over Kate's toppled form. She opened her mouth to shriek, but the intruder reached down with rough, claw-like hands and plunged her head beneath the surface. Water gushed into Kate's still-open mouth. She could feel the air being flooded out of her by the water that was only too eager to replace it. She struggled but could not escape. She opened her eyes.

The rippling water distorted the wide, unblinking eyes of her attacker, causing them to appear as fluttering petals of white. She stared into those weepy shapes and somehow came to understand that she was dying.

Freed of distractions and all the ties that bound him to his old life, Neil blindly groped his way out of Kate's apartment, and eventually, out of the building itself.

Behind the building was a small wooded ravine. Neil intuited that he was to go there and wait, which he did.

The shrubs and brush seemed to bend and wind about him like welcoming arms.

Neil understood that in a short while there would be panic inside the nearby building, and then a desperate hunt. But he was not afraid. He understood that he was safe, protected.

The voices in his ear whispered how crucial it was for him to be patient, and to be still; oh so very still. Neil understood the guidance of these Spirits of Place. He imagined himself shrinking, growing stiff. The voices promised further guidance.

He imagined his response to the voices and had faith that They understood his willingness to honour Their wishes. For even now, as he hunched down inside the vault of the night, They began to reveal nature in its purest form: leathery leaves that drooled gems of rainwater, a soft bedding of fog that crowned the heads of poison fungi, the near-neon hue of so many hidden flowers. Even the sky, black and choked with clouds though it was, held the promise of renewal.

Neil's sense of rejuvenation was ecstatic. Although his lungs seemed to be refusing him air, he knew bliss. His slowing heart began to feel like a knot of wood inside his chest, but Neil was enraptured.

He was nothing.

He was in bloom.

A Cavern of Redbrick

EE NOW AS the boy sees. Bear witness to a Summerworld, a place sparkling with clear light and redolent with the fragrance of new-mown grass and where the air itself hosts all the warmth and weightlessness of bathwater.

It is the first morning in this Summerworld and, knowing that autumn is but a pinpoint in the future, Michael stands on the porch of his grandparents' country home and allows the elation to erupt inside him. He then mounts his bicycle and rides headlong into the season.

The town whisks past him in a verdant smear. But Michael holds his destination firmly in his mind's eye.

The gravel pit on the edge of town has long been his private sanctuary. He has escaped to that secret grey place more times than he can possibly remember. It is his own summer retreat, one of the many highlights of spending the summer with his grandparents in the little village of Cherring Point.

Visiting the pits is technically trespassing. His grandfather, who was appointed by the government to maintain and occasionally man the place, has often told him to keep away from it. Thus Michael keeps his mild transgressions to himself. Clearly he isn't the only one to sneak into the secluded area. He isn't the one who has cut the hole into the chain-link fence that distinguishes the property line, though he does always make sure to re-cover this portal with the brush that camouflages it.

Michael consoles himself with the logic that he really never disrupts anything in the pits. On his bike he would race over the mounds, which he likes to imagine as being the burial sites of behemoths. He loves watching his tires summon dirty fumes of gravel dust. Often that instant when his bike soars past the tipping point at the mounds' summit, Michael feels as though he is flying.

It is his private ritual of summer elation; harmless and pure. ·

Except that today, on his inaugural visit of the season, Michael discovers that his ritual ground is no longer private...

His initial reaction to seeing the girl beyond the fence is shock, a feeling that gives way to an almost dizzying sense of disbelief.

At the far end of the lot is a large redbrick storage shed, its door of corrugated metal shut firm and secured with a shiny silver padlock. Michael has often fantasized about all manner of treasure being stored within those walls.

Standing on the shed's roof is a girl whom Michael guesses to be no older than he is. She is dressed in a t-shirt only slightly whiter than her teeth. Her straw-coloured hair hangs to the middle of her back. Her bare feet are uncannily balanced at the very summit of the shed's pitched roof, yet she does not teeter or wave her arms to maintain this daring balance. She is as stationary as a totem.

Michael can feel her eyes upon him.

He veers his bike away and rides the paths above the gravel yard for a while, cutting sloppy figure-eights in the dirt while wrestling with whether or not he should retreat. What exactly is she trying to prove standing on the shed that way? What if she tries to speak to him, to shake loose his reasons for coming here? What if this place is in fact *her* special place? Perhaps *he* has been the real outlander all this time.

Michael veers his bike cautiously back to the hidden gap in the fence, hoping, foolishly, that the girl will flee.

He crouches low on his bike and glides to where the brush is thickest.

"What's your name?"

The sound of her voice chills Michael. He wonders how she has spied him. Does her position on the roof make her all-seeing?

Like a surrendering soldier, Michael rides out from behind the greenery, clears the entrance to the pits and eases his bike toward the shed.

"How did you get up there?" he asks.

"Do you live near here?"

Michael frowns. "No. My grandparents do."

"You're not supposed to be in here, you know."

"Neither are *you!*" Michael spits. He feels a strange and sudden rage overcoming him. Somehow his childish anxiety over seeing an interloper in his sanctuary pales beneath a fiery anger, something near to hatred. It erupts with such sharpness that Michael actually feels himself flinch, as though he's been shocked by some hidden power line. Why should the girl anger him so? He wonders what it is about the nature of her innocuous questions that makes him despise her.

He pedals closer and is opening his mouth to say something, just what Michael isn't sure, when a searing glint on the girl's body forces him to screw up his face.

Shielding his eyes with one hand, Michael gives the girl a long and scrutinizing glare.

And then he truly sees her...

Sees the flour-pale and bruise-blue pallor of her skin, sees the nuggets of crystallized water that form in her hair, in the folds of her oversized T-shirt, on her rigid ill-coloured limbs. Her eyes are almost solid white, but instinctively Michael knows that blindness is not the cause.

When she again asks Michael what his name is, her voice rises from somewhere in the gravel pits and not from her rigid face, for the girl's jaw remains locked. For a beat Michael wonders if she is frozen solid.

To answer this thought, the girl suddenly raises her ice-scabbed arms as if to claim him.

Michael's actions are so frantic they must appear as one vast and hectic gesture: the shriek, the rearing around of his bike, the aching, desperate scaling of the gravel mound, the piercing push through the tear in the fence, the breathless race across the fields.

Michael rides. And rides.

The distance Michael places between himself and the gravel yard brings little relief. Not even the sight of his grandparents' home calms him. He rushes up their driveway, allows his bike to drop, then runs directly to the tiny guestroom that serves as his bedroom every summer vacation.

Burying his face in his pillow, Michael listens to the sound of approaching footsteps.

"Mikey, you all right?"

His grandmother's musical voice is a balm to him.

Michael lifts his head, but when he sees the reddish stains that mar his grandmother's fingers and the apron she's wearing he winces.

"What is it, son?"

He points a bent finger and his grandmother laughs.

"It's strawberries, silly. I'm making jam. I saw you come tearing up the road like the devil himself was at your heels."

Michael wipes his mouth. "Grandma, do you believe in ghosts?"

Her brow lifts behind her spectacles. "Ghosts? No, I can't say that I do, Mikey. Why?"

His account of the experience reaches all the way to the tip of Michael's tongue, but at the last instant he bites it back. He shakes his head, stays silent.

His grandmother frowns. "Too much time in the sun, dear. Why don't you lie down for a while? I'll wake you for lunch."

Michael nods. His grandmother's suggestion sounds very good indeed. He reclines his head back onto the pillows and shuts out the world.

He doesn't realize he's dozed off until he feels his grandmother nudging him. Perspiration has dried on his hair and skin, which makes him feel clammy. He shivers and then groggily makes his way to the kitchen to join his grandparents for sandwiches.

"What happened, sleepyhead?" his grandfather teases. "You didn't tire yourself out on the first day, did you?"

His grandfather receives a sardonic swat from his grandmother, which makes Michael laugh.

"He probably just rode too long in the heat," she says.

"Oh? Where'd you ride to?"

"Just...around." Michael bites into his sandwich, hoping that this line of questioning will end.

"Mikey asked me a little earlier if I believed in ghosts." His grandmother sets a tumbler of milk down in front of Michael as she settles into her chair.

"Ghosts? What brought that on?"

Michael shrugs. "Nothing. I was just wondering."

He cannot be sure, but Michael feels that his grandfather's glare on him has hardened.

Michael remains indoors, the only place he feels relatively secure, for the rest of the day. He helps his grandmother jar up the last of her jams and wash up afterwards. He watches cartoons while she prepares supper. His grandfather is outdoors, labouring on one of the seemingly endless projects which occupies so much of his time. He is a veritable stranger in the house. Last summer Michael had tried to assist him with the various chores, but he got the feeling that his grandfather found him more of a burden than an aid. So this year he takes his mother's advice and just stays out of his grandfather's way.

Though he's never been mean, his grandfather does give off an air that Michael finds far less pleasant than that of his grandmother. She is always cheerful, brimming with old family stories or ideas of various things that he could help her with. Grandma's chores never feel like work.

After supper Michael's mother phones to see how his first day went. He is oddly grateful for the deep homesickness that hearing her voice summons; it means that he doesn't have to think about what he'd seen that morning. His mother says she'll be up to visit on the weekend.

The late morning nap and mounting anxieties make sleep almost impossible for Michael. He lies in his bed, which suddenly feels uncomfortably foreign, and wrestles with the implications of what he has seen, what he has *experienced*, for the encounter was far more than visual.

Standing in the presence of that girl, whatever she had been, made the world feel different. Just recollecting the event made Michael feel dizzy.

Maybe his grandmother is right, maybe he has been riding too hard under the hot sun. After a time Michael understands that the only way he can put the incident behind him is to return to the pits, to test what he'd seen or thought he had seen. His teacher last year told him the first rule when learning about science and nature is that you must repeat the experiment. If you want to know the truth about something you have to do the same thing more than once. If the results are the same, then what you've found is something real.

Tomorrow he will go back. He will find the truth.

The girl is nowhere to be found. Michael rides out after breakfast, despite his grandmother advising him against it. He promises her he will ride slowly and in the shade, and that he'll be home to help her with lunch.

Michael is so elated by the absence of the ugly vision that he plunges through the rip in the chain-link and begins to scale and shoot down the gravel mounds at a manic pace. Dust mushrooms up in his wake. Michael feels unfettered from everything.

The sound of an approaching vehicle startles him to such a degree that he almost loses his balance.

Glancing up to where the country lane meets the gate of the gravel pit, Michael spies his grandfather's pickup truck. He per-

forms a quick shoulder check, panicked by the distance that stretches between him and the hole in the fence.

His grandfather steps out of the cab. Realizing that he has no
time to escape, Michael hunches low and pedals behind the farthest
gravel mound. There he dismounts, crouches, and is punished by
the thundering heartbeat in his ears.

The gate is unlocked, de-chained. The pickup truck comes
crawling down along the narrow path, parking before the shed. Michael doesn't hear the engine shut off and he wonders if his grandfather is just waiting for him to come out from behind the mound
so he can run him down.

But then the engine is silent and is soon followed by the rum-
bling sound which signifies the corrugated metal door being
opened. Has the ghost-girl flung the door open from the inside?
Perhaps she has attacked his grandfather. Michael swallows. With
utmost caution he creeps to the edge of the mound and peers.

It is dark inside the shed, so dark that it looks boundless; a deep
cavern of redbrick. Michael can just discern the faintest suggestions
of objects: power tools, equipment of various shapes, overfilled
shelves of metal.

The only item that stands out is the white box. It glows against
the gloom and puts Michael in mind of Dracula's coffin. But the
sight of its orange power light glowing like a match flame confirms
to Michael that it is nothing more than a freezer.

The shed's corrugated door is drawn down. His grandfather
must have chores to attend to in the shed. It likely won't take him
long to locate whatever tools he needs. Michael steals the opportunity to rush back to the tear and escape.

He races out to the bridge above West Creek. There he settles
into a shady spot, dangles his legs over the bridge's edge and studies
catfish squirming along the current.

Near noon, Michael mounts his bike and rides back to his grandparents' home.

The pickup truck is parked in the driveway. He takes a deep
breath, praying that his grandfather hasn't seen him making his
escape.

"I'm home, grandma," he calls from the foyer.

Entering the kitchen, Michael is startled by the sight of his
grandfather fidgeting at the counter.

"She went into town to run some errands," he says.

"Sit down, your lunch is ready."

Michael does as he is told. His grandfather plunks down a bowl of stewed tomatoes before him, along with a glass of milk. He nests himself at the far end of the table and chews in silence.

His stomach knots. Michael chokes down the slippery fruit in his bowl.

"I suppose I should have had you wash your hands before we sat down," his grandfather remarks. "You're pretty filthy. You've got dust all over your clothes and hands."

Michael freezes. His grandfather's gaze remains fixed on the food in his dish, which he spoons up and eats in a measured rhythm.

When his bowl is empty, his grandfather sets down his spoon and lifts his eyes to Michael's. "I have a confession to make," he begins. "You know yesterday when your grandmother brought up the topic of ghosts? Well, can you keep a secret, just between us?"

Michael nods.

"You swear it?"

"I swear."

"Cross your heart?"

Michael does so.

"All right then. I wasn't being honest when I said I didn't believe in them. The fact is I do. I saw a ghost once myself."

"You did?"

"Yes. Well, it was something like a ghost. I think what I saw was actually a jinn."

"A jinn?"

"A jinn is a spirit, Michael. Legend says they are created by fire. They can take all kinds of forms; animals, people. But they're very dangerous."

"What did the jinn that you saw look like?" Michael asks breathlessly.

"It was in the form of a young girl."

Michael feels his palms growing damp. "Where did you see her?"

"In the woods, not too far from here. I think she was planning to burn the forest down. That's what the jinn do, they bring fire."

"And did she?"

His grandfather shakes his head.

"So what happened?"

His grandfather tents his hands before him. "They say the only way to combat the element of fire is with ice..."

And with that, a silent tension coils between child and elder, winding tighter like a spring. Michael is confused, curious, and scared. He doesn't know what to do or say.

"Young boys get curious, and when they get curious they sometimes discover things that give them the wrong impression of what the world is like. There are always two sides to things, Michael," his grandfather advises.

"There is the appearance of things and then there is what lies beneath. I want you to remember that, boy. Don't base your opinions of the world on how it appears. Always try to remember what lies beneath. Sometimes the things that appear to be the most innocent are the most dangerous, and vice versa. It was a long time before I knew this, so I want you to learn it while you're young. You understand?"

Michael nods even though he does not at all understand.

The sound of his grandmother turning into the driveway brings Michael a relief that borders on gleeful.

He runs to her. His grandfather rises and dutifully clears the table.

The remainder of the day moves at a crawl as Michael searches for a way to probe his grandfather further about the jinn. Is this what he has seen? No, what he's seen looks more like a spirit born of ice. Either way, the woods that surrounded the old gravel pits are obviously haunted, and that means they are dangerous. By bedtime that night Michael has resolved to never again visit the gravel pits. He will find other ways to amuse himself.

He has almost managed to convince himself that everything is right with the world when the girl appears again, this time inside his grandparents' house.

It is the dead of night and Michael is returning to his bed after relieving himself. She stands in the hallway, her flesh phosphorescent in the darkness. The nuggets of ice sparkle in her hair like a constellation of fallen stars.

Michael is bolted in place. His jaw falls open as if weighted. He looks at her but somehow isn't truly seeing her. In the back of his mind Michael wonders if what he is experiencing is what lies beneath the surface of the girl and not merely her appearance.

The girl neither speaks nor moves. She stands like a coldly morbid statue, with one arm jutting toward the wall of the corridor.

Michael's gaze hesitantly runs along the length of the girl's extended arm, and her pointing finger. Is she indicating the unused phone jack on the wall? Michael turns back to face her but before him there now stretches only darkness.

He lingers in the vacated hallway before finally crouching down to investigate the phone jack. It is set into the moulding, which Michael's grandmother always keeps clean and waxed. Michael clasps the jack's white plastic covering and tugs at it. It pops loose.

Within it Michael discovers a pair of keys. One of them is larger than the other and has the words 'Tuff Lock' engraved on its head. The smaller key is unmarked.

A creak of wood somewhere inside the house acts as a warning to Michael. He hurriedly recovers the jack and slips back to his room where he lies in thought until the sun at last burns away the shadows.

Only after he hears his grandfather fire up his old pickup and drive off—Is he going back to his secret redbrick vault at the gravel pits?—does Michael leave his room.

His grandmother is sitting on the living room sofa.

She seems smaller somehow, almost deflated.

"Morning," Michael says, testing her mood.

"Good morning, dear," she replies. Her tone is distant, a swirl of unfocused words.

"Where's grandpa?"

She stands. "He had some chores to do. Are you hungry?" She advances to the kitchen without waiting for Michael's response.

"You all right, grandma?"

She forces a chortle. "I'm fine, Mikey, just fine. Your grandpa just seemed a little out of sorts this morning and I guess I'm a bit worried about him, that's all."

Michael feels his face flush. "What's the matter with him?"

"He didn't sleep well." She seems to be attempting to drown out her own voice by clattering pans and beating eggs in a chrome bowl. "Your grandpa has bad dreams sometimes, and when he does he wakes up very cranky and fidgety."

"Oh."

When they sit down to eat, Michael wrestles to find what he hopes is a clever method of interrogation. He needs so badly to know...

"Does grandpa ever talk about what his bad dreams are about?"

"No."

"Do you ever have bad dreams?"

"Almost never, dear. I think the last time was a couple years ago when there was some bad business here in the village."

"What happened?"

"A girl went missing." She speaks the words more into her coffee cup than to Michael, but even muffled they stun him.

"Missing?"

His grandmother nods. "She was one of the summer people, came up here with her family. I'd see her walking to and from the beach almost every day by herself. Then one day she went down to swim but never came back. Must have drowned, poor thing. They dragged the lake but she was never found. A terrible event. Felt so bad for her mother and father. That's why your grandfather and I never let you go to the beach unsupervised."

"Do you remember what she looked like?"

She shrugs. "Thirteen-years-old or so. Blonde hair, I recall that much."

Michael excuses himself from the table. His jimmying open of the phone jack is masked by the noises of his grandmother washing the breakfast dishes.

"Think I'll go for a ride," he tells her.

"Be careful, dear. Have fun."

Throughout his race to the gravel pits Michael senses that the village is somehow made out of eyes. He passes no one, but is terrified by the prospect of encountering his grandfather at the pits.

The area is equally abandoned. The cavern of redbrick sits snugly locked, illuminated by a hot dappling of sunlight. He enters the breach in the fence and fishes out the pair of keys from his pocket.

He marries the one labelled Tuff Lock with the padlock that bears the same engraving. The lock gives easily. The clunking noise startles a crow from its nest. Michael cries out at the bird's sudden cawing, wing-flapping reprimand. He quickly looks about, terrified of being caught.

The gravel mounds are as ancient hills, silent and patient and indifferent to all human activity. Michael removes the padlock and struggles to raise the corrugated door. It rattles up its track, revealing the cluttered darkness.

Like an ember, the orange light of the freezer gleams from the back of the shed.

Michael feels about for a light switch but finds none.

With great care he makes his way to the light. He is like a solider crossing a minefield. Every motorized tool, every stack of bagged soil, is a danger.

He reaches the freezer. Its surface is gritty with dust.

He sees the metal clamp that holds its lid shut. It is secured with another padlock. Before he's fully realized what he is doing, Michael inserts the smaller key and frees the open padlock from its loop. He can hear the freezer buzzing and he wonders if he is truly ready to see what it contains.

'You've gone this far,' he tells himself. He pulls the lid up from the frame.

Frost funnels upward, riding on the gust of manufactured arctic air. Like ghosts, the cold smoke flies and vanishes.

A bundled canvas tarp reposes within the freezer's bunk. Its folds are peppered with ice, its drab earthy brownness in sharp contrast to the white banks of frost that have accumulated on the old freezer's walls. The tarp is secured with butcher's twine, which Michael cannot break, so instead he wriggles one of the canvas flaps until his aching fingers can do no more.

But what he has done is enough. Through the small part in the bundle the whitish, lidless eye stares back at him, like a waxing moon orbiting in the microcosmic blackness of the canvas shroud.

Michael whimpers. All manner of emotion assails him at once, rendering him wordless.

A shadow steps in front of the open shed door.

Michael spins around, allowing the freezer lid to slam down. His grandfather has caught him. Michael sees his future as one encased in stifling ice.

But the figure in the doorway is too slight to be his grandfather.

Michael then sees the ghost-eyes staring at him from the dim face. A face that is brightened by rows of teeth as the girl grins. She bolts off into the woods.

"Wait!" Michael cries. He stumbles across the littered shed, but by the time he reaches the gravel pits she has gone.

What do I do? Michael keeps thinking as he locks both freezer and shed. He needs help.

His confusion blurs the ride back to his grandmother.

It also makes him doubt what he sees once the house comes into view. His grandfather's pickup is once more in the driveway. Beyond it the entire house is engulfed in flames. Neighbours are rushing about the property, seemingly helpless. Michael speeds up to the lawn, jumps off his bike and attempts to run through the front door.

A man stops him. "No, son! We've called the fire department.

Stay back, stay back!"

Ushered to the edge of his grandparents' property, Michael can see the window of their bedroom. The lace curtain is being eaten by fire, allowing him a heat-weepy view of the figures that are lying on the twin beds inside.

He sees his grandmother, who appears to be bound to her bed with ropes. Next to her, Michael's grandfather lies unbound, a willing sacrifice. The large can of gasoline stands on the floor between them. The pane shatters from the heat.

Michael feels his gaze being tugged to the trees at the end of the yard, where some kind of animal is skittering up the limbs with ease.

In the distance, sirens wail their lament.

Tending the Mists

UNI'S FIRST THOUGHT after she had turned off the main road and begun negotiating the thin lane of sand was that the village of Isted likely housed more stories than could ever be conveyed. This inkling was born out of the fact that, to Muni's eye, Isted appeared to have grown out of the wilderness that surrounded it. The long-neglected houses huddled among the old growth poplars as though they were kin to them, the stationary watermill could have been part of the glacial rock formation that served as its base. Even the narrow walkways that wended between the few buildings nearest to the beach were populated by copses and shrubbery and fauna (three hares frolicked on the steps of the former bank).

Zelia, in contrast, seemed wholly unfazed by the incongruities of their surroundings, by its air of long-standing abandonment. She sat in the passenger seat, her hands resting neatly upon the book in her lap. Muni felt her gaze being pulled, almost magnetically, to the affliction that marred her sister's left hand. Shame moved through her like a furnace blast.

"Where are we supposed to park in this place?" Muni asked. She hunched over the steering wheel and slowed the vehicle to a timid, tedious pace.

Zelia pointed ahead with her good hand. "The other guests are just using that path there as a lot," she said.

Once the car had stopped Muni remarked, "How on Earth did Lucy ever find this place?"

"I helped her," replied Zelia.

"Well how did *you* find it?" Muni asked. She was so intent on hearing her sister's answer that she exited the vehicle without grabbing her purse.

Zelia had collected it for her. She handed off the bag before mutely walking past the row of stationary vehicles. Muni noted with surprise the variety of provinces represented by the license plates.

The lanes were all that distinguished Isted from the nameless un-tampered wilderness from which the village had been hewn. These lanes were few and narrow; scarcely more than footpaths. To Muni they were as dead riverbeds whose course was still detectable: wending down the sloping hill that leads to the sea.

Ordinarily the sight of a beach brought Muni feelings of plac-idness, even a sense of rejuvenation. But this particular scene left her feeling cold, bloodless. The water mirrored perfectly the pallor of the overcast sky and there were no seabirds or greenery to be seen. The current worked the water into an ivory lather as the waves crashed against the rocks that lined the shore.

Muni's gaze pressed further, out across the cold dishpan-drab water, out to where the pale thing squatted.

The island was small, so slight that it looked to stretch mere inches from one end to the other. It was more akin to an iceberg, but not only because of its size. Like the beach, the island appeared bar-ren. Its colour was singular: the harsh white of sun-bleached bone. Its form was tapered, rising up from the water and culminating in a stout flat top. It reminded Muni of the Mayan ruins she had seen many years ago in Mexico.

"See the steps?"

The sound of Zelia's voice made her flinch. Her sister was point-ing past her, toward the edifice that looked less like a structure and more like some meticulous outgrowth of the land itself. Muni was put off by the fact that Zelia was pointing with her unpleasant hand. She did her best to look beyond it, out to the island which now struck her as a sort of microenvironment, a site that sat within a larger habitat but was not part of it. It was, she thought...isolate. Though it was seemingly bereft of life, it was not of movement.

At her sister's mention, Muni could now see the faint suggestion of steps carved into the chalk-like rock. She could not say whether they were actual steps or just a natural anomaly, nor could she guess whether they were designed to sublimate a climber or lead them downwards. It was a truncated pyramid whose stairs seemed to lead nowhere.

A pillow of fog swayed lazily over the seam where island and sea intersected. The whitish tufts blurred the boundary between the two.

There then came a sound; a murmur of voices.

"There are the others."

This voice was much clearer and closer. She turned her head to
see Zelia walking away, down the narrow path and toward the crowd
of welcoming strangers.

The building before which the tiny throng had gathered bore a
faded sign that simply read 'Inn.' Muni pressed politely past a few
people in order to join her sister.

Zelia was already engaged in conversation with what appeared
to be old friends, or was introducing herself to new ones. To Muni
the crowd was a swarm of unknown faces. She waited patiently to be
introduced but Zelia did not do the honours and no hands were vol-
unteered for her to shake. Muni did not truly absorb the fact that all
the strangers were female until after they began to disperse. Many
of them slipped through the Inn's open entranceway. A few made
their way along the various paths that snaked this way or that.

"Who were those people?" Muni asked once she was relatively
sure they were out of earshot of the others.

"Guests," was her reply.

"We should get settled," Zelia advised.

"Settled?" cried Muni. "What do you mean?"

"I mean settled in our room at the inn."

"What about the wedding?"

Zelia began to speak but paused as if thinking of a different
response. "We have to wait for the ferry," she said. "The next one
doesn't come to mainland until tomorrow morning."

"Tell me you're joking."

Her stony expression conveyed her earnestness.

"We have no luggage!" Muni cried.

"It's fine."

"I don't even have a toothbrush! And my outfit! It's for the wedding! What am I supposed to do, sleep in it and then show up tomorrow unwashed and in a rumpled dress?"

"I said that it's fine." Zelia's tone was almost mockingly calm.
"Let's go get settled in our room."

Muni remained on the path, enfeebled by rage. She watched her
sister glide through the inn's open doorway. She half-expected her
sister to gesture for her, or at the very least offer her a backward
glance, but Zelia had already allowed herself to become subsumed
in the circle of chattering women.

Finally she turned on her heel and began to march back toward

their car. Though this was hardly the first time she had ever defied
her older sister (even if that seniority amounted to just thirteen
minutes in the delivery room), Muni couldn't recall a time she'd
been so furious, so bent on retribution.

She would not abandon Zelia to the strangers of Isted, but she
would not join her either. Not now. If she was to be marooned here
for the night, she would at least get some necessities from the nearest town. This would allow her time to cool down and hopefully
instill worry and remorse in Zelia during her absence.

Her reach into her purse brought on anxiety, then a boiling hatred.

The keys were not there. An impression of Zelia handling her
purse passed swiftly through Muni's memory. Had Zelia taken the
keys?

She heard laughter coming from behind her and turned to see
another small cluster of strangers emerging from the woods. There
were four of them in total, two elderly, one barely in her teens, and
one who looked to be about Muni's own age. They were carrying
large baskets. Their laughter and conversation, which was in a language Muni did not speak, ceased when they passed by her.

Muni stood by the vehicle and watched the women as they
strolled back to the inn. Reluctantly, resignedly, she then followed
the same path.

She stepped through the open door and into a cramped lobby.
She scanned the cluster of foreign faces in search of her sister's.

Zelia was standing at the far end of the lobby, chattering with the
women from the woods. They were showing her various strange-
looking root vegetables that they'd been carting in their baskets.
Muni wove her way through the crowd.

"I'm sorry, I'm sorry!" Zelia gushed. Muni hadn't even had a
chance to confront her. "I slipped the keys into my pocket by mistake," she continued, without producing Muni's key ring. "I got us a
room. Come on, I'll show it to you." Zelia excused herself from the
circle without bothering to introduce Muni.

Muni followed her sister up the spiral staircase. The upper corridor was bustling as various women milled about, moving in and
out of the opened doorways. The room to which Muni was led reminded her of a college dormitory. It was stuffy. One folding cot was
leaning against one wall while another was opened and blanketed.
A table with a metal water pitcher stood on the opposite wall. A
hurricane lamp sat on a second table along with a box of matches.
There were no other furnishings. Zelia had apparently already set-

tled in, for her purse and her book (which was lying face down) were both set upon the open cot.

"I can't believe you're making us spend the night here."

"I'm not making us do anything."

"Don't we have to register?" Muni asked.

"With who?" answered Zelia.

Muni advanced to the window. Their room had a view of the lake and of the island that reposed within it.

The mists were stretching. The mists were pressing nearer to the mainland.

"We're going to start preparing supper in the kitchen," Zelia said. She was already standing in the corridor. "I'm sure the ladies could use your help peeling some of the vegetables."

In the time it took for Muni to formulate a sharp reply, her sister had fled. Turning back to the window, Muni watched a few of the younger girls from the wedding party as they milled about the tiny paths, weaving between the buildings, setting items down here and there.

The inn's lobby was all but vacated when Muni made her way down the creaking spiral steps. The air was redolent with spices. Through the opened doors of a dining hall Muni could see several women arranging place settings and removing dust covers from tall stacks of chairs. Beyond this hall, in a room still hidden behind closed doors, there were voices and the telltale noises of kitchen work.

Outside the inn the first chilly breezes were blowing in off the water. Muni undertook a directionless stroll. She believed that she needed time to think but after a few moments came to realize that she was thinking of almost nothing at all.

She eyed the handful of buildings and was struck by how they were more akin to facades or incomplete set-pieces rather than actual structures. But it was not artifice that lent the houses and the little places of business this air, rather it was time itself. They had eroded into ghosts of themselves.

When a teenage girl appeared from behind the stairs of what had once been the town's post office, Muni yelped with surprise. The girl walked briskly on a diagonal course. Muni watched her slip into the inn.

Muni resumed walking toward the beach. A second cluster of women passed by her before she finally reached the shore. This second group was at least visibly friendlier than the others she had encountered this afternoon, for all four of them offered Muni warm smiles and nods as they passed.

The beach was a thin band of stones, many of which were haired with seaweed. She was nearer to the white island. Ironically, frustratingly, it was even less visible than it had been earlier, for now the fog bank that padded it had thickened as the day was winding down, more than thickened; it had begun to rise, ascending to occult the details of the carven steps. The bank had also pressed much closer to the mainland. Its lace-pale edge was now just a few yards from the shore.

Out there, just above the fringe of the mist, something stood upright. Muni placed her hands on either side of her face. She squinted her eyes. A tree? Is that what poked up from the top of that stepped pyramid? If tree it was, it was one long dead. It was a forked limb; two branches jutted up from the trunk like a pair of ruddy horns. Had this object been there earlier today or had it just been placed there, Muni wondered?

She began edging her way to the water in the hope of gaining a better vantage point.

Her foot met with something firm, something that was also half-hidden by the fog.

A downward glance revealed a slab of angled darkness. Muni wondered if the top layer of the pyramid had somehow become dislodged and had floated across the lake.

It was a raft, one held in place by several iron spikes which had been driven into the shore. The raft's shape, combined with its faint overlay of eager mist, gave the impression of a marriage bed dressed in fine white sheets.

Muni heard arrhythmic clunking noises, faint as paws on cobblestone. She had to crouch to confirm that the source of the sound was the variety of dolls that had been attached to the raft by rope, by nails. The raft entire was wreathed in effigies. Each poppet, though wildly different in terms of aspect, appeared to have been carved from the same warty root matter. Flowers had also been tacked to the waterlogged boards; flares of colour to combat the oppressive drabness of old wood, fog, and a dimming sky.

She wondered if this raft was going to be used in tomorrow's wedding ceremony, and if so, in what manner? Muni was then struck by just how little she really knew her cousin Lucy. She had, after all, never even met her fiancé.

Zelia was waiting for her when Muni re-entered the inn.

"They're about to dish up dinner," she explained. "And Lucy is inside. Raj is with her if you'd like to meet him."

The dining room was furnished with two banquet tables, very rustic and very long. Metal folding chairs had been tucked underneath them. Everyone sat where they pleased. Muni felt a wave of relief when Zelia took the chair beside hers before remembering that she was still angry with her. Lucy was seated at the head of the opposite table. Raj was across from her. His face was kindly and, Muni thought, unusually handsome.

Each guest was served a uniform entrée: an oblong slab of some form of root vegetable bake and a slice of homemade bread. Muni found the bake to be too heavily seasoned with anise but the bread quite good. Tin cups brimming with mulled wine were presumptuously set before each diner. The drink smelled heady and sour, yet even the youngest girls were imbibing.

One such girl was demonstrably interested in getting Muni's attention. She was a plain-faced child whose hair was very long and in dire need of brushing. After draining her tin cup of wine the girl made her way down the table.

"Well hello there, little one," Zelia said warmly. She leaned in close enough to make the girl giggle. "Are you excited about the wedding?"

The girl nodded, then, with a child's brazenness, she reached a dirty finger toward the very noticeable scar that afflicted Zelia's left hand. The girl poked the waxy tissue more than once.

"Would you like to know how I got that scar?" asked Zelia. Though the question was directed at the girl, her eyes were fixed on Muni.

Muni mouthed the word 'don't.'

Zelia's lips hitched into a hybrid of a smile and a smirk.

"You see that lady there?" she began. The girl nodded. "Well, she is my twin sister. Do you know what that means?" The girl gave another affirmative sign. "Good. Now, this scar you're looking at, it wasn't there when I was born. Can you guess what *was* there?" This time the girl shook her head.

"Zelia, stop," Muni protested, "I'm serious."

"I have, or rather I *had*," spat Zelia, "what doctors call hyperdactyly. That means I was born with six fingers on my left hand. See how my sister is wearing white gloves, even though it's summertime? That's because she only has *four* fingers on her left hand..."

The girl's eyes widened. "You're frightening her," said Muni.

"You can't tell because my sister hides this fact. She wears gloves and stuffs tissue into the empty finger sleeve. Now, when we were still little girls we had a very stern father. A downright *nasty* father actually. He insisted that my sister and I become 'corrected.' Well, little Muni here was so thrilled about being able to have a normal hand that she couldn't wait to get a transplant. My father and my sister had a doctor steal my finger and try to sew it on to her hand. But it didn't work. In a few days it turned all black and had to come right off..."

The little girl had gone running back to her caregiver but Zelia hadn't noticed. She was now relaying the taboo history for Muni's torture. She was staring stone-faced at her sister who was now on the verge of tears.

"Why?" was the lone word Muni could manage.

Zelia raised her afflicted hand and then ran the scarred heel down her own cheek like some twisted gesture of seduction.

Muni rose and exited the dining hall. Having no desire to return to the beach, she opted instead to climb the groaning steps and hide inside her room. At least there she might find some semblance of privacy.

She closed the door, or tried to at least, but realizing that the locking handle was hanging uselessly from its joint only compounded Muni's sense of impotent fury. She grabbed her sister's purse and used it as a makeshift doorstop. The room now nominally secured, Muni sat down on the open cot and tried to collect herself. She wanted very much to leave. Perhaps she could speak to Lucy, tell her some fabrication about being sick and needing to get back to the city.

Struck by inspiration, she began to search Zelia's purse in search of her car keys. They were not there. She deflated further still. Somehow she knew that pleading with her sister to take her even as far as town to get away from here would be poorly met. Perhaps this protracted wedding was something she was simply fated to endure.

Night was beginning to fall; a fact that brought Muni a strange sense of relief. It meant that she was that much closer to the ceremony and therefore that much closer to leaving Isted. The voices and laughter from the dining room below suggested that it was going to be a very late night for many of the revelers. But there was no law that said Muni would have to join them. She needed to be alone tonight.

She fiddled with the hurricane lamp's turnkey and glass shield. Finally she had the room bathed in a cozy glow.

It was now only a matter of occupying her mind until she felt sleepy. She toyed momentarily with the idea of taking another walk but the darkness and the unfamiliarity of the outer woods caused her to dismiss the idea. She looked to the coffee table book that Zelia had left face-down on the mattress.

Muni removed her shoes, positioned the pillows and arranged herself in a comfortable reading position before she'd even glanced at the title: Echoes in Stone: Haunted Houses & Ghost Towns of the Maritimes. The book had no dust-jacket. Its earnest cover of white typeface on black cloth reminded Muni of the dry academic works she'd been forced to plod through while earning her Bachelor's Degree. But a quick fanning of the slick pages ended this similarity, for Echoes in Stone was heavily illustrated with black-and-white photographs.

Books have a way of betraying their most cherished passages. In this case, the sewn binding had been particularly worn out from repeated readings. Muni scarcely had to open the book before it fell open to the chapter on Isted.

The first detail to leap up at Muni from the page was the sepia-toned photograph of what the author called 'the high street.' The very inn where she was lying was plainly visible. For an instant Muni was claimed by the fantastic and absurd thought that if she peered into the photograph of the inn's window with sufficient focus she would be able to spot herself upon the folding cot. A stifling cold passed through her.

The next detail about the book was the amount of attention her sister had lavished upon it, for not only had this chapter been read enough times to hurt the binding, its pages were festooned with notes. Zelia's frantic handwriting covered the margins and even tattooed the photographs of the half-ruined houses...and of the island. Muni tried to decipher her sister's notes, but they were incomprehensible to her, not because of poor penmanship. Were these words even English, she wondered?

She turned instead to the actual text:

On 5th June, 1859, Admiral Tiberius Baker sought refuge for himself and the crew of his ship the Queen Victoria in the seaside village of Isted. They had been on manoeuvres for several weeks when a bout of fever forced them to come ashore. Baker's journal, which was secreted in the captain's cabin on board the Queen Victoria, describes in horrific detail a variety of travesties which the captain claimed to have witnessed seeing being committed by the members of this isolated village. Tales of murder, cannibalism, and other grisly and sensational events shocked and fascinated the readers of English newspapers once the Queen Victoria was rescued at sea. Baker had apparently committed suicide while on board the ship after hastily departing Isted without any of his crew. His diary was later discovered and excerpts were published in the tabloid journals of the day.

According to Baker, his crew was initially welcomed warmly by the villagers of the remote agrarian and fishing community. They were, he wrote, 'a deeply religious people' but the specifics of their faith were alien to Baker's own sensibilities.

He and his mates convalesced in Isted for a fortnight, during which the captain made laudatory notes about their hosts.

But his entry dated 21st June displays a radical shift in tone. His warm, effusive entries begin giving way to terse points of suspicion, even paranoia. He begins to question

A sudden noise from the dining hall below caused Muni to jolt, to gasp. She had grown used to the murmur of women's voices. But this last sound shot above the din. It was the sound of a man screaming.

Or had it been? Right now the dining hall was a cacophony of chairs being dragged along the wood floor. Perhaps what had startled her had been nothing more than a heavy furnishing being moved.

She sat up, noting with unease that the choir of conversing voices was now silent.

A floorboard popped. Feet scuffled. There was the thumping of a child's feet running through the main hall.

Muni rose and tiptoed to the door. Though frightened, she was also ashamedly rather titillated by this experience. Until she heard the voices outside her window.

She crouched down and did her best to spy without being spied herself. The glare from the hurricane lamp made it difficult to see into the night. Muni extinguished the light and looked out once more.

It was a parade of plain white dresses moving along the darkened path. The figures were also veiled in the same pale fabric, reducing them to amorphous spectres animated by some unfathomable need. The women passed along like a great albino snake. Muni was quite sure she could hear them singing. They were moving toward the shore.

Muni rushed to the exit and kicked Zelia's purse to one side. She pulled the door back with great caution and care. She pressed her ear toward the darkened landing and she listened, listened.

The inn was silent. Lowering her head, Muni could see that both the main entrance and the doors of the dining hall were ajar. She made her way out into the upper landing, down the spiral staircase, and out into the mist-plumped night.

She regretted not putting on her shoes the moment she stepped outside. She considered ducking back inside to get them but the inn had suddenly assumed an ominous air. Muni could think of nothing worse than being alone in there.

There were fires on the beach.

Not wishing to be spotted, Muni stepped off the path and began to cut through the woods. The uneven terrain was made doubly treacherous by the blanket of fog. Muni winced and cursed every time she passed over something sharp, something cold and wet, something blunt.

She did not need to reach the shore in order to see. Her being on the high ground gave her a good vantage of the awfulness.

The women had moved into the water. They had formed an almost perfect rectangle within that bedding of fog. The bonfires glowed like the primal light of nascent worlds, of new and horrible terrains being scorched into being.

There were also noises of primacy: the churn of parting water, shrill caterwauling like the calls of hell-birds. There were masculine bellows, first for help, then to vent physical agony. These later cries froze Muni's blood and raised tears.

The singing continued; that awful razors-on-glass wail. And along with it came the deep churn of the lake being disturbed.

When the singing turned to elated screams Muni's eyes knew to focus on the great shape that had rendered the veiled women feral.

It was a mammoth stag. Its antlers seemed as large as a pair of dead trees that wore the fog like yuletide snow. The beast was fighting heroically to not only press against the water but also against the earthly pull that was trying to drag it back onto all fours. It was marching on its hind legs. Its forelegs were like ropes of muscle. The buck's unnatural posture also afforded a flame-lit view of its phallus, which was stimulated, swollen.

Raj was splayed upon the raft. Muni could now see that several of the women's white veils were stained red.

She turned. She ran wildly. She screamed, screamed.

The only thought Muni could keep in her mind was to get back to the room, to search Zelia's purse for the car keys. She could escape if she could just keep running.

Her leg connected with something in the fog, something hard enough to snap the bone. The pain was bright and searing, yet Muni experienced only a second of it before she fell forward and her skull smacked against a boulder.

The room she awoke in was warm and punishingly bright.

Turning her aching head to one side, Muni was stunned to see Zelia's purse lying on the floor by the open door to her room. The second cot was still folded up against the wall. The matchstick she'd used to light the hurricane lamp was lying curled and blackened upon the un-swept floor.

In her grogginess Muni thought, prayed, that perhaps the memories were but a nightmare, but the nauseating pain in leg flared and reminded her of her flight and her fall.

"Hello?" she croaked. Had the monstrous women actually deigned to rescue her?

The spiral staircase beyond the door began to groan. Muni held her breath as the heavy footfalls grew louder. Muni bit her fist.

The man who entered the room was rugged-looking.

"How..." was the sole word Muni managed to utter before her voice escaped her completely.

The man crossed the room. Then, without comment, he picked her up out of the bed.

Muni struggled to resist, but neither her questions nor her swats broke the man's stoic march down the stairs. He carried her into the dining hall like a groom crossing the threshold.

The hall was once more filled to capacity. There were numerous conversations in languages Muni could not understand. The smell of cooking made her sick. She surveyed the room and all the guests fell silent. Today, in the hot still afternoon, the hall was filled with males, from fresh-faced boys to crooked geriatrics.

They looked at her and then began to rise en masse.

Outside the sun shone down, heartless to Muni's predicament. She screamed and struggled, but her injuries left her hobbled. She screamed her sister's name.

The raft had been scrubbed clean and adorned with fresh poppet figures and flowers.

Two men lashed her down while the rest began to sing. Their song was sonorous and ugly, like earth tremors, like encroaching thunder.

Despite the sun, the mist rushed forward from the island with dizzying speed. By now Muni was hoarse and could only whimper as she heard the telltale splashing of an approaching figure.

She shut her eyes to avoid seeing that awful stag again.

The beach turned quiet. Still, Muni refused to open her eyes.

For several minutes the only sound was a symphony of faint scraping noises. She squinted one eye open. The men were dragging their blades against whetstones.

A figure then glided into her periphery.

'Mother Mary...' Muni thought, for the feminine shape conveyed the same grace and maternal energy. She was tall and veiled in endless layers of mist which hung from her like a nun's habit. Muni lifted her aching head to follow the shape as it moved to one side.

The sparse island was plainly visible in the distance. Muni noted that the steps were no longer capped by a forked tree. In its stead there sat a vast black cauldron. Its brew sent fresh mists into the afternoon.

"Help me, sister," Muni pleaded.

The figure raised her arm. Muni waited for some kind of blessing, until she was able to look closely at the hand.

The sixth finger was once more intact. The figure then gestured for her acolytes to do what must be done.

Fume

THE YEARLY RITUAL commenced in its customary fashion: Clark awoke shortly after dawn, prepared himself a pot of coffee from which he poured a generous cup, and took up his post on the front porch of his smallish wooden frame house.

He nestled into the nylon folding chair, sipped from his mug, and stared contently at the gravel road that edged his front lawn. The road was vacant now, but shortly the caravan would begin; the glorious exodus of the summer people. The hamlet of Beech Point invariably swelled every year, usually around Victoria Day, as city folk sought refuge from the urban blight that held them. Clark, by contrast, was a year-rounder, one of Beech Point's permanent fixtures. It had been this way for the past twenty-two years. Prior to this, he had himself been one of the summer people, those who breached the hamlet for a day or a week during the fair weather in order to swim in its waters, repose on its beach, rest in its campgrounds or rent one of its few cottages. But that was all a very long time ago and Clark preferred his current position as one who kept Beech Point exactly as he liked it.

The first cup of coffee had sufficiently revived him, so Clark allowed himself to be indulgent for the refill; stiffening the java with a shot from the metal flask he kept secreted in the leg pocket of his cargo trousers. He swirled the mug a few times and then drank, savouring the sting of the first of the day. 'Corrected coffee' was how he referred to it. He never could understand why the neighbours reacted negatively whenever he'd offered to correct their cup during the various morning encounters he'd had with them over the years. A few of the locals had reacted so priggishly that Clark had to remind them that it was perfectly legal. If there was one thing Clark knew it was law and order.

The slow parade began sometime between Clark's second and third corrected coffee. The warmth he felt in his belly was soon mimicked by his heart as he watched the foreigners' cars gliding past his home and toward the highway. He waved at one or two of them. A Rove Ranger carted off a family of three. The young girl in the back seat was sobbing, her wailing muted by window glass and distance. Clark watched her clinging to a beach toy (a red inflatable dolphin) as if doing so might enable her to cleave to summer, to her vacation that was being inexorably left behind. She glanced at Clark, who couldn't resist waving bye-bye with one hand while using the other to toast her with his mug. He saw her frame begin to shake more wildly. He polished off his drink with great relish and began to whistle an improvised tune.

The exodus stretched into the afternoon. Clark had traded his mug for a blue plastic tumbler, and the coffee for a mere finger of cola. He made it a habit of keeping a mental roster of the summer people in order to keep track of any stragglers that lingered beyond Labour Day. This list included few names, save for those who'd happened to bother Clark during his morning reposes or his pre-dinner constitutional around the main loop. In truth these were nearer to reconnaissance missions than strolls, at least in Clark's mind, for they gave him the opportunity to inform cottagers about the by-laws concerning bonfires, or campers about music and raucous laughter after dusk. If he happened upon litter or dog feces, Clark had no compunction about knocking on the front door of one of the rental cottages and handing the waste to whomever answered it. Who were they to argue or resist? This was his home, not theirs.

The last car to leave held the two women who'd occupied the yellow hilltop cottage since the first of July. They were not old enough to be retired like Clark was, so he came to deduce that they must be school teachers. And very likely lesbians, though not the style he liked.

Clark's gurgling stomach informed him that dinnertime was not far off. He rose cautiously from his chair and reached for the heavy oak walking stick that he always brandished during his daily march.

Twenty-two cottages in total lined the main loop of Beech Point. Of these, only nine were owned by year-rounders. There were other permanent residents, but they either owned chic houses out on the bluffs or on the waterfront, or they were dwellers of the double-wide trailers that filled the trailer park at the village entrance. Clark didn't really count either class, for they never deigned to mix with him. So he carved off the edges of Beech Point like the stale heels of a loaf of bread. He kept the middle for himself.

His inspection of the rentals was as displeasing as it had been in previous years. This tenant had left too many trash bags by the roadside; that one hadn't closed all the window shutters properly; yet another hadn't bothered to give the lawn a final mowing.

Good riddance to them all.

Having compiled a mental list of which indiscretions needed to be reported to which landlord, Clark wended his way back toward home. The shadows were beginning to dim the western bluffs; to creep down from the tree limbs like swiftly spun cocoons. Stomach pains reminded Clark that he had been deprived of solids for too long. His head was also beginning to ache. He fished out the small bottle of aspirin from one of the pockets of his cargos but was disgusted to find it empty. He clutched his walking stick by its middle and began to clear the bend in the road in a series of wide, angry strides.

What he spotted in the gulley that fed off the main loop created an internal conflict. Clark found himself having to gauge what was more important to him, his physical needs or his duty to the village. A crude (and illegal) access had been forged through the brush that distinguished the Beech Point Campgrounds from the road. Bushes were rendered crêpe-flat, tree boughs snapped, soil bored into. It was as if a vast slug had erupted from the soil and surged wantonly for the main road.

Clark would have almost preferred some form of mutation to the ugly reality, as clearly this destruction was by human hands, for mixed in with the snapped branches and trampled plants was an unpardonable amount of trash: liquor and beer bottles, foil bags made greasy from the potato chips they'd contained, soda cans, candy wrappers, apple cores, peach pits.

Like a trail of criminal evidence, this band of waste and damage led down into the ravine to where a small (and illegal) camp had been erected. There was a crude fire pit and a length of twine stretched between two beeches. Clark wondered if it had been used as a clothesline, or perhaps for hanging small game. A half-shelter tent squatted a few feet from the fire pit.

He stepped off the main loop and advanced toward the camp, calling out "Hey!" He had just cause in reprimanding whoever was responsible. County bylaws stated clearly that overnight camping was restricted to designated sites, and fires were strictly prohibited.

Though sight had been the first of Clark's senses to be assaulted by this indiscretion, as he padded toward the tent his nostrils were brutalized by a potent stench that seemed to hang over the camp like a drapery. It was stifling. For a moment Clark feared he would lose what little he had in his stomach. Fortunately battling nausea was a skill set in which he was well versed. He shut his eyes and breathed through his mouth and managed to stave off the bile.

"Hey!" he called again after re-opening his eyes. He tapped the half-shelter with the rubber-tipped end of his walking stick but received no response. Confident that he had every right to investigate further, Clark peeled up the triangular flap that formed the tent's door. He got down on one knee like a suitor and peered inside.

The smell was obviously radiating from inside the half-shelter, for it was so strong here that Clark had to shield his nose with the back of his hand. The tent's interior was surprisingly dark. He squinted to confirm that the wrapped form lying within was that of a sleeping person.

But even in the dimness it was clear that this shape was too still to be slumbering. Clark leaned in, resisting the instinct to inhale through his nostrils. The occupant of the tent was less a figure than a bundle, for it had been swaddled within the same green material that the tent had been cut from. The face was completely covered and the limbs (Clark assumed) were tight against the sides of the body. He could not see twine, pins, or any other means of securing the fabric in place. As far as Clark could tell the bundle was being held by some sophisticated means of folding, as a chef may demonstrate when making some complex pastry.

It could have been the conspiratorial play between the half-shelter's shadows and the sun's late afternoon beams, but Clark thought he could distinguish a pair of breasts swelling up from the chest area. Involuntarily, he licked his lips. He also involuntarily inhaled a waft of the stench, which immediately caused him to scuttle back from the half-shelter and heave the day's libations onto a weedy patch of clay.

The nausea passed swiftly and left clarity of mind in its wake. Clark understood that he had in all likelihood stumbled upon a corpse. Whether the camper had died in their sleep or from foul play had yet to be determined, but all the elements—the secluded site, the swaddled body, the overpowering scent—clearly indicated death. All that was left to do now was confirm his suspicion before making the call to the authorities.

Clark fancied himself as one impervious to fear, a bastion of reason that came from a full and constant understanding of his surroundings. Discovering the body had thrown him momentarily, but now his mastery was restored. He crept back to the half-shelter's mouth and drew back the flap. He noticed how peculiar the material felt, not like nylon at all, or canvas, but more like a great leaf, waxy and almost brittle to the touch. He tugged lightly at it. The flap did not tear.

The reposing body, disappointingly, was not endowed with tantalizing curves as he'd initially thought, for the figure now appeared smooth and genderless, though doubtless this was at least partially due to its verdant shroud.

Bolstering his nerves, he reached inside the tent and attempted to jostle the still form.

The shroud was smouldering. Clark felt as though he had just attempted to scoop out furnace coals with his naked hand. Crying out, he snapped back his hand to assess the burns on his palm.

His flesh was unmarred.

Reaching in again, this time armed with his walking stick, Clark jabbed at the body. It moved with ease, rolling like a papier-mâché construct. He'd been had. This was not a body at all, but a forgery, a joke of which he had been the butt. Fuelled by embarrassment and rage, Clark yanked the swaddled thing from the tent and hurled it clear across the campsite. It landed amidst the shrubs and grasses, which provided it with instant camouflage. But Clark refused to allow the effigy to exist. Its creator, whoever they may be, was mocking his concern, his allegiance to order.

Tramping forcefully toward, Clark felt a rich satisfaction when he raised his boot above the cadaverous bundle. He brought his foot down with power, finality. The shell popped immediately, caving in around Clark's leg.

The fume came rushing out with speed and ferocity. It must have been sealed under extreme pressure inside those folds of delicate flora, for its escape was a concentrated fist of air. Like a furnace blast in both temperature and power, its impact knocked Clark clean off his feet. It also scalded the flesh of his face and legs and arms. Lying dazed and pained after having been burned and flung, Clark stared glassy-eyed at the mass of shimmering hot air that was flailing, twisting, and pulsing above the deflated wrapping that had held it captive. Were these manic flitting motions some kind of elemental victory dance, Clark wondered?

The stench was now omnipresent, though this broad distribution did nothing to weaken it. Every shallow breath Clark stole stained his nostrils with the pungency. But after a few involuntary whiffs he was able to determine that the smell, despite its potency, was not one of rot.

This was not an assault of death and decay, but of Life. Clark could now discern thin but unmistakable traces of jasmine flowers and fresh mint leaves. Also teasing his nose were the scents of new-mown grass, earthy root vegetables nesting in moist black earth, hot milk... even (he believed) the coppery perfume of menstruation. It was like the concert of suggested tastes and aromas that a fine wine affords the trained palate. Its ugliness and brashness was the result only of its sheer concentration, its purity.

He studied the weepy fume. It blistered and stretched the very atmosphere of the campground. In a beat it would stretch to the summit of the poplars that framed it, and then with equal swiftness it would spiral down into a dense little seed of coiled heat.

Only when the fume began to sweep over the campsite toward him did Clark experience dread.

It was directly above him now, hovering like a ghost. Veins that coursed with prismatic light ran through the blob and also defined its edges. Otherwise it was transparent, but wavy and lilting. Its heat was overpowering, burning off the precious oxygen that Clark was now gasping to draw in. Subconsciously he was frantically stockpiling air in order to scream, to give vent to his terror and confusion at the apparition.

But the air refused him. And when Clark next opened his mouth to inhale, it was the fume that took advantage of the gap. It charged down his throat in a rapid gust. He could actually hear the tissues and tendons crinkling into cinders inside him. His chest swelled like a caricature of overabundant pride. The fume snaked down further, baking his stomach, turning his blood and his bile into a bubbling soup.

Clark emitted a low, weak rasp, but not of his own volition. A hush like stirring coals filled his ears.

The trees about him began to spin and in time they went black.

By the time his surroundings faded in without fading out again the trees were obscured by the blue haze of evening. The fever that afflicted him was so aggressive Clark could actually feel the contagion coursing through his body like wildfire. He imagined his innards being blackened and melted in the fever's wake, like old growth trees after a forest blaze. His lungs felt as though they were impacted with embers.

'Gas attack,' was a phrase that raced through Clark's mind end-

lessly, bearing with it a mounting sense of helplessness, hopeless-
ness. Had some maniac left a chemical bomb for a random victim?
Had the world's chaos finally reached Clark's sanctuary?

Each breath was agony, so Clark resolved to cease inhaling in
a desperate attempt at relief. But as he lay on his side, holding his
breath, Clark discovered that his respiration did not cease. The
wilful refusal of oxygen could not silence the desiccated rasping
rhythm from sounding in his ears, could not halt the expansion
and contraction of his blazing lungs. But if this was not air he was
breathing, what was it?

The scent too, that cloyingly dense signal of too much in bloom,
was now a constant. Clark could smell it even when he didn't inhale.

He was beginning to fade and he knew it. He could feel the black
void staining the edges of his mind and the corners of his eyes like
a puddle of spilt ink. Soon that awful night would hold him once
more in its thrall, and Clark feared that this time there might be no
return from it. Help was needed.

He forced himself to sit up; a process that was far more painful
and slow than it ought to have been. Finally he was upright, then
erect. A little while later he was walking.

The climb out of the ravine was the most tedious. The main loop
was easier, but only slightly. Sweat flowed in steady streams and his
legs were constantly threatening to buckle. He passed by the cottages that were now abandoned by the summer people. Never had
he felt more alone.

Finally his cottage came into view. Clark reasoned that since his
home was closer than the next occupied home on the main loop he
could slip inside and phone for an ambulance.

He could just barely work the key into the lock of his front door.
Once inside he made it as far as the living room sofa before becoming utterly inert. The telephone sat in waiting atop the wooden stool
beside the paisley armchair; mere feet from where he was laying,
but to Clark the distance seemed an impassable gulf. Vertigo spun
his psyche like a top and kept him on his back. His eyes involuntarily closed. He tried to cry for help but what escaped his chapped
lips was a feeble peep that was no word at all.

Resisting the fiery illness felt useless, even risible. In fact, Clark
almost started to laugh. But the tingling pulse of imminent sleep
pressed more deeply upon him. He felt his limbs go heavy and dull
while his mind began to lose its cumbersome anxieties. Although he
knew he may never wake again, Clark submitted himself to slumber.

Awaken he did, but slowly, and into a state of sheer delirium. The cottage was dark. The combination of night without and all the curtains drawn for privacy's sake amplified the blackness. Clark reached out to the coffee table as an aid to push himself into a sitting position, but his hand slipped off the tabletop. His palm was soaked. Reaching again, Clark dabbed the table with his fingertips, confirming that its surface was wet. He must have left a half-empty glass on there and had knocked it over in his sleep. He reached with his other hand to use the living room wall for the same brace.

It too was soaked with liquid. The wood panelling felt clammy and soft, like hands that had been clasped too long in anxiety or in prayer.

A droplet of moisture struck Clark's brow and splattered there. It was cold and foul. Listening intently, he could hear the soft patter of other droplets striking the carpeted floor, the living room furniture, even his own body. Stretching his arm back above his head, Clark located the table lamp but could not tell whether it was also soaked or whether the moisture was on his hands already. He switched it on and for a few seconds the disaster that was his living room was made apparent.

Condensation was rushing through the ceiling tiles and down the walls. Clark couldn't believe his horrid luck that a pipe would choose to burst when he was all but immobilized. The beige carpet was several shades darker due to saturation, and the wall paneling looked as though it was already warping and splitting. His favourite armchair was ruined and the stack of war encyclopaedias and crime novels were swollen.

Beads of water fell from the cradled receiver of the black telephone. Clark reached for it uselessly, desperately. The lamp shorted out with a pop, adding a whiff of ozone to the musk of flowers and menstrual blood and mould that permeated every inch of the cottage. Clark lay in the darkness and listened to ruinous rhythm of the water.

The sound must have lulled him, for grogginess permeated his mind when he opened his eyes. It was no longer so impenetrably black inside the room; the murk of sunlight filtered through heavy draperies lent his surroundings a small measure of contrast and shading.

The heat was unbearable, almost asphyxiating. It was as if Clark's fever had externalized itself to infect the very atmosphere. His clothing was soaked, as was the sofa that braced him. The

stench was unquestionably still extant but Clark found it less offensive, likely due to his overexposure to it.

The rasping, clattering, wet rattle of breath continued to sound
inside his skull, even when he refused to breathe. His lungs forced
into stillness did not prevent Clark's chest from rising and falling,
did not halt the rank fume that escaped his throat.

He could see it now, passing from his lips and into the air, rippling like a mirage over sun-cooked asphalt. Veins of phosphorous
colour ran through the fume; spectrums of prismatic light.

He was heating the cottage, Clark reasoned. Or rather the contagion within him was. He felt hollow, like a chalice from which all
wine had been poured. Whatever was filling him now was something foreign, something incorrect and offensive. His head rolled
feebly to one side, and it was then that Clark discovered the growth.

He laughed, even though doing so caused a coughing fit. But
responding aptly to the absurdity of his hallucination was worth
the burning and sharp pain in his throat and lungs. The fume and
the fever had conspired to create the image of a vine right there in
Clark's own living room. He was impressed by the vividness and
verisimilitude, for it was a very organic looking shoot. It jutted out
from a crack in the wall panelling and coiled sunward. Its green was
lush and cool-looking. Tiny pale flowers decorated the stalk here
and there, as fine and as clean as bridal lace.

His arm, which seemed to have no strength left whatsoever, fell
from his side. When his hand struck the floor it was subsumed by
something soft and dewy. Clark grazed his hands across the low
pile carpet, but what he felt against his palm was the gentle bristle
of grass.

The scent was a permanent thing in this new—or perhaps most
old—world. This was the musk of life unbridled, Being and Becoming at once; the orgia of Nature that never knew the raping thrust of
progress nor the blush of the mortal's morality.

The maddening patter of falling moisture was no longer audible.
Instead there was a concert of fainter, more idyllic sounds: the hush
of wind-nudged leaves, the trilling of various birds and something
Clark could not quite identify; something distant but queerly musical. It was not the call of bird or beast, nor was it the intrusion of
human endeavour.

Music, yes. But not of man.

He sat up, but only long enough to note the dense forest that
now filled his cottage. The wan light that illuminated it was not that
of sunlight through curtained windows, but was the glimmer of a

fledgling day attempting to permeate the lush veils of leaf and shrub and old growth trees. Night was dying its protracted but inevitable death and soon dawn would be upon him. Perhaps he could make sense of this in the daylight. Perhaps the rays of the sun would simply burn away this impossible woodland like so much morning fog.

Enfeebled by shock, Clark fell back onto the sofa, which was unyielding and cold and firm, like a headstone. He rolled onto his side, and although he had no explanation for the slab of moss-laden rock that now sat where his living room sofa had been, Clark was unfazed. He was dying, or perhaps was already dead. Had he any belief in the afterlife this would have qualified, but he did not.

He closed his eyes and reclined upon on the flat rock.

The music persisted, its crescendo swelling but its source still sounded incredibly distant.

Now there was additional music, much nearer and every bit as sweet.

Clark opened his lids and confirmed what his brain and his groin had suspected: the sound was the bright giggling of women. They were before him now, five by Clark's estimation. Their ages varied as wildly as their body types, but each one, from young woman to sagging crone, was beautiful and stirred in him the blazing fume of want. They were naked, but their nudity did not clash with the world, which surprised Clark. For him, nudity and arousal had its proper time and its private place, but this was markedly different. Their uncovered flesh was as an expression of this strange place, the canvas upon which the invisible presences expressed themselves.

They were watching Clark giddily, expectantly. He wondered what he was supposed to do.

"Are you Him?" one of the women, the youngest one of about twenty, asked. Clark lifted his hand. Speech eluded him.

"Are you Him?" echoed another.

"Of course He is!" announced the crone. "Look at His feet!"

They advanced and were upon him.

Clark was beside himself, for all he could see and feel was wave after wave of the women's hair, their lips, and their tongues, marking every inch of his body. His bliss was so great it bordered on panic. He wanted to scream, not out of fear or passion, but simply to vent all the paradoxical feelings that were now battling to claim his heart and brain.

In unison the women rose up, still tittering and whispering to one another.

"Come and catch us!" one of them called, and just like that they were fleeing, leaping and racing through the forest.

Clark stood, immediately stumbled and fell to the ground. His vision was murky and the burning in his lungs and head had not subsided. Now his legs felt misshapen and new. He pulled himself upright and tried to follow the women, but he found that the only way he could keep erect was not to walk or run, but bound; to move in great leaps over stones and logs and brush.

The music was nearer now, Clark noticed, the strange piping. He perceived the silhouettes of the women. They were dancing, whirling and lolling in a clearing. Beyond the great ledge there was only sky; vivid and rich in colour, like the prismatic light of Clark's infected breath in the darkness, yet expanded to rival the aurora borealis. It was a new dawn, one apparently endless and ever-renewing.

Half-blind and utterly drained, Clark fell into the clearing. The women laughed uproariously, but there was no malice in their expression.

"Need...help..." Clark wheezed, "...please..."

An especially buxom woman strode forward, plucked something from the bough of a nearby tree, and moved to Clark. She knelt beside him and pressed a waxy, fragrant bulb to his lips.

"Eat," she cooed.

Clark bit down into the unidentifiable fruit. His mouth was instantly filled with a juice so sour it made him heave.

"Stop..." he pleaded. "Make this...all this...stop."

The woman rose, the chewed fruit dripping in one fist. "Are you saying you wish to go back? Back to that dead world?"

"Please..." A roar filled the air, a grating sound, like something enormous being forced into motion.

The light began to fade...no, not fade, but be shut out. A great heavy veil was being drawn across the beautiful dawn. It was as a great gate being shut and bolted.

The darkness was there when Clark sat up upon his carpet. The cottage had restored its customary gloom. He crawled toward the telephone stand and after a few botched attempts managed to dial 911.

His convalescence in hospital took longer than Clark would have liked. The doctors concluded that he was suffering from some aggressive flu virus. He told them nothing of the fume that was swaddled in greenery or of the visions that had plagued him. His physician warned him that some of the negative effects of his illness could be long term. Clark later discovered this to be the case, for food had lost its flavour and drink brought only hangovers and no pleasure.

The sight of women, no matter how attractive, only reminded him of his new and likely permanent impotence.

Upon release from the hospital Clark sought new lodgings in the city.

His apartment was clean and modern. He cleaned his home fanatically, but no matter how diligently he scrubbed and scoured, a stray spider would still manage to spin a fine web here and there, or the dust of inexorable time would find unreachable nooks in which to mass.

These threats to order were both constant and evasive. They crept in as faintly as the distant piping one hears at the shining gates of dawn.

Goatsbride

M ARIETTA CAME TO the Fallows to wait once more for the ghostlights. Although they would manifest for her that day, she had no inkling that this would be the last time she would see them.

Her pilgrimage unfurled under the blaze of mid-afternoon. The ghostlights appeared in their customary manner, boiling up out of the aether itself; tiny splatters of luxuriously coloured light, their centres the purple-black of heart's blood, their edges wreathed in a gaudy gleam of chartreuse. They were suspended in midair like Yuletide baubles hung with spider's skeins.

The uncomfortably cold, soaked earth of the Fallows began to climb up around the holey leather that covered Marietta's feet as she stood stone-still in the field, gazing. Although only her lungs and eyelids were moving, and, even then, scarcely, Marietta nonetheless felt as though she were cart-wheeling forward, spinning through the borderless country inside herself.

After so many visitations, she was well accustomed to such sensations, but thrilled to them all the same. She pressed her eyelids closed, watching the paler suggestions of the ghostlights cascading through the fleshly veils of her eyelids.

She was straining to hear the sound of his leap, or his terrible bellow that had long ago inspired all the local shepherds to usher their flocks elsewhere. (Marietta was, to the best of her knowledge, the only one who still visited the Fallows.)

But these heralds of his arrival did not come.

Opening her eyes, she was puzzled by the grim vacancy of both the field and the woods that framed it.

All at once, the landscape felt altered. Even the ghostlights shifted their pattern. They began to manically twirl and flex.

Then they began to drift, leaving thin trails of putrid fog in their wake.

Marietta followed them to the far end of the field.

The ghostlights seemed to swarm together in order to create a kind of constellation. The atmosphere thickened with a rare new gravity, which pulled Marietta's gaze to a mud patch that stretched drably beneath the brightly churning orbs.

The ground here drooped in a lazy slope; forging a ditch that distinguished the Fallows from the copse that grew dense and wild alongside it.

There, heaped upon the dirt like a flung bale of hay, was a nightmare in flesh and fur. Marietta's senses were so offended by the sight that she reflexively turned away, counting off enough heartbeats to melt the phantasm into nothing more than the twisted boughs that had been made to breathe only by her own imagination.

But when Marietta opened her eyes she realized that her attempt to banish the shape had been in vain.

The leaping one was still lying broken in the mud. The shock of discovery tainted the atmosphere with a numbness as cold and grey as a stone marker.

Talons of sorrow pushed deeply, deeply into Marietta until, punctured, she could only collapse at the side of her great love.

The crooked one's jaws were moving, but no sound escaped his mouth. When Marietta's sobs softened at last, the only noise she could discern was the delicate plash of ichor against stone.

She could but watch as the vital fluid emptied itself from the various wounds that brightened the leathery skin of his trunk, mottled the blackish wool on the wayward contours of his grand legs. Emerging from the tangles of fur was his great livid serpent of muscle, its skin the hue of an overripe plum. Marietta found herself staring at it in a shameful-yet-unbreakable trance. As this snake flexed, the black pit of its eye widened, releasing a reedy sine, a sound not unlike a song. The vivid ichor even spilled from this throbbing hole, mingling with the oh-so-mortal drabness of the earth.

Marietta believed that the thing was beseeching her with its unworldly eyes. Their irises were the blue of a frozen sea; their pupils, vertical slit-like things, cauldron-black and omniscient. A filmy membrane winked across them in rapid sweeps, pushing the grit and sludge to the rim of the reddened sockets.

She wanted so much to question him, to learn what had happened and how. But Marietta knew that, although her lover's plump tongue had many uses, speech was not among them.

Had the others found him? Had they traced him to the great ruddy cave where he slumbered, and then beaten him, cut him with blades, pierced him with arrows?

The grove suddenly dimmed. At first Marietta wondered if time had disappeared (Hours always melted much more swiftly when she was with him), but she realized that the darkening was the result of the ghostlights winking out in tedious succession.

Now their colours existed only in the vital ichor that bled out of the dying god, and seeped into the earth that seemed to be climbing around his gnarled hands and the scuffed lustre of his cloven feet.

New forms began to halo the failing old one: flies that had come not to crown him, but to sup on the outpouring streams of his life-blood. Marietta swatted away as many as she could, but, soon, they were legion. They swarmed in swiftly. After lapping up the vivid ichor, the bugs came away intoxicated. Their flight paths were visibly meandering, their pace logy. Never had they suckled a blood so rarefied.

Marietta traced her hand along the sharply jutting bone structure of his face. Through the filthy moss of his beard, a deep, silent oval of agony widened.

I'll come back, Marietta sent to him. *I'll come back with help or with wine, or a song. I'll come back with something to cure you. They'll come looking for me if I don't get back to the village, but I will come back to you. Please stay with me. Please.*

The girl knew no sleep that night. When, upon sunrise, she returned to the Fallows, she discovered that even the gory remnant of her great love had vanished.

She shirked her chores in order to spend the lion's share of the day scouring the meadows and the dim groves and the shadow-moistened caves. In her pouch she had a small ration of wine and some salt to titillate a waning palate. But he was nowhere to be found.

Even the lurid pond of his blood had been subsumed by the soil.

Marietta lowered herself onto the site of his expiration, too gutted to even weep.

❧

The invasion commenced the very next morning. Great ships appeared, carrying people with ghost-pale flesh and a faith that was alien to these ancient woods.

The imprint-free villages of pitched canvas were razed, as swiftly as fired bullets, as inexorably as the descending blade. What swelled in their stead were structures forged from gutted forests. The ruddy contours of his great organic temple were smothered by chapels of chastity, of symmetry. His sighs and shrieks were bridled by a faith that wrestled to keep all ecstasies infuriatingly aloof until after one's flesh had turned respectably cold.

The Fallows were upturned and transmuted into a golden carpet of wheat. Harvests sprouted and soon after sown as the interlopers put down deeper roots.

Marietta lingered, not for family ties, but to keep vigil in the place that had been his, been theirs.

She earned her keep by carrying out the meagre toils of one of the prominent families in the village. She slept on a cot in the barn and prepared their meals to their unique specifications. She scrubbed the smoothed wood of their floors and washed their dishes of clay. When their stiff clothing looked too lived-in, Marietta mended them with a silver needle and thread.

But, at night, when the austere ones were slumbering, she would bear a lantern back to the former Fallows and would call his name into the darkness.

Did these people even sense the one who had called these rustic hills his own? Had they any hint of the forces that churned beneath their pathways and their churches and their snug homes?

Surely, some among them would ache for it, could they but discover the Source...

Marietta wished and, ultimately, the ghostlights returned...but in a changed state.

In the early harvest of the year, during one of Marietta's rare afternoon visits to her paramour's landmark, she discovered that the ghostlights were now colouring the wheat itself.

It had been a rainy season and the crops that had sprouted were not golden, but whitish and blotchy with a peculiar fungus: blue and green and flecked with a black that made Marietta think of the vault that held the stars; the darkness that had been the nativity of her great love, whose birth had heralded the primal dawn. And now his sovereign blood was flowering once more, chthonic and musty and raw.

The people were so desperate to maintain their comfort that they chanced the possibility of toxicity rather than deny themselves a bountiful table.

They cut the grotesque shoots and ground them. Though the resultant grist was pasty and smelled of unturned roots, they baked it into their loaves, which were devoured with thanksgiving to their Maker. Such were the gifts bestowed to the true.

Fittingly, it was a young woman who first felt the ichor burning within her. She would awaken with strange stories of nocturnal flights through eerie woodlands and of somatic memories of the touch of an inhuman lover.

Marietta would often comfort the daughter, encouraging her to keep such fancies to herself, to rest, and to, of course, eat heartily of the bread and wheat gruel she prepared for the girl daily.

The keepers of the stringent faith soon learned of similar night-rides from other girls in the village. Superstition grew rampant as reports of a great horned form emerging from the woods to hold congress caused great alarm, then persecution, and finally executions.

Twenty girls found death at the end of a rope. Men of reason pleaded with the authorities that the true problem was a blend of superstition, adolescent fancy, and a tainted crop from the previous autumn. *Ergot* was the name some gave it: a strange mould that had infected the girls with sickness, with vivid nightmares.

But by then the ghostlights had ignited the blood of the chaste. This sanguinary pyre heralded the long awaited Return...

The clan who had conspired to put an end to the diabolism was small but among the most fanatical. They went out to the Fallows, now stripped, where the girls had claimed they had seen It.

There they waited, without benefit of fire or food. In a blackness as cold as the deep sea, they waited.

The ghostlights were the first manifestation they witnessed and, even then, with unbelieving eyes.

Then, seized with Panic, they saw the goatish shape as it came bounding from an ugly patch of woods and into the clearing.

Nothing, they thought, could be more ineffable than the awesome bent giant who was now lumbering toward them, reeking of dread-sweat and olde lust.

But, one by one, they glanced upward to see the face of the unclad woman who rode upon the creature's back.

More dreadful than the appearance of the Beast was the face of its Bride. Her aspect: the living emblem of Rapture untamed.

Weaned on Blood

ROTHER BALDEMAR STOOD beneath the quarry-rock wing of a flying buttress, studying the forest that seemed to stretch and deepen with the setting sun. It was his first night within the cloister of the Trappist abbey and he hoped the nagging uneasiness he'd been experiencing since his arrival was nothing more than a passing symptom of his unfamiliarity with his new home. Though he was not expecting to spot one of his fellow monks emerging from the shadowy forest, he was quite puzzled by the degree to which this innocuous sight had managed to unsettle him.

The monk hurried across the open field, his hood drawn up. He stopped at the birdbath, (which was presently vacant as the local swallows and finches were all wisely nested until morning's light) where he scooped up several handfuls of rainwater. He rubbed his hands together vigorously and then shook them dry. The faceless brother then knelt before the large cross with its carven Christ and performed what Baldemar deemed to be a somewhat trifling genuflection.

A deep metallic thunder purged these judgments from Baldemar's mind as the great bell summoned all the brothers to Vespers.

Baldemar spent the bulk of the following day conversing with his fellow monks in between their requisite observances and chores. This particular Trappist abbey may have been new to him, but monastic life was not, and this fact brought a measure of comfort to Baldemar, in fact it nourished him.

Nourished him until sunset.

As to what exactly was impelling him to creep back to the shaded perch of that same cloister, Baldemar was unclear. Some force, which he hoped was purer than mere suspicion or unseemly curiosity, returned him to the outer rim of the property.

There he waited well into the night.

If Baldemar was housing any deep-seated feelings of guilt over being suspicious of his brethren, they were dashed the very moment he saw the same robed figure fleeing again out of the woods and cutting across the yard.

Although once again disguised by his upraised hood, Baldemar's keener study made it obvious that this was a different monk from the previous night. He was noticeably taller and did not have the somewhat distended belly of the original brother. This fact notwithstanding, the monk's actions were identical: the hasty march across the grass, the frantic washing of the hands with rainwater, the cursory genuflecting before the large cross upon which hung Christ in radiant alabaster.

Once this night's mysterious brother had entered the abbey, Baldemar decided to approach the birdbath.

The Vespers bell tolled as if to hurry him. The scene around the basin was quite dim, but there was light enough in the gloaming to illuminate the still-unsettled water. A few faint streaks swirled about the otherwise transparent pool. Baldemar reached out to touch these eel-like contaminants, but stopped himself just short.

With heartfelt need, he looked up to the crucified effigy and crossed himself before rushing off to prayer.

"My plans for the morning?" Baldemar echoed as he passed the wooden bowl of steaming gruel to Brother Jerome, "I thought I'd take a walk through the woods. I've not yet explored the area."

He offered Brother Jerome a long assessing look, hoping for some type of reaction, but none was forthcoming.

"A splendid idea," Jerome returned. "I can show you the nicer paths if you wish."

After breakfast the two men passed through the tended shrubs that distinguished their cloistered grounds from the verdant church of nature. The sun irradiated them, casting the whole scene into something like an etching. They strolled and spoke of matters secular and of matters of the Catechism. Baldemar was charmed by the landscape of his new home.

After a time the two monks found themselves stationed at the nexus of four crossed paths. Baldemar innocently and unthinkingly began down the northerly path. Brother Jerome gripped his elbow with what Baldemar felt was unnecessary force.

"That path gets rather treacherous," said Jerome. "I suggest we take this one here. It's much more pleasant."

Baldemar heeded the wisdom of his brother and onward they went, past moss-contoured stones, imperial oaks, and all manner of scuttling and lively fauna.

"Tell me," Baldemar said as they neared the conclusion of their hike, "do the brothers often use these trails?"

"Oh, yes," Jerome replied. "A picturesque area, is it not?"

"Indeed. As a matter of fact, I've been thinking it might be nice to wander through here after dark. To hear the crickets and see the moon on the trees."

"I must advise against that," replied Jerome. "There have been several coyote attacks in recent months. Those beasts tend to hunt at night. We've had to dispose of more than a few rabbit carcasses on the grounds. You'd be running an unnecessary risk venturing into these woods after sunset."

The leisurely tone of the morning did not stretch into the afternoon, for Baldemar was busy with chores and study. Though he felt duplicitous for doing so, he ventured once more to his cloistered spying space and waited and watched until the Vespers bell rang.

This time when one of his brothers appeared from the woods Baldemar rushed forward to meet them.

The approaching monk did not appear startled. In fact, he nodded and bade Baldemar a good evening as he dipped his stained hands into the basin of rainwater.

"You've cut yourself!" Baldemar declared.

The brother gave him a nonplussed look.

"Aren't you taking a rather sizeable risk by hiking with the coyotes about?" Baldemar continued.

The monk peered intently at Baldemar. "Are you the new arrival by any chance, the brother who has joined us from across the Atlantic?"

Baldemar nodded.

The brother slowly pointed his finger heavenward, where the bells resounded. "We shall be late for Vespers if we don't hurry."

"One moment, please," Baldemar pleaded. "Earlier today Brother Jerome informed me that walking those trails is dangerous after dark because there have been a number of coyote attacks. Yet for the past three evenings I have seen with my own eyes brothers rushing out of the woods at dusk and each of them pause here at this bath to do as you've just done; cleanse their bloodied hands, then genuflect and cross themselves before rushing off to Vespers. Why? What is it that you're all doing in those woods?"

"I suggest you speak to the Abbot, brother," he said. "I'm afraid I would be speaking out of turn."

The knock on his door roused Baldemar. He noted that the sun had yet to fully rise. He hurriedly donned his robe and answered it. Jerome was standing in the corridor.

"I have been given a charge by the Abbot himself," he stated. "I'm to accompany you to the cleft. Please meet me in the courtyard immediately."

"The cleft? Whatever do you—"

Baldemar's inquiries were ignored. Jerome was already rushing down the corridor toward the abbey's main doors. Baldemar prepared himself quickly and raced outside.

There was a chill in the air. His breath appeared in plumes of frost as he approached Brother Jerome. "Will we not miss Lauds?"

"We have the Abbot's permission to forego Lauds today. Come." Jerome began to walk. Baldemar had to rush to keep pace.

They entered the woods. Baldemar spouted many questions but received no responses.

When they came to the crossroads, Jerome marched purposefully down the northerly way. Baldemar reminded him about the trail's unsuitability, but Jerome was impervious. The path coiled further into the woods until at last opening into a small glade.

Baldemar found its atmosphere disheartening: the carpeting of half-mulched leaves from prior autumns, the scattering of whitish boughs, the ominous crevasse that cut wide and deep into the granite floor.

He noticed something resting by the edge of the deep cleft; a tiny bowl that sat next to a small and less identifiable object. Together these two gave the stone slab the appearance of a great rustic table set for a solitary meal.

His advancement toward the stone was halted by Jerome. Baldemar opened his mouth to question when he saw Brother Jerome press a finger to his mouth. There was a low, hushing breeze.

He lowered his hand and used it to silently beckon Baldemar, who followed down to the bowl and the slender, jagged implement lying beside it. Jerome once more signaled for silence, then, with visible caution, or possibly reverence, he lifted the bowl.

That the bowl was not carved of wood became apparent by the color of its outer side. Its hollow was wine-dark. A thin pool of the staining fluid sat shimmering at the bottom. There appeared to be carvings on the inner bowl; a dancing woman, a smirking mask in angled clouds, an alphabet both crude and queer.

Memories of Baldemar's pilgrimage to the friar's ossuary at Cimitero dei Cappuccini bubbled to the fore of his mind. His mind conjured pristine images of the fleshless monks, their skeletal frames still chastely concealed by their hooded robes. Baldemar had meditated long and thoroughly upon these human relics, his ancestors of faith if not by blood. His memories were vivid enough to confirm by first sight that the bowl Jerome was now returning to its stone table was in fact the cap of a human skull.

The smaller object was a splint of keen stone. Strands of bleached grass had been wound and rewound along one end to form a cord-wrapped dagger handle.

The architected silence of the two monks was suddenly broken by a susurrus that echoed up from the cleft.

Baldemar thought little of this, until he saw Brother Jerome's expression.

With sacramental care Jerome replaced the ugly stone next to the even uglier bowl. He then rose, clutched Baldemar's wrist, and led him on a frantic dash back to the main path.

Within seconds the hushing noise from the cleft had ceased, but Jerome's pace did not slacken until he emerged from the edge of the wood and was back on the monastery's manicured lawns.

Baldemar, still lagging several paces behind, stumbled out onto the grounds just as Jerome was making his way to a bench by the cloisters.

"Perhaps you'd be good enough to explain yourself," Baldemar said breathlessly. He sat down next to Jerome.

"I'm sorry, brother, truly. I could not risk your curiosity impelling you to investigate those woods too late in the day. As you can see, it's perilous, even in the morning light."

"I saw no danger, brother," replied Baldemar. "I saw some unpleasant objects and you running for your very life, but I don't understand what any of this means."

Jerome wiped his mouth. "The brothers," he began, "the ones you've noticed coming out of the woods at eventide, were engaged in holy work. But it is holy work that is... unique to this monastery."

Brother Jerome tugged back the sleeve of his robe, revealing numerous slashes along his forearm. Many were still scabbing, while others were whitish scar tissue.

"It's our charge, Baldemar. Know that. Under ordinary circumstances the Abbot would have explained it all to you and walked you through the rite the way he did with myself and many others, but when he learned that you'd already spotted the brothers out here instead of being in the hall for Vespers...well, he couldn't risk you going off to investigate at the wrong time."

"What are you saying?"

"Years ago...*many* years, long before our time or even the Abbot's, there was a woman who lived in the village nearby. She was, I've been told, a very kindly and righteous person, a spinster who used to say she only had room in her heart for God. Rather late in this woman's life she announced, much to everyone's shock, that she was with child. Because she had the reputation of being somewhat eccentric, naturally the townsfolk didn't put much stock in her admission, until she began to show signs of impending motherhood. This led to her becoming something of a pariah in the village.

"This situation was unpleasant enough, but it was her insistence that her pregnancy was an immaculate one and that the child growing in her womb was the Second Coming of Our Lord that led to the woman being persecuted by the villagers. They accused her of blasphemy and hounded her tirelessly to leave the village. But she refused to go. She assured her neighbors that they would all be falling to their knees when her child was born."

Jerome shook his head. "Poor soul. She was so clearly troubled. The Abbot at the time tried to counsel her, but she refused to let go of her delusions.

"One day she collapsed while washing her clothes in the creek. A physician came and examined her and told her that he could find no heartbeat in her womb. There were several tests, I gather, and the doctor concluded that the woman's child would be stillborn. Worse than this was the fact that she would have to carry the child in her womb until it was ready to...pass. So tragic...What was in her womb was a stone baby. Her child actually calcified while in her womb. What she eventually gave birth to was a lifeless stone."

"God have mercy," Baldemar whispered.

"When the woman learned that her child was not the Messiah reborn but in fact something lifeless and hard, she went mad. She burned her hovel to the ground and fled into those woods there. Some of the brothers formed a search party, fearing that she would commit suicide. They found her alive."

Jerome closed his eyes and swallowed before he finally continued. "She was sitting on the ledge of the cleft. There was a great deal of blood on her clothes. She held something in her cupped hands; her stone baby. Seeing her in such a condition naturally one of the brothers ran to fetch the local physician. She was rocking back and forth, humming a lullaby, as if the poor creature in her hands was a living baby. One of the brothers approached to offer her comfort, only to discover that the Lithopedion was suckling at the woman's hand."

"It was *alive?*"

"Not alive, not truly. But not stillborn either. It was...an in-between thing."

"You say it was suckling her hand. You don't mean...?"

"The creature was weaned on blood. The brothers tried to reason with the poor woman, but her mind was beyond reach. When the physician returned she attacked him and some of the brothers. She claimed that the hatred of the locals had poisoned the Christ child she was carrying, and that now the village was cursed to suffer under this abomination she'd been punished with. The brothers tried to stop her, but she dove headlong into the cleft."

Baldemar rubbed the back of his neck. "An awful and tragic legend, but I still don't see what this has to do—"

"The brothers assumed she had died from the fall," Jerome said, speaking over him. "But the following day the physician went missing, and later three other villagers. The woman's hatred and her affinity with that monster of stone had mutated her into something that could no longer be called human. She was a jaundiced, twisted thing, with flaming eyes and long claw-like fingernails. She dwelt in the cleft. The Abbot hid in the area to study her movements. He discovered she had kept the bodies of the missing villagers, and every night she emerged from the cleft with her baby and allowed it to drink by the light of the moon. She had pried the skullcap from the body of the physician, the first to die, and she carried it with her to collect the nightly meal of blood from the cadavers. She'd pour it over the stone child in her hand, singing songs in her strangled voice, cooing as the thing drank.

"The Abbot made a last drastic effort to end the violence against the village. One evening he confronted the woman. Before she could attack him, he took a sharp stone and nicked his own wrist and offered his blood. She collected it into her skull bowl and used it to feed her child, then crept back into the cleft, singing her lullaby.

"The killings stopped that very night. But the Abbot knew that if the woman were ever in need of blood she would think nothing of taking another innocent villager. So he returned for the next few evenings. At each eventide he cut himself. And each night after moonrise the woman slithered up from the cleft and fed her child. In time other brothers took over the task. Now the woman leaves the stone dagger and the bowl at the top of the cleft. And every evening each of us in turn gives some of our blood."

Baldemar was at a loss for words.

Jerome's face took on an air of disappointment. "Recall Job 39, Verses 28 and 30," he advised. "'She dwelleth and abideth on the rock, upon the crag of the rock, and the strong place...Her young ones also suck up blood: and where the slain are, there is she.'"

He rose and walked way; a blunt gesture that informed Baldemar that their discussion was over.

For many hours Baldemar struggled to come to grips with what he had been told. Should he accept this? Could he accept this? Surely the authors of the Book of Job knew a thing or two about metaphor and fable. Not everything in the Bible was to be digested as reportage on a physical reality. This reasoning did little to temper Baldemar's unease.

At dusk it took every ounce of his resolve to resist spying from the cloisters, but he was successful.

There was no sign of Jerome at Vespers, a fact that troubled Baldemar until he finally caught sight of Jerome on his way to his quarters for the night.

Baldemar looked down and noticed the fresh linen dressing that was wound around Jerome's wrist. Jerome opened his mouth as if to speak, but said nothing. The two men went their separate ways to retire for the night.

It was still dark when the idea struck Baldemar with all the force of an unbridled charger.

He sat up in his humble bed, his brain reeling. It would require deception, this freshly-hatching plan of his; not a great amount, just a tincture. And the end result would surely justify the means.

At breakfast he marched up to Jerome and announced that he

wished to make payment at the cleft that evening.

Jerome appeared stunned. "Well...I...I certainly admire your enthusiasm, brother." He spoke *sotto voce*. "But novitiates to this custom are required to first attend the offering solely as a witness. We believe the creature in the cleft needs to feel that she can trust each brother before she will accept his offering."

"Very well," said Baldemar. "I submit myself to be witness to tonight's offering."

Jerome's gaze was one of deep assessment. "So be it," he said at last, though his words were heavy with misgiving. "This evening's offering is to be given by Brother Anthony. I'll inform him that you will be joining as witness. Meet him on the front steps right after supper. You must obey his every command and only speak when spoken to. Do you understand?"

"Yes."

The day crawled past. Baldemar spent much time in prayer and contemplation. His soul oscillated between fiery certainty of his plan's virtue to a cold and stony fear about the danger he was placing himself before.

The chapel was not fully vacated until the late afternoon, at which time Baldemar slipped in and completed his task as quickly as his trembling hands would allow.

By suppertime he couldn't bear the idea of eating anything. He sipped a cup of water then hastened to the front steps.

Brother Anthony arrived after what seemed an interminable wait. He nodded his longish head at Baldemar, mutely acknowledging him and the task ahead.

They set out to the forest.

The cleft appeared much larger and deeper and blacker to Baldemar. The skullcap and dagger were at their customary stations. Anthony raised his hand for Baldemar to stay. He scurried with impressive stealth and silence to the granite feeding ground. The fibrous sleeve of his robe was peeled back.

Baldemar winced when he saw Anthony boring the crude dagger tip into the haired meat of his forearm.

Libation for the child of stone seeped out in a seductive rivulet. One by one the dark fluid fell like red-black pearls from a snapped necklace, like the eager water of spring squeezing through the rift in a winter-long encasement of ice.

Anthony set the skullcap down with care. He tugged a white swatch from his pocket and lashed it around his wound, pulling the tourniquet tight with his teeth.

The pair of them moved from the woods.

The sun was still struggling to stay afloat when they reached the basin of water. Anthony went through the final gestures, nodded again to Baldemar, and hurried off for the last of evening prayers.

Baldemar did not follow. Once he was reasonably sure that all eyes were on God and not him, he tore across the lawn and back into the woods. The gloaming was beginning to deepen, light perishing about him as embers in a hearth.

Before he actually reached the cleft, Baldemar concealed himself behind an oak and listened. There were no sounds of movement. He peered out and saw that Anthony's offering had yet to be poured from the skullcap.

He tugged the cord around his neck and drew up the wineskin he had hidden under his robe. His pulse was manic and deafening in his head. His legs and hands were almost useless. He rushed over to the cleft, snatched the skullcap, and flung its contents into the nearby thicket. The splashing sound sickened him. He wrestled with the wineskin's cork until it popped free.

The sacramental wine sloshed down his robes and over his sandaled feet. Too frightened to care, Baldemar poured the wine into the skullcap and whispered, "*Hic est enim calix sanguinis mei, novi et aeterni testament: mysterium fidei, qui pro vobis…*"

He set the skullcap down and tore up the path, hiding once more behind the oak tree.

The orange and purple glimmer of twilight gave way to night-blue. Baldemar waited and silently prayed. No matter what the outcome of this endeavor, he hoped that his brothers and God Himself could see that his intentions were pure.

If no one arose from the cleft, he could prove to Jerome and the others that they needn't maintain this barbarous ritual. If there was some poor lost wretch down there, the priority should not be sustenance but salvation. Tonight the stone baby and its mother would partake not of mortal blood, but the blood of the Messiah.

When the noise began Baldemar craned back his head, assuming (or wishing) that it was simply the oak leaves fluttering under the press of the wind. When he discovered that the boughs were still, his mind clambered for a new explanation, no matter how outlandish. But it soon became woefully clear that the sound was a rasping, dry, shallow breathing. It seemed to bleed from every inch of the forest, surfacing like dewfall on the foliage and the stones. It spilled out from the depths of Baldemar's own soul, breaching the levee that had been so scrupulously maintained by his conscience, his faith. It was deafening him, drowning him.

He felt his gaze fall to the cleft. Infirmed by shock, he could but stare at the crooked fingernails that were wriggling up from the crack in the stone like a spout of muddy water. The long misshapen nails became fingers and hands and arms, all robed in grubby, reeking flesh.

She was lanky, a chain of bones layered in flesh raw as dough. She was impossibly tall, but her swaying, unsteady movements made it seem as if her body had been lengthened on the rack, stretched rather than grown to such a height. Her hair was as dark and tangled as the roots of the forest's old growth trees. Her eyes resembled shucked oysters and were evidently just as sightless.

The stone baby was cradled in her flaccid hands. By the light of the moon Baldemar could just see that it was something gray, something weed-swaddled.

The woman scooped up the offering bowl and tipped it until the sacramental wine, the blood of all blood, baptised her calcified child.

Baldemar had to remind himself to breathe, so eager was he to witness the purification.

The cry met him with all the force of the spear that screams for annihilation. It was piercing and crippling, conjuring in the mind the snarling mewl of fighting cats and the desperate frustration of a newborn's cry. The night was swollen with its wail.

Traumatized by the awful sound, and terrified of his possible fate, Baldemar turned and fled, manically, desperately.

Only once did he dare a backward glance. He was expecting to see the woman charging after him, her claws eager to puncture his heart.

But she was a lump of quivering rags lying on the stone slab. Her hands seemed empty. Had the wine's purity dissolved her offspring?

The woman shook and wailed her deep irreconcilable maternal pain into the night.

The trees seemed to part for Baldemar once the abbey's grounds came into moonlit view. He wanted to feel great relief once he crossed the threshold, but he was numb.

He went to the basin, knowing that the pooled rainwater could not cleanse him. He washed nonetheless, cowering as he stood in the crooked shadow of the cross.

Rigid by what he had glimpsed or merely thought he had glimpsed, Baldemar forced his gaze upward. His eyes were stained by the sight of the thing on the cross, with limbs like withered corn husks and a head of mangled stone.

The Lithopedion had grown to maturity in mere seconds.

It slipped free of the nails that had kept it in thrall.

Baldemar watched its beak fall open before it clamped fatally onto his throat.

He hoped his indiscretions had not tainted his blood. He closed his eyes as the creature slaked its thirst, draining him as though he was a living grail.

Tinder Row

S CAVENGING GULLS LURED Reid to the ghosts. Not nearly as appealing as the Sirens of myth, their shrill squawks
had the impatient tone of orders for Reid to hasten along
the boardwalk. He attempted to shoo the avian pests by
kicking a mashed beer can into their cawing huddle, but
succeeded only in tripping himself up. A quick grip of the boardwalk's railing allowed Reid to both regain his balance and to look
unobstructed at the cold, ash-dull sands where the pair of ghosts
was stationed.

The first was a woman. Reid recalled her name the selfsame
instant he looked upon her face. They'd both been teenagers the
last time he'd seen her, but it was Agnes. Of this Reid was certain.
Her unmistakable eyes—irises the violet of bruises; two shards
of wet stained glass—stared out from a face long wrung of its
youthfulness.

Life had apparently been no more lenient to her in adulthood
than it had been during those awkward years when her epilepsy,
near-pathological shyness, and family's unfashionable penury had
branded Agnes with a modern equivalent of the pariah's scarlet
letter.

Reid was able to appreciate a summary of her cruel fate by the
ragged mummery she had draped over her unwashed flesh, and by
the pitiful and drawn mask that was her face. He nearly buckled
under his own sorrow. He regretted his decision to spend a summer
Sunday revisiting his hometown. Facing such melancholic echoes
from the past, Reid relished the penance of the railing's splinters
sliding into his skin. He was almost overwhelmed by the impulse
to rush down to Agnes and embrace her.

The second ghost beneath the boardwalk was more abstract. Agnes was actually holding it, shield-like, before her fragile-looking frame.

TINDER ROW

It was a sign composed of water-stained cardboard, marred with hectic letters in graphite.

Reid had never forgotten Agnes, not completely, but Tinder Row was a place he had not thought of, perhaps wilfully, for many years.

The reality of what this woman's life must have been like for her to be deliberately hunting after Tinder Row was almost unfathomable.

"Do you need help?" Reid heard someone call; realizing too late that the strangled voice had been his own.

Agnes pointed dumbly at her sign.

"All right," he said. "Okay."

Only after compulsive promises that he would not harm her, and that, yes, he would take her to Tinder Row, did Agnes follow Reid to the café at the head of the pier. Her pace conveyed reluctance.

Once they were seated Reid began plying the woman with food. Though she initially claimed to want nothing, her stubbornness shrank once the hostess heaped their table with hot roast beef sandwiches and au jus, thick-cut sweet potato fries, and fresh coffee.

Reid was pleased at the way his near-feral companion tore into her meal. He reasoned that it was likely the first decent one she'd eaten for a long time. He tried to feel magnanimous but inside there was only numbness.

After gobbling two servings of dessert Agnes asked if they could leave now. Reid tried to stall her with the offer of a drink. When she refused, he momentarily fretted about her storming off. To balm this, Reid finally acquiesced, assuring Agnes that he would now carry her to her destination.

Even the keenest eye could not have detected anything remarkable about Tinder Row. By strict definition it was a dead-end street near the town's main viaduct. Though Reid held memories of his grandfather working at a Tinder Row plant where vegetables were canned in iodine water, they were very old memories, made to seem older still once Reid witnessed the vacancy and erosion of the various structures.

Only one of the drab dun brick buildings still managed to fight against anonymity by bearing a sign, but it was so rusted and weather-bullied that the only partial words Reid could scry through the red-brown stains was '& Sons Inc.' The other buildings all flaunted even greater neglect. Tinder Row was a set of elegiac grey-brown rectangles, like an avenue of mausoleums in a churchyard, each one long-hollowed.

He was surprised at the total lack of vandalism here. Back in the city such unmanned sites were ripe for graffiti and shattered windows, but Tinder Row appeared to have been left unmolested by everything but the tariffs of time.

Agnes, without comment, suddenly rolled down the passenger-side window and tilted her head into the gap. The car was driving at just over thirty kilometres an hour; motion enough to imbue her dreadlocks with the illusion of life. Reid imagined her as a Gorgon aroused. Agnes appeared content.

"I love the sound of crunching gravel," she said. "It reminds me of walking on snow." It was the most jovial she had sounded all afternoon. Reid wondered if she somehow drew vitality from the barren Row.

The further they cruised down the road he sparser the buildings became, until finally an open patch roughly the size of a football field stretched out from the edge of the gravel road to the viaduct in the distance. Agnes said, "You can let me off anywhere along here."

Until then Reid's hesitancy and unease toward Tinder Row had been an amorphous, wispy feeling; one that had all the timidity of a childhood nightmare recalled in adult life. He could remember something about the place having a dark reputation in the town, but until he witnessed that fallow field, the threat had been abstract. The combination of seeing the place afresh after so very long and of hearing Agnes once again expressing her wish to be there caused the power of the place to impress itself on him. Here, a field, then a quickened heart-thump later: Tinder Row.

The lore bubbled up near enough for Reid to recall it with almost crystal clarity. "Please," he muttered to his passenger. "Please don't do this."

Agnes already had the door handle in her grip, and with a clunk the door was popped open. Was she going to dive headlong out of a moving vehicle? Was the woman that depleted?

His foot found the brake pedal. The vehicle slowed but had not reached a full stop when Agnes pulled herself out of the car. Reid almost cried out to her, but the woman had already recovered from the stumble she suffered when her boots hit the gravel road. She was now walking into the field. Reid shifted the car into park and shut off the engine.

Agnes had left the sign marked Tinder Row in the car's footwell. It was no longer of use to her. Neither, Reid thought, was he.

He took in a sharp breath and glanced at the Row, hoping on some primal level that someone or something would feed him a solution, a suggestion of what to do next. Reid knew Agnes was in peril, even if the particulars of the threat were still a bit fuzzy for him. Nevertheless, there was danger here. Of this much Reid was somehow certain. Why else would his pulse have suddenly begun to dash, his mouth to become so parched?

His hands fumbled to unclasp the seatbelt. Reid rose out of the cab and called out, "Agnes!" His cry echoed ever so faintly as it passed through the small viaduct at the far end of the field. In his boyhood this very tunnel had roared with mechanized thunder as trains passed through the town day and night, carrying steel and grain and lumber on their backs. Now the tracks lay rusted and bearded with weeds, and the only sound to shake the dust from the tunnel's throat was Reid's own trepid voice.

Agnes had wandered almost halfway across the field. She appeared to Reid as more silhouette than solid. He was certain that she'd heard him call out but, as far as he could discern, she'd not given him so much as a backward glance.

Reid took a few steps toward the hem of the road. The toes of his loafers poked over into the tangles of sun-bleached grasses that marked the edge of the field. He noted what looked to be blackened pine needles carpeting the ground.

Dusk was encroaching but had yet to begin the rubric of night. Distance from the lake made the air here relentlessly arid and hot. There was no breeze to speak of, and the whole area was almost unnaturally quiet. Reid stood and listened, but the only noises he heard were the clicks of the car's engine cooling behind him. Distance muted Agnes' movement into something as soundless and graceful as a wraith's.

The field seemed much smaller than Reid had remembered it... or rather imagined it being. Only now did he realize that in all the years he'd heard rumours about Tinder Row, he had never actually ventured past the cut-off that led down this lane to the field.

Grass grew here only in random patches. And although the blades were tall they were also the unhealthy yellow of old bones rather than being verdant. They seemed almost artificial, like setpieces from a play that folded years before. A few tufts of milkweed drifted past Reid's periphery, tricking him into seeing moths in flight.

Ahead, Agnes laid herself down amidst the blades.

Reid felt a surge of helpless panic. It was as if he'd just witnessed an undertow dragging Agnes beneath a lake's surface. He was half-expecting her to emerge. When she did not, Reid crossed the threshold and began to move through the field.

The ground was firm and almost perfectly flat. The black needles snapped and crunched beneath his feet. The grasses barely reached to his knees, but Reid still felt as though he was navigating his way through something like a corn maze. He was so jittery about venturing to the heart of Tinder Row that he found himself constantly looking backward. Both doors of his car had been left open, which gave the vehicle the look of a bird frozen in flight. Reid looked ahead and was relieved when Agnes came into plain view.

She was reposing in a tiny clearing. Only after he'd gotten near enough did Reid realize that the clearing was shaped in the contours of a human being. There was a space for the head to rest, and the grasses swept in a contour to afford shoulders and a trunk and legs. The casket-like pocket wasn't quite small enough to fit Agnes snugly, but must have been tailored enough to make her feel at home, for her eyes were closed and she did not as much as flinch at Reid's noisy approach.

"What are you doing?" he asked her. Agnes did not respond. Her smudged face was complacent. Her bosom rose and fell with deep, well-measured breaths. She was distant.

"Look," he coughed, "I...I'm not too sure what it is you feel you need to do out here, but this doesn't look like the safest place for a woman to be alone, so I'm going to wait for you, okay?"

He received no response. More confused than perturbed, Reid made his way back to the car. He shut the doors, rolled down both windows, and waited.

In time the gloaming began to dilate, pushing the daylight to its farthest margins before snuffing it utterly. But Reid hadn't noticed nature's dimming. He was absorbed in his own reverie.

He was reflecting back on Tinder Row...

'Soul-moulting' was the term Reid had heard in relation to the mysteries of this place. It was said that the soil on Tinder Row was thin; not in its physical compound, but rather its spiritual aspect.

The ground on Tinder Row was not piled high enough to keep the Underworld interred. Here, it was said, was a passage. The Row, or something in the Row, acted as a carriage to whisk the wanting off to the realm of Spirit.

As to the specifics of this process, theories were legion. Reid's grandfather used to feed him a healthy dose of bedtime story dread when he was a boy, telling him that on Tinder Row ghosts sprouted up like weeds whenever some despondent local laid his or her body down among the strange grasses. Inebriated high school gossip birthed a different mythology, one of a monstrous force that had the ability to crack the body like a lobster's shell and fish from it the person's immaterial essence.

None of the speculations felt apt to Reid. If soul-moulting was the street parlance for what took place on Tinder Row, surely it made more sense to envision the process as the celebrant lying down and resolving to forfeit their cage of bone and blood. Like unnumbered saints, ascetics, and martyrs before them, here in the fields these wretches envisioned themselves as symbolically shedding their soul, like a serpent sloughing its unneeded skin.

But, Reid pondered further, if this process was only 'mystical' to the one engaged in it, what truly occurred was...what, death by starvation, exposure? Is this what Agnes had in mind for herself, a prolonged and agonizing death by lack of food and water while he sat by and watched?

Reid could feel his feelings toward the woman changing. Somehow the thick waves of pity and sorrow he'd been working through began to mangle. What arose was an unruly fire of righteous indignation. Who was she to put him through such a trying ordeal? Who was she?

Reid pulled himself out of the car and engaged in a full-out march across the field.

Agnes's position had not changed. Something about this fact instantly dampened Reid's ire. The woman was visibly waiting, waiting. Was she as Siddhartha, anticipating some grand enlightenment; Tinder Row her bodhi tree?

But it was clear to Reid, even if it was not to Agnes, that nothing positive could ever be gleaned from such a place. Neither enlightenment nor liberation gestated here. Here was neglect and decay, and little else besides.

"You really..." He'd had the words only a moment ago, but Agnes still lying-in-wait had wiped Reid's mind clean. He cleared this throat and started anew. "I don't think this a good idea at all, Agnes. Why don't...why don't we go get a cup of coffee or something? This place...it doesn't seem safe. I don't want to leave you lying here alone any longer."

She did not even flinch. One hand resting on her hip, the other flung up beside her head, she slept; her breaths shallow and metronome-even.

A breeze passed over them. The grasses shivered, but not from cold. The stones of the viaduct emitted a low sigh.

Reid knelt down beside her. He reached out to touch her wrist, but stopped just shy of actual contact.

"Look," he began, "I'm not going to pretend to understand what your life has been like, but no matter what you're going through it's not worth just lying down and giving up. I remember how brutal high school was for you; the way the other girls mocked you at every turn, and how the boys....how the boys did even worse. But you cannot have *nothing* to live for.

There must be someone or—"

"There's no one," Agnes mumbled. "I'm alone."

The sound of her voice, meek as it was, kindled his hope.

"But you *aren't* alone." He righted himself. "*I'm* here. Come on, let's just go, okay?"

Her mouth pursed back into corpse-like stiffness.

"Hey, I agreed to bring you out here, I didn't agree to just leave you lying in this grubby field alone in the dark, so come on, get up and we'll go somewhere and talk."

When she still refused to respond, Reid literally threw up his hands. "Okay, suit yourself. But I'm not leaving you alone. I'll wait back at the car. When you're done...doing whatever it is you came here to do...I'm taking you back into town."

Back at the car, the worries welled up rapidly: What if she had already choked down a bit of cyanide while he'd been musing? Was there a glass shard or a rusty razor secreted in the folds of her dress that Agnes planned to slice her wrists with?

His decision was firm: he would take her back to town, even if he had to drag her there by force.

Reid exited the car and was about to begin the task of collecting Agnes, but he halted.

Tinder Row was now clotted with indigo dimness, which imbued every inch of the field with the glamour of motion, of malice. He blinked rapidly to fight off tonight's recurring problem with his eyes; that of seeing spots flitting about in his periphery.

Only now the flecks were no longer restricted to the margins of his field of vision, they were weaving every which way, and despite Reid's efforts to banish them, the specks did not dissipate under his concentration. Instead they increased.

Looking as far a-field as possible, Reid realized that nightfall was not the sole reason for Tinder Row growing hazy and dim: innumerable spots had swarmed where Agnes was, or perhaps had been.

It resembled a sprawling black storm cloud that had somehow been dislodged from the sky and now lay twitching and squirming on Tinder Row, trying to coax itself back into flight. Reid wondered if Agnes in the throes of another grand mal seizure could be the cause of this motion, but somehow he knew this was inaccurate.

If insects they were, they were unlike any Reid had encountered, not only because of their dizzying numbers—billions would have been Reid's guess, given the shape and scope of the frenzied mass— but also because, despite their legions and their frantic activity, the entire swarm was surreally silent. These squirming spots neither chirped nor buzzed. The only sound at all was a breezy hiss that was borne solely from their motion.

Reid began to advance, and as he did he noticed the peculiar scent in the air. It smelled vaguely of vanilla, or of baking bread; a cosy fragrance, one that seemed to embrace, to lull.

Agnes was interred beneath the bugs, her body cocooned in the pulsating mass. Now close enough to see them more clearly, Reid was bewildered by the appearance of the insects. They were similar to hornets, only much plumper. Their wings were teardrops of amber cellophane. The fuzz that covered their bodies was milk- white. The only marking each one bore was a bruise-like blotch of chartreuse and purple and grey. Their backs resembled the eye of a peacock's feather. Huddled together to task, the insects resembled a carpet of mould, omniscient and spreading rapidly across the grasses and over the woman that reposed there.

The shock that had rendered him momentarily helpless ebbed ever so slightly, allowing Reid to cry out Agnes's name and try to swat the hideous things away. His revulsion spun through him like a heated coil, causing his skin to draw tight across his bones.

When his fumbling and timid attempts to banish the insects failed, Reid held his breath, squinted his eyes shut, and brought his foot down on a patch of the huddled mass. They did not crunch beneath his sole as he'd expected. Instead they popped, as though their bodies were but sacs.

The hushing sound ceased. When Reid looked he discovered that the hornets had grown perfectly still.

For a long moment the only motion in the field was Reid's heaving chest. He called to Agnes once again, but the body beneath the quilt of bugs now seemed smaller, whittled down to a size too scant to host life.

The insects once more became active, but their attention was no longer on Agnes, it was on Reid. They scuttled down off of Agnes and began to advance across the field. Like a puddle of curdled milk, the bugs spread white and wide toward him. If they were angry at him for depleting their numbers they did not exhibit it in the customary way. Their movements were tediously slow, almost Zen in their assurance of purpose.

Reid glanced up quickly, enough to see that Agnes's already ragged clothing had been reduced to mere strips. Much of her body was missing far more than fabric.

Reid stumbled backward, tripping on his own feet. When his hands reflexively reached out to cushion his fall, something pierced his palms. Wincing, Reid pulled himself up and began to run. He could not bring himself to turn around, for the insects were now hoisting themselves skyward. Their stained-glass wings beat the air, fanning their perfume closer and closer to Reid.

The sight of his car parked in its jackknife position in the lot brought no sense of relief, for Reid could feel the swarm at his back, their wings causing his clothing to ruffle.

Worse than the chase, more unbearable than even the threat of extinction, was the sound his pursuers suddenly unleashed: They started singing.

Their song was thin and high-pitched, yet it was closer to a human choir than a flock of birds. There was a meaning to their song, Reid felt, but he did not wish to decode it.

His aching hand rummaged through the pocket of his trousers. The instant his fingers tugged his car keys free, Reid jammed his thumb down on the red alarm button.

The car horn began to beep at a persistent rhythm. The head- and taillights began to blink. He prayed it would disorient his stalkers long enough for him to flee.

With much speed but little grace, Reid flung himself into the cab. He started the engine, managed a frantic U-turn, and tore down the gravel road before even disengaging the car alarm.

The speedometer read 94 all the way along Tinder Row; Reid didn't even think of slowing down until he was back on the main road that wound toward town. He was mindful of his pace for the remainder of the drive. The last thing he wanted was to be stopped and questioned. What would he tell them?

What *could* he?

He hankered for a drink in the worst way but dared not enter a bar or a liquor store for fear of being seen. Even a cup of coffee at a diner was a luxury Reid would not allow himself.

Though he knew it would take him the better part of the night to reach the city, Reid wanted nothing more than to go straight home, to hide from his own memories.

He would find a way to put this night behind him. He had to.

After driving in circles around his hometown, Reid finally veered onto a country lane where he could park and think with little risk of intrusion.

Flashes of the awfulness simmered in his consciousness, pecking and pulling at him. Though he was frightened and confused, these feelings paled against his shame.

Try as he did to reason that Agnes had gone to Tinder Row in search of expiration, or moulting, the thought did nothing to console him. Her face, like a cracked china doll's, could not be wiped from Reid's mind's eye. Those lavender eyes watched him, pleaded wordlessly with him.

She had been through so much, and when she had reached her lowest rung, all he had done was nudge her off the ladder of life.

Then there was the appearance of foul play. Someone would surely find Agnes, or what remained of her. Even a location as seldom tread as Tinder Row was bound to be breached in time.

There had been witnesses at the boardwalk that had seen him escorting Agnes. And the waiter would unquestionably remember a well-dressed man dining with an obvious transient.

Any investigation would point back to him. It was only a question of time.

To say nothing of the metaphysical questions; the what and why and how of those monsters in the field. What had happened to Agnes?

Reid needed to know these things as well.

Daylight had broken by the time Reid doubled back and returned to Tinder Row.

He was relieved to find the place customarily empty, yet its dimensions seemed to have swollen. Only half-certain that its new vastness was merely the taint of his guilt and fear, Reid wondered if Tinder Row was nourished by the pain of others. Did sorrow enrich the soil and cause the terrain to grow? Did the insects act as Psychopomps, carting the disheartened from Tinder Row to the some Elsewhere?

His shame and his terror over being implicated in whatever had happened to Agnes overpowered whatever fears he had for his safety.

He made his way to where she had been lying but found nothing. There were no telltale spatters of crimson, no scraps of clothing, no signs of struggle. The blades of yellow grass stood bolt-straight. The body-shaped indentation remained, perhaps inviting Reid to nestle into its contours. Reid then realized that what littered the ground, what had stabbed into his hands last night, were stingers.

He began to search the field.

There was nothing to be found but for some bleached and shapeless trash here and there until he reached the mouth of the viaduct.

The initial clue was not a visual one, but an olfactory one: the sweet, almost inviting scent sat heavy in the blackened tunnel, clinging as surely as stale cigar smoke, or the funk of sex on motel room sheets.

Reid stood under the viaduct's great frown of an archway and for a space he did nothing but listen. He had to strain to hear anything that might exist beyond the thumping of his heart, but Reid was confident that the tunnel hosted no sounds of movement.

Perhaps the scent was merely a sign that the abominations left in their wake. The creatures were likely long departed, returned to whatever distant sphere they belonged. Agnes must have been taken with them, perhaps piecemeal. Either way, Reid hoped she had found whatever it was she'd been questing after.

He risked a forward step and was immediately embraced by a cool, sunless respite from the August morning.

The fragrance inside was heavier, but not cloying. Its near-sickly-sweetness was offset by a refreshing coolness. The shadows made dripping sounds all around Reid, undoubtedly from the condensation that had collected on the viaduct's ceiling.

Reid lifted his hand; his flesh was almost spectral in the dimness.

His fingertips found the oily stones of the tunnel wall, which he then used as both a support and a compass to navigate his journey to the far end of the viaduct. His clumsy, ill-measured steps spat tiny rocks against the rail tracks and the wall. The ping of their impact was unnervingly loud.

When he reached what he believed to the midpoint, Reid regretted not bringing a flashlight, for the glow of the entrance was now well behind him and the exit was not yet near enough to assure him.

The darkness made mischief with his perceptions, dilating the viaduct into something akin to a primordial cave from which escape was impossible. Though the tunnel had not wavered from its arrow-straight design, Reid began to perceive bewildering bends that drew him ever-wayward from his plan. The distance he'd travelled also seemed not merely obscured by the lightless passage, but to have vanished altogether. A barb of superstitious thought began warning Reid to be wary of the ground suddenly dropping out from beneath him.

A sliver of sunlight suddenly came into view, and not a moment too soon. For Reid was now practically employing the jutting wall stones as pulleys to drag himself to his destination.

He would take the long route back, outside in the daylight. This would be his reward. After he'd searched here for Agnes he would return to the car by going across the field, where nothing was immune to the sun's glaring scrutiny. He would drive away, would leave this place forever. There was likely nothing left of Agnes, and therefore nothing to bind him to her demise.

The tunnel's far mouth was now visible, as was the shape that lay slumped against the tunnel wall. The glimmer of sunshine lent partial illumination to what Reid first perceived as a heap of newspapers. Trying to bring the lump into clearer view was taxing; a series of squints and leans and shielding his eyes with his hands; a process that succeeded only in making Reid dizzy. The contrast between the untrammelled daylight and the heavy darkness was too great.

A few more steps made the object appear larger and nearer, but no more identifiable. It was a great mound of brownish tissue which looked to be several feet long. The whole surface was ruffled, like a shredded cardboard carton.

Reid let out something halfway between a sigh and a laugh. He shook his head, offering wordless kudos to the viaduct for a well-played illusion.

But the folly of shadow and light could not furnish an old cardboard box the overwhelming architecture of such an elaborate structure, this geometric wonder into which a great cavity had been smoothly bored.

Something inside this hole glinted, catching Reid's eye like a magpie's. Whatever it was looked gelatinous, jewelled. It resembled a bloodied fish eye staring ruby-lidless from the bottom of the hole.

The sweet scent was strong here, so strong that Reid nearly choked. His sweat was beginning to cool on his skin, making it clammy. His tongue was coated with the panic-taste of metal.

Unwittingly, Reid called Agnes's name. His voice thundered through the tunnel, scaring him.

As if in response to his beckon, the brown thing twitched. Reid cried out and backed away. From his new vantage point he recognized the structure as a great hive. Just as he recognized the tiny strips of the dress that brightened the otherwise drab construct.

Bidden by something deeper than his own desires, Reid extended a thin finger toward the hive's shoulder.

The entire construct caved at his touch. The deep red gel it housed in its mouth slipped loose. The crimson sac popped the instant it struck the rocky ground. Liquid splayed out in a steaming glistening mess over the gravel and the unused rails.

Not daring to step over the mess he'd wrought, Reid stumbled back through the darkness. He wanted very much to run, for within the tunnel a great force had begun to swell. It grew so intense that the rails now palsied under Reid's fine leather shoes.

It was not the roar of a steel beast plodding along the track, but a cacophony of motion, an anthem of predatory movement as the sleepers within the hive came vomiting out.

Reid wondered if he had fallen into the void, for he felt truly weightless. His feet kicked wildly but met only air. His senses returned long enough for him to realize that he had not fallen but was instead being lifted. He opened his mouth to shriek, but what emerged was something nearer to a song.

Wormwood Votaries

ILLNESS AND FEAR had been the stalwart companions of Langdon's youth. He was November's creature; a child of that drab term that hangs between autumn's vibrant beginnings and the jeweled austerity of winter. Because it was an in-between time, Langdon had always perceived himself to be something of an in-between creature. During those crucial formative years, this perception brought him only pain.

Whenever he had been surrounded by his peers on the playground, Langdon would realize how at odds his world was with that of the other children. Whenever he'd spoken, his comments had invariably seemed inappropriate, either in timing or in tone.

Loitering at the fence that distinguished the schoolyard from the city at large, Langdon used to press his back to the wire mesh and stare out at the noisy huddles of children who had all seemed so eager to either stomp over the world in order to leave some kind of imprint, or they were hungry to reduce the external world to a mere backdrop against their near-autistic imaginary life.

Langdon felt eternally condemned to hover somewhere between these two tribes, the aggressors and the escapists, for while he was neither athletic nor boisterous, he was also not a refugee from reality. He never once sought the sanctuary of make-believe. Perhaps this was because for as long as he could remember Langdon had felt a delicate reality evolving within and around him, maturing as he himself did. Presences that Langdon could not see but certainly felt moved over him like insects of ice, ones that climbed the rungs of his spine and left a delicious chill in their wake.

On quiet, solitary afternoons he could almost hear a distant chorus of whispering that teased pleasantly at the whorls of his ears.

These presences left hints at the back of his mind, like trinkets on the doorstep of a superstitious homestead.

Often this process of visitation brought on an ugly vertigo that spiralled out from the base of the boy's skull and made him feel as though he was spinning like a top while yet remaining perfectly still.

The only way Langdon knew to stop this feeling was to grip the nearest solid object and brace himself until the hurricane passed. But even this act of self-preservation betrayed him, for the boy took to studying his hands and wondered if those were really his fingers and just what were fingers anyhow and what a queer thing it was to saddle one's self with a sack of fluid and bones in the first place...

It was not uncommon for the boy to see the lunulae of his fingernails stretching out like ten tiny waxing moons.

"I got a bottle of that *Bourgogne* you like," Langdon boasted as he entered the house's foyer. He wiped his left foot once, again, and a third time before removing the loafer. This ritual was repeated with the right before Langdon set the shoes in the dead centre of the rubber mat where they lived, their toes pointed true north.

He trotted up the main stairway and entered the bedroom with the bagged bottle held up proudly, as though it was some hard-won trophy.

The alteration to the room's order was so drastic that it actually stole Langdon's breath, made him feel physically violated.

"How do you like it?" Nancy called from the bathroom. Langdon turned to see his wife stationed before the medicine chest mirror, stretching her face in order to apply eyeliner.

"You moved it." His voice was a melodramatic gasp.

"I know."

"Why, Nancy?"

"Because I practically froze every night this past winter and I don't intend to broil now that summer's here. Covering the vent defeats the purpose of having a heating and cooling system. And it's a huge waste of money. Besides, I think it looks nicer this way." She passed by him and gave him a consolatory peck on the cheek. "Relax. Your side of the bed is still the same."

Langdon's attention was locked on the exposed furnace grate that was set into the carpeting. It seemed to be mocking him with a metal-teethed grin. Tufts of accumulated dust dangled from the grill like soft stalactites.

The numbness of shock began to melt away, and soon Langdon felt a tide of steely dread rising inside him. He breathed deeply, willfully, in order to keep the tide from breaking his emotional levee and drowning him.

Would he hear them again, he wondered? See them?

If only Nancy knew what she had set in motion; Langdon could practically hear the long-dormant gears of some great machine groaning to life, moving everything widdershins, everything inversely.

The chiming of the doorbell caused him to jolt, which obliterated his reverie.

He peered over the landing and saw the first guests, backlit by late evening sunbeams. Company continued to arrive in a steady stream. Langdon hastily changed into a fresh dress shirt, which he buttoned all the way up to the collar. He hoped, likely in vain, that the simple pleasures of spouse and old friends would enable him to forget about his benighted youth.

But just to be safe, he unlocked the wheels of the bed's frame and rolled the king-size slab over the vent.

On his way out Langdon gave the handle of the bedroom door three deosil turns before making his way to the dinner party downstairs.

The first time Langdon experienced the Votaries he was but a child, enrobed in the gauzy blur of influenza and lying in his snug bed. From there he passively watched as the root of his being plucked itself free with disturbing ease.

This other-Langdon began to roam, leaving his body behind it as an escaped prisoner would shackles.

All the reassuringly familiar sights of his bedroom began to smudge and fade as Langdon saw what this other self was seeing. It was as if he had a vine of pale light coiling lazily out of his forehead, his chest. This cord was the only thing that reined in his other self, for the blurry discarnate form felt riled and eager and hungry. The further the other-Langdon pulled away from the boy's prostrate body, the more disoriented the child became. He gripped the sides of his mattress, felt his limbs go rigid.

He then heard them, the whispers. It was an onslaught of staccato voices, none of which were distinct or familiar or indeed even decipherable. It was a mere jumble of pleas and beckoning calls, as though detuned shortwave radios had been scattered throughout the house.

Somehow, the other-Langdon became aware of the one unifying quality of these manic sermons: they were all emanating from somewhere below. They came slithering up through the floor vents like blasts of manufactured air.

In addition to having keen hearing, this amorphous other-Langdon seemed to be made out of eyes, for the child found himself able to see everything at once: his parents slumbering peacefully in their bed, the moon-paled furnishings of the living room, the second-hand (which, Langdon noted, was spinning the wrong way) of the clock on the kitchen wall, and lastly the open basement door.

When this sprawling net of sight stretched to include in its gaze the descending basement stairs, Langdon tried to protest. But the boy's jaw felt fused shut. He could only twitch and sweat as his consciousness pressed through the darkened door frame and began to lurch with tortuous patience down each of the wooden steps, toward a chamber Langdon had always loathed, for it was a dank place, cool and musty with neglect. And it was dark, even at high soon in mid-summer, always...dark.

The portico-red walls of the stairway had been decorated with a row of paintings. Each picture was housed in a frame so ornate it was ugly. They hung from the crumbling plaster by thick wire.

The paintings were unnerving. Langdon was struck by the fact that they all looked as though they could have been fashioned by a child, even though there was a strange sophistication to their execution. They were the kind he would have loved to have painted had he possessed artistic talent.

They were of churchyards that basked in greenish light, of stalking wise-looking beasts of wood, of rigid candle flames that jutted up to lick the clefts of buxom women of shadow. The one that captivated Langdon the most had transformed the frothy thunderheads of a raging storm into the whorled face of a demon. Its colours were vivid, the paint slathered on thickly. He could see hairs from the painter's brush lying trapped within the smears, as though the artist had painted the canvas while in a frenzy.

"That's Stormbrow," explained one of the chattering voices. It was female and it emerged from the din like a leaping fish breaking waters. Langdon was able to discern "He cloaks his sermons in thunder..." before the woman's words sank back into the susurrus.

The other-Langdon pressed nearer to the basement.

Had that been the voice of his aunt Thora, the lying boy wondered?

Unconcerned by these attempts at recognition, the other-Langdon pressed down the final few steps.

The cellar was awash in a wan absinthe-green glow. It seemed to pour forth from the hull of a great furnace, as though the source of the light was trapped there like a caged comet, a buried star.

The greenish shimmer spotlighted four piles of boughs. Langdon wondered if these had been cut from the ash tree that grew in his backyard. He had scaled those crooked limbs often enough to be able to read their knots and bends like a kind of Braille. These cut switches had been bound in what his aunt Thora had called faggots. They were piled neatly beside the great iron furnace. The axe that had been used to chop the wood rested in the corner, its burnished blade gleaming.

Strangely, Langdon was unfazed when he discovered that the basement was occupied.

By the time the final dinner guest departed, the wine had gone to Langdon's head enough to make him more amorous than frightened. He and Nancy bantered and flirted like two teenagers while they cleared the dining room table and loaded the dishwasher.

Afterwards Langdon boiled tea and settled next to Nancy on the sofa. The television was on but neither of them paid it any mind. In no time they wordlessly opted to relocate to the bedroom.

Their copulations were frantic and hotly impersonal. The exertion and his drunkenness allowed Langdon to sleep deeply until sunrise.

He planned to spend that Sunday engaged in yard work. After a cup of strong black coffee he was ready to mow the lawn.

Pushing the mower across the grass, Langdon was irked by the debris that was continually snapping under the blades.

He crouched down and found that the litter was ash wood, despite not having such a tree growing anywhere in the neighbourhood. Langdon righted himself and chewed his lower lip.

"Boo!" Nancy called sardonically from behind him. "Aw, you didn't even flinch."

"I saw you," Langdon answered.

"How? Do you have eyes in the back of your head?"

Langdon marched into the house without saying a word.

He paced from the kitchen to the living room and back again, all the while dreading the moment that Nancy would come in after him, armed with questions about his behaviour. Could he even articulate what was unnerving him? Did he himself even know?

Twenty-four hours ago Langdon had had everything successfully slotted in its proper place. Perhaps he had grown overconfident in his ability to keep life contained, for it was now unravelling with such swiftness, such ease. He questioned whether his current predicament could actually have been touched off by something as slight as nudging a piece of furniture a few feet from its long-standing niche. Could one exposed duct really have opened such a floodgate, ushered in such misrule?

This question rattled around Langdon's head like a loose bead.

But the bead was soon threaded with others of a similar kind, which caused a radiant picture to bloom at the back of Langdon's mind. A chill crept down his back, awakening what his aunt Thora had referred to as his Eyes of the Spine. (*Was this what she had meant, that confusion and terror could stretch the senses to a newfound height, a greater sensitivity?*)

Langdon no longer saw the living room wall at his rear. Instead he viewed himself standing as an adult in aunt Thora's drape-dimmed sitting room. He had spent so many afternoons there as a boy, the times when his mother had to earn their keep and he was too sick to attend school.

A fire crackled in the hearth. Aunt Thora was seated in her wing-back chair, facing the flames.

The mantle was bare, save for a lone piece of statuary. The mere hint of it in the murky room was enough to make Langdon's heart ache with nostalgia. This statue had been one of those trinkets that childhood fascination elevated to the status of a magical fetish.

It was a small sculpture, approximately six-inches in height, and was of white marble carved in the shape of a faun. The figure's goatish legs were bent, its face leering. The cheekbones were so pronounced they were blade-keen. The eyes were without pupils, the mouth was frozen in mirthful laughter, or possibly a feral bellow.

The statue's base was of simple wood, which Langdon now viewed as being ash. He could not truly tell whether he was imprinting the memory with his mature perspective, or indeed if this was even a memory at all. A small copper plate was affixed to the base, upon which the following quote was engraved:

> The chasm was merely one of the orifices of that pit of
> blackness that lies beneath us, everywhere...

It needs no earthquake to open the chasm. A footstep, a little heavier than ordinary, will serve...

—Hawthorne, The Marble Faun

The vision duly faded.

And then Langdon heard the whisper.

Its egress from the furnace vent was soft and languid. As to the speaker or the nature of the message, Langdon could not ascertain. Fear propelled him out of the house and back into the yard where he found Nancy raking up the last of the ash boughs.

"What are you doing?" he asked, still breathless from the chase.

"Helping," Nancy replied. She pointed with pride to the fruits of her labours. The ash sticks were all tidily bound in several faggots and lined up against the house.

On the fateful night of illness, the other-Langdon had entered the basement and witnessed a trio of figures standing in the centre of the room. Each of the three was frozen in a unique but equally aberrant pose. One was twisted as a withered root, another stretched their left arm heavenward, the last was bent in a scythe-like curve. Masks rendered them anonymous. These masks were nothing more than pouches of crushed velvet with no openings to afford the wearer vision or breath. Each pouch was a different colour (earthen for the hunching one, bone-white for the one with the scythe-like body, midnight blue flecked with stellar glints for the one who reached skyward) and each was secured by a drawstring knotted around the neck.

The poses shared only one trait: each figure had an extended forefinger pressed to where their mouth would be; the universal signal for silence. They resembled condemned criminals who had somehow managed to escape the gallows.

Even though they were not facing him and even though they were masked, the boy somehow knew he was being watched. Did the lack of eyes somehow make them all-seeing, just as Langdon now was?

They lingered like great birds upon a taxidermist's shelf. Each figure was dressed in the same top and trousers, shapeless and genderless. These garments were similar to surgical scrubs, but were the colour of sackcloth.

Langdon would spend much of his subsequent life pondering what Spirits inspired their strange raiments, their unshakable asanas, their ego-killing masks, but that night he could only feel his childhood reality stretching to a painful parameter hitherto unreached.

Then, from behind him, came the voice, so familiar to him, aloof and yet so curiously stalwart.

There was no question that it was Langdon's aunt Thora.

"To get inside you have to see with the Eyes of the Spine..."

And with that phrase, the ever-growing sense of sight was obliterated. Langdon felt himself spasm a single time. The motion wiped away basement and green light and hooded visitors.

Langdon's next memory was of waking up in his own bed as his mother pressed a cold compress against his fevered brow.

Within a month Langdon had already begun to spin a cocoon for himself that began to immunize him against whatever significance his encounter with the Votaries might have held. This immunization occurred so subtly that Langdon hardly noticed it. Being young, he was driven to distraction, by the flavours of comfort food and by Christmas tinsel and by the canned laughter on television sitcoms. Later these simple pleasures were overpowered by the exotic promise of sex, later still by the allure of home and hearth.

The years passed and Langdon gradually found himself perceiving through a lens that hazed most things with a rosy wash and that filtered his memories through an equally pleasing mesh of positive nostalgia. Hormonal changes and improved nutrition had eliminated his boyhood torpor. By the time Langdon reached manhood he was so numb to the Votaries that he felt no memory of them whatsoever.

Perhaps this is understandable, for he was a married man now, living in a house of his own, one with a newly-thatched roof and a little garden walkway paved with imported river rock. Copper pots hung from the kitchen walls and Nancy perfumed the foyer daily with fresh potpourri of her own recipe.

Langdon knew how to keep order. It was all just a question of caution, of never allowing that foot to fall too heavily, as aunt Thora's marble faun had warned (or possibly dared) him.

The order was all so very much Fated, so very much as it was meant to be.

❧

Langdon kept apologizing profusely for being sick on the back lawn. Nancy would hear nothing of it and helped him into bed.

"You're burning up," she told him as her alabaster hand was pressed against his ruddy brow. "I think this is the first time I've ever seen you sick in all the years I've known you. I guess you're overdue."

"I guess," he replied. He shut his eyes and felt the illness pressing in all around him.

"I think I'll sleep for a bit," he told her.

"That's a good idea."

She left him.

The hot June day was made beige and gloomy as it filtered through the drawn curtains. It was the kind of illumination Langdon had known so well during his boyhood, when a never-ending cycle of ailments initiated him into an altered perspective on life.

It had been so long Langdon had almost forgotten what sickness felt like—the buoyant expansiveness, the vague sense that the world at large was somehow unreachable, the mind's gallery of images blossoming free as wildflowers in spring.

Drifting now, eyes shut, Langdon observed with mounting interest the environment that was flowering beneath him.

Lying on his back, he allowed his occulted eyes to open. His consciousness pressed through mattress and floorboards, down, down, until it hovered like a perched bird above the basement.

The Votaries were there, waiting for him. Langdon could not be sure, but there seemed to be a distinct air of reverence for him as he joined them.

Everything was softened by fever. His body was lying isolated in the bedroom while this other-self traipsed chambers that were stationed between memory and future, subjectivity and terra firma. All was as it should be.

He studied the Votaries, who bowed to him.

A wingback chair sat facing the far wall. The greenish fire from the furnace gave the impression of a regal woman seated in the furnishing as though it were some kind of throne. Langdon was suddenly overcome with a joy so great his physical self began to sob. Had she been teaching him something about his true lot in this world? And had he repaid her by embracing vulgar convention?

Shame shot through him. He willed himself nearer to aunt Thora, but somehow his attention would not sway from the ash faggots lying by the furnace. Langdon wondered if they were the ones from the yard. He watched as the Votaries in turn lifted each of the bundled boughs and fed them into the furnace. Two faggots remained, one of which was then retrieved by aunt Thora, who, the other-Langdon noted, was now masked in a similar pouch. Hers was of many colours, first the black-red of stale clotted blood, then the milky lustre of polished opal, then a shade of grey so banal it seemed to Langdon almost elegiac.

After aunt Thora's bundle had been slid into the furnace's green fire, only one bundle of ash boughs remained. Beside it the axe gleamed. Langdon hesitated for a brief flash, wondering if he had the fortitude to meet this requisite.

The Votaries clustered in a semi-circle around the furnace.

At once they removed the hoods from their heads. There were no heads.

From the neck of one there sprouted a gnarled mandrake, from the second, a jawbone jutted up crookedly from the severed stump, the third was a smear of light, like a candle flame.

The three magi of this secret faith reached upward to where Langdon's fleshless self loomed like sentient mist. The Votaries' gestures could have been either beseeching or reverential.

Langdon felt as though the sum of his life was being super-heated until only the essential salts remained. The presence of his aunt, of the Votaries, the verdant glimmer of the furnace, the cool dank perfume of the neglected basement...they all radiated a sig-nificance, a meaning, that was diamond-brilliant, diamond-hard. They coalesced to form a skeleton key, one that unlocked Langdon's existence, showed him that his all his endeavors and trials, all his passions and times of heartsickness or laughter were but a wayfar-ing from this, the occulted nerve-centre of his true life, the one that had been crackling secretly beneath the surface, like the vents that lie hidden in the floor.

Aunt Thora squatted down by the ash boughs, the axe held tightly in her spindly hands, waiting to birth her nephew into the sidereal garden she had tended all her life.

Nancy's attempts at CPR had been confused, panicked, and ulti-mately fruitless. Although the paramedics had arrived only a hand-ful of minutes after she'd made the sputtering, shock-laden 911 call, they were unable to revive Langdon.

"He just had the flu," she kept telling them as they wheeled his covered body out of the house.

"Unfortunately these kinds of things sometimes happen," one of the medics had told her.

Lost, Nancy made the phone calls and answered questions.

It was very late in the night before loneliness finally sank its teeth into her. She was lying on the living room sofa, sobbing into the silent house.

When her cries were answered, Nancy shot upright, listening.

From somewhere below came the blast of a shrill trumpet. Distant and haunting, it sounded once and died.

Her back was to the living room window, yet Nancy's mind's eye saw the image so perfectly reflected in the grimy pane: a hooded figure loomed just beyond the glass. It calmly peeled away its vague mask to reveal a gleaming wormwood star, one whose fey radiance was somehow familiar.

The Old Pageant

E DIDN'T WANT her to know how physically taxing he'd found the long drive to the woods, how tedious the prospect of unpacking now seemed, or how repugnantly primitive he found their accommodations to be upon their arrival. The holiday had the potential to be far too special an occasion for him to sour it by sulking.

The cabin had been in her family for decades, though the moment he spied it—an oblong box slumped between leprous-looking birch trees—he wondered why she didn't regard the cabin as a skeleton from her family's closet instead of a prideful heirloom.

After an anxious struggle to fit the copper key inside the ancient lock, the door gave, allowing the pair of them to be assaulted by the stench of long-trapped air. The dark had evidently grown so accustomed to the cabin's interior that it stubbornly refused to part for the sunbeams that the man and woman ushered in.

Shutters were peeled back, windows were pried ajar. She stripped the ancient white sheets from the beds and took them outside and hung them from the birch limbs so that the breezes might push out their mustiness.

They cleaned and unpacked and traded off-colour wisecracks. The supper they cooked together was hearty and its aroma managed to mask a bit of the cabin's cloying staleness.

After eating he delighted her by finding the detached wooden footboard that had once braced the lower bunk bed she'd slept on as a girl. It had been wound in a shower drape of translucent plastic and stored behind her grandmother's dormant sewing desk.

Her grandfather had carved (with visible skill and obvious love) an inscription into the wood:

Here lies Diana
Each and every summer
Dreaming...

She cried and ran her fingers along the grooved words as though they were Braille.

"I have another gift for you," he told her in a voice whose shakiness surprised him.

He was almost fearful of producing the ring case from his pocket.

Ultimately he opened the case and he asked her.

She accepted and they both began to shed fresh tears, but ones of happiness.

He uncorked the bottle of pinot noir. She stole a sip from the brimming glass he handed her. She then set it on the windowsill and told him not to move a muscle. Her purring tone thrilled him.

Leaning against the deep washbasin with its antiquated hand pump, he watched with increasing anticipation as she pushed together a pair of slender cots, draped a quilt across their bare mattresses, and stripped the dusty clothing from her body.

She giggled at his suggestion that they shut the door and windows, assuring him that they were all alone, no one within earshot. In fact, no one within walking distance.

He went to her.

The ferocity of her climax proved to him just how isolated they were, for she had always been painfully aware of the neighbours. Birds actually rustled free from a nearby tree, startled by her passionate cries.

Buoyed by his *petit mal*, he lay back in the humidity, hoping that the encroaching dusk would cool him.

"Well, we've officially christened this place," she beamed. She held up her left hand to admire the glinting star that now ringed her finger.

He asked her if she was happy.

"Very," she told him.

"When was the last time you were up here?"

"Not since I was eleven, the summer before my grandma died."

"How come your family never sold it? If the cabin wasn't being used, I mean."

She shrugged.

"It had been in the family for so long, no one ever thought of getting rid of it. My great-grandfather built this cabin with my great-grandmother. They actually lived here for a few years. Eventually they moved to Olympia where my great-grandfather had landed a job doing...something, I can't remember what it was. They used to spend their summers up here with their kids. Then my grandparents vacationed here with their kids, then on to my parents with my sister and me. And now us." She pecked his cheek and he smiled and tipped back the bottle of pinot noir.

"Did you like coming up here when you were a girl?"

"I loved it."

Her tone was richly sincere, if a shade melancholic.

He placed his head against her breast and asked her to tell him what it had been like. He was city-born, city-bred. Nature was to him as it should be to all: utterly bewildering, daunting in its autonomy.

"My grandmother used to take my sister and me on these marathon hikes where she'd point out all the different plant types. Or she'd try to teach us how to identify a bird by its call, things like that."

She began to chew her plump lower lip and he asked her what was wrong.

"Nothing."

His bladder had been throbbing for several minutes. He rose and muttered some euphemism for relieving himself which she did not find as funny as he'd hoped. He excused himself from the cabin.

Without, the countless boughs were now garlanded in fine shadows, ones that linked oak to ash to sycamore to yew as though it was some kind of dark ligament. Mosquitoes formed a buzzing fogbank. The temperature seemed to have jumped from humid to chilly with no temperate phase between.

He moved a respectable distance away and relieved himself on some spiky foliage. He experienced a sense of being not just isolated, but marooned.

Something skittered out from one thicket and was almost immediately subsumed by another. The cracking of twigs and the hushing spasms of leaves turned threatening.

He turned and ran back to the cabin, catching himself just before he came thundering through the front door. After regaining his composure, he crossed the threshold with artificial nonchalance.

She was cross-legged on the cots, her torso now covered in one of his loose t-shirts.

"You sick?"

She shook her head.

"You look pale."

He uncapped a bottle of water and handed it to her. She took it but did not drink. He nudged her sardonically.

"What's going on? I step out for a moment and when I come back inside it's like you're a million miles away."

"I'm sorry."

She entwined her fingers with his and kissed the back of his hand, then said:

"I guess this place has more memories than I realized."

"Bad ones?" (Wisely, he was treading lightly.)

"I think seeing the night beginning to fall outside reminded me of this stupid game my older sister invented called *Something Scary*."

"Um...okay..."

They both laughed a little bit.

"It sounds so stupid now, I know, but at the time that game really got to me."

"What's the goal of *Something Scary*?"

"To scare the piss out of whoever you're playing with, what else? Like I said, it sounds stupid."

"No, don't say that. Given that you were both kids at the time and stuck out in the boonies I can see how a game like that would have worked."

"Oh it did, believe me. But...*Something Scary* wasn't what got me upset just now. It was remembering something my grandmother introduced us to, another game."

"Oh?"

"See, *Something Scary* was just a typical kids' game. My sister and I would sit in the dark here and whisper little ghost stories to one another. Mine were never that good at all because I spooked really easily, so I always played it timid. My sister, she was good at it though. I mean *really* good. The funny thing is, later on I learned that most of her stories were just retellings of *Tales from the Darkside* episodes that she used to watch after my parents had gone to bed. Sometimes they were just old urban legends. Still, she knew how to tell a story."

"That seems to run in your family."

She rolled her eyes.

"No really! I've told you that your life sounds so much more interesting than mine. You've got storyteller instincts."

"Regardless, I remember one game of *Something Scary* where my sister said there was a decrepit hermit who lived in these woods. According to her story, the man's wife had gone out to fetch water one night many years ago but she never came back. So every night the man went out searching for his lost love. But of course after so many years the man had lost his mind, so if he saw any woman in the woods he would *make her* his wife. He'd just drag her away into the trees and she'd never be seen again. Any female had to fear being in these woods after sunset. And I had to try and *sleep* with that in my head! God, I fucking *hated* that story."

"That is pretty creepy. But what about the game your grandmother taught you?"

She cleared her throat needlessly.

"Almost every summer night we played *Something Scary*. My sister insisted on it. Until the summer I turned eleven."

"What happened that year? Did you outgrow being afraid?"

"You can't outgrow that. At least I know I can't... but not because of *Something Scary*; because of *The Old Pageant*."

"*The Old Pageant?*"

"That was the so-called game my grandmother introduced to my sister and me. We'd been playing *Something Scary*, whispering quietly, or what we believed was quietly, to ourselves. There was a rustling of cotton that terrified us, but it was only our grandmother rising out of her and grandfather's bed at the other end of this room. She shuffled over to us. I remember how her white cotton nightgown and her long white hair both seemed to glow in the dark. Without so much as a word she carefully unbolted the cabin door, pulled it open, then waved for my sister and me to come with her. We went out with her and I admit I was pretty excited at first. You know, being out at night, it was like an adventure. But the more we walked the less I liked it. I asked my grandmother how far we were going to walk. I remember that none of us were wearing shoes and that my feet were freezing from all the dew we'd traipsed through. I kept asking my sister if she knew where we were going but she wouldn't answer me. Finally my grandmother stopped us."

He'd forgotten to breathe for so long that his lungs actually ached. After gasping he asked where they'd been led.

"It was a really thick part of the woods, well off any of the marked trails. My grandma gestured for us to be very quiet. I could hear crickets and bullfrogs. My grandma pointed above her head and told my sister and me to listen closely."

"What did you hear?"

"Creaking, a very low creaking. At first I thought it was the thicker boughs of the trees being rubbed together by the wind. You hear that kind of noise all the time out here. But this was actually my grandmother. She was making this low creaking sound in her throat, but it was *perfect*. You'd swear it was the sound of wood grinding in the wind. My sister laughed, I remember that because it was the only time I ever saw my grandma get angry. She grabbed my sister's face and told her to be very careful because the three of us were tempting fate being out there in the dead of night. She said that if we weren't careful there would be things from the woods that would take our place in the world. When we came to learn *The Old Pageant* we had to treat it with respect. By then I couldn't get that awful creaking sound out of my head. I put my hands against my ears. I probably started to cry. My grandma put her arm around my shoulder and took my sister and me back to the cabin."

He could feel his brow knitting in confusion, and quite possibly in anger.

"Why on earth would your grandmother have done that to you two?"

She lifted her hand to stop him.

"I know, I know. But what amazes me is that I truly hadn't even *thought* about that night until we got up here. But that night wasn't what scared me earlier tonight. It was something that happened the next night, or a few nights later. Hell, I might have only dreamt it."

He gripped her hand and kissed the back of it, giving the engagement ring a playful twist to remind her that this was a happy occasion. "We don't have to talk about this anymore. I didn't mean to upset you," he told her.

"No, I need to get this out. That other night...my grandma woke only me. When we got outside the cabin she told me that my sister didn't understand. *Only you felt it, my Diana*, was how she put it. We went walking, the two of us, even further into the woods."

"And did you hear the creaking?"

"I didn't hear anything; no crickets, no wind, nothing. It was perfectly still. My grandma took my hand and led me down to this old tree. And she told me to watch while she imitated this tree. She started that horrible creaking sound again, only this time she began to twist her arms and her fingers until her shadow was exactly like that of the tree. And I mean *exactly*. She seemed to be getting taller too. I know that sounds insane, believe me, but I felt dwarfed by her..."

"Shadow-play," he assured her.

"Sure, but..."

"But what?"

"Then a sound came from the tree beside my grandmother. It was a newborn baby crying."

He felt his skin constrict and go cold against his spine. His eyes were watering.

"A what?"

"A newborn baby. I swear to Christ. It was coming from the tree and then when I turned around to face it, the tree's bark was all swollen and pink. And then my grandmother stopped that creaking noise and all I could hear was that awful, shrill crying. It echoed through the trees. My grandmother whispered to me not to be afraid, that this was just the tree taking part in The Old Pageant. We mimic them, they mimic us. She went over to the tree and actually started singing to it...a lullaby...Oh fuck, why did I have to remember this tonight of all nights? After all these years..."

"You were a kid! You were dreaming or sick. And I don't mean to speak ill of the dead, but it sounds as though your grandmother might have been a little touched in the head."

He hated himself for prodding further but he needed to know what happened next, for he felt oddly cheated.

"Nothing," she told him. "I don't even remember our walk back to the cabin. The next day was just like any other as far as I can recall; swimming at the lake, colouring books, Go Fish, the usual. That autumn my grandfather got sick. My sister and I never came back to the cabin."

"Until now?"

"Until now."

They drank the rest of the wine and did everything they could to pretend Diana's memory had not brought to their holiday an elusive yet very present affliction. He wondered about being amorous again but it somehow felt improper.

She drifted off.

Though exhausted, sleep evaded him.

A grave moon illumed her old footboard. Its inscription, coupled with the way it was propped against the basin, made the slab of polished cedar look more like a headstone than a bed piece.

Here lies Diana

He looked over at her. She was breathing shallowly. Not wishing to disturb her, he slipped out onto the porch.

The night was still but, mercifully, not as silent as the one she'd described to him. He could hear the crickets and bullfrogs.

He also heard the groan of wind-bullied wood.

Something stark flitted in his peripheral vision.

He craned his head to the left, and for a beat all was right with the world again, for he was assured that what he'd glimpsed was merely the white sheets trembling upon the limbs of the birch tree with its equally spectral-looking bark.

But then he realized that the rest of the forest was motionless.

It was not wind that stirred the trunk, or the sheet that billowed like a crown of crone's hair, like a bridal train.

He backed up until he hit the cabin wall. He turned to call Diana's name, but the figure that he viewed through a pane sullied with moonlight and grime was not one that would have recognized him.

Fabric licked the side of his face. It was now near enough to touch him.

One of its limbs was brightened by a distinct and concentrated glint. Was it wearing the engagement ring to mock or punish him?

His eyes squinted shut instinctively. He raised his boneless arms and held them in mimicry of ancient boughs. He prayed his novice pageantry would fool it.

The Stiles of Palemarsh

"SAYS HERE YOUR reservation is for two, Mr. Morrow," remarked the concierge.
Ian Morrow neither needed nor wanted reminding of
this fact, and he couldn't help but feel that the overfed
man at the reception desk was taking perverse pleasure
in grinding this verbal salt into his wounded pride. The man even
went so far as to spin the computer screen around to evidence his
claim. The chunky, archaic monitor creaked on its nest. Ian didn't
bother to look at it.

"It was originally for two," he muttered. "But I'm here alone."

"Can't give you no discount," the concierge returned, jerking the
monitor back into place. "Set rate, you know."

"I'm not asking for one," Ian said curtly. The tone was so unlike him that a feeling of shame painfully twisted his insides. He
snapped his credit card onto the reception desk and tried to avoid
further eye-contact.

"It's a very fine room; plenty of space, nice soft bed. Air-conditioned of course, which is a blessing on days like this, yeah?"

"Sounds perfect, thanks."

The concierge nodded noncommittally.

June heat waves were hardly uncommon for Ontario, but Ian
(naïvely, he now realized) had expected his Welsh destination to be
ideally temperate. Perhaps this was because, to hear Cari describe
it, Wales was awash in milk and honey. But then, anything, no matter how banal, could be made to sound fantastical if Cari's mood
was in an upward cycle. Honeymooning "across the pond" in the
village of Palemarsh had been her idea, as had been the June wedding date, the traditional Welsh vows, and the marriage site of Saint
Tudwal Church.

Her familial roots stretched well past the new world boundaries

of Canada and ran deep in Wales. Ian had been happy to indulge
Cari in this area, having always felt only a tepid kinship with the
stew of British and European cultures that informed his own family
bloodline.

Wales and her family's connection to it had been but one of
Cari's many fixations. Ayurvedic medicine, the silversmith's craft,
speed reading, and so many more had each been her primary fascination at one time or another. But their allure would bleed out
whenever she experienced the inevitable emotional downturn.

Her depressive phases were unquestionably worse than her
manic ones. Unnerving or frustrating as it was to be awoken by Cari
compulsively waxing the kitchen floor at three in the morning, or to
try to keep pace with her breathless chatter, Ian would have happily
taken them over seeing his lover become the grey, maimed creature
to which her downward cycles reduced her. In those tedious spans,
Cari could scarcely do more than sink into their bed or, at best,
their living room sofa. She would stare sightlessly, her chapped lips
twitching reflexively and mutely every now and again as though she
was a beached fish.

Throughout those interminable low days and nights, Ian could
almost comprehend the impulse to consent to a loved one receiving
electroshock therapy. Without the merest wisp of sadism, even, he
was confident, in the roiling deeps of his subconscious, he would
have signed any waiver, accepted any radical therapy. He simply
wanted Cari to be free again, for that was precisely as he viewed
her: as one prematurely interred in a vault of negative forces. But she
was in there somewhere. He knew she was. If only the controlled
electric surge could press into her temples, if only those sparks of
unthinkable wattage could pierce through that catatonic shell and
bore out the woman he loved.

Ian unlocked the handsomely carved door with the key the concierge had given him.

The suite was much slighter than its online photos had suggested, and one step into the room made it clear that what the Welsh
considered air-conditioned differed from what Ian was accustomed
to. He flung his suitcase onto the bed, causing the box spring to
squeak like startled mice. He experienced a mild, if ironic, relief
that he would be using this conspicuous furnishing for sleep and
nothing besides.

Upon the mirror-backed desk, a complimentary bottle of cham-
pagne stood between a pair of long-stemmed flutes. A tented card

offered its congratulations. Ian couldn't help but feel mocked by the display. He wrung the foil from the bottle's neck and uncorked it. He took a swig, and then tossed the card away without reading its inscription.

Glaring out the window he saw a sloping meadow whose grasses bowed and were righted in turn by the wind. Cari's relatives were somewhere beyond those glens and orchards. The thought made Ian's insides chill. He then randomly flashed back to the curt exchange with the concierge and once more felt pangs of guilt.

He needed to clear his head. From his luggage he fished out his runners, a pair of shorts and a t-shirt. Humidity be damned, he needed a run.

Crossing the crowded lobby made Ian feel the burn of self-consciousness, imagining as he did that every pair of eyes was upon him, mocking his athletic attire and the pale flesh of his exposed legs.

Palemarsh's high street was, Ian wagered, about as close to bustling as the village ever knew. Figures moved in and out of the charming, if antiquated, shops. But Ian found displeasure in their company. He felt that they, too, were studying him, judging him. As he passed the window of the furniture maker's and the butcher's, faces seemed to draw toward the glass as though he was a flame and they moths. A delivery van and a pickup truck rattled over hills that were paved with ancient, uneven cobblestone. The motion distorted Ian's perception of the driver, for the face was an inhuman smudge.

He began to jog faster, and his legs, stiff from the transatlantic flight, throbbed painfully in protest. There was the temptation to pause in order to stretch them, but Ian adjudged that he deserved this punishment.

Rounding the corner, he welcomed the sight of a dirt road that led away from downtown Palemarsh and into a more bucolic setting. Briefly he noted the road sign, Wheat Sheaf Lane, before the town gave way to old-growth trees, and farmland. Ditches lined both edges of the lane, reducing the road to something only nominally wider than a footpath. Ian followed the gentle bend, wincing as the water that sat pooled in the ditches created a greater and more pungent humidity. Every time he moved beneath a taller tree he felt gratitude for a fleeting scrap of shade, even though such respites only made the long stretches of open sun-soaked road all the more uncomfortable.

Eventually all shade was behind him and he found himself flanked by sprawling fields of what he assumed by the colour to be wheat. Yet they looked more bleached than golden, and the shoots were limp, as if wilted or trampled. Were they harvesting dead grass here? Motes flitted above the flat fields, and these desiccated visions alerted Ian to his own parched throat. He reached down to pluck his water bottle from its belt clip, then realized that in his emotional state he'd neglected to bring anything to re-hydrate himself.

All at once the distance he'd run dilated into something hopeless, a journey of a mythic scale. His pace began to slacken and his head began to swim, so much so that Ian only became aware that he'd been sharing the road with a hatchback car when the driver laid down on her horn. It let out a thin peeping noise, keen as a shrieking child. The vehicle veered around Ian, who was also trying to leap clear of it. He stepped too near to the ditch and quickly found himself lying face-first in the mud. Pain flared in his ankle.

As the woman sped off, she extended an arm out the driver's side window and gave Ian a gesture that he presumed was meant to both chastise and offend him.

With care, he righted himself then limped over to the wooden fence that distinguished the lane from the open field. The beams creaked when Ian leaned against them. Looking down at his clay-spattered body, coupled with the unfortunate knowledge that his ankle might be sprained, nearly brought Ian to tears.

'Why am I here?' he asked himself. 'What am I *doing*?'

Drawing in a calming breath, Ian willed himself to be centred.

'I'll walk back to the hotel,' he thought. But the pain in his left leg instantly shot down this solution.

He needed assistance: water, a drive back to the inn, and possibly medical attention. Glancing over his shoulder, he noticed the barn at the far end of the field. There was likely a farmhouse somewhere on the property as well, but the less distance he had to walk the better.

A wooden step-stile was arched over the fence. Ian cautiously scaled and descended it on the other side.

Dried grasses crunched beneath his runners as Ian, slowly yet impatiently, crossed the field. The sun pressed beams of white light and heat against him. Seeing the condition of the barn quashed his thin hopes for assistance, for the structure was nearly dilapidated. Gaps stretched open between several of the wall boards, giving Ian the impression of extracted teeth. The interior appeared empty.

"Hello?" Ian cried.

Silence.

But a figure then stepped out of the murk and into the sunlit mouth of the barn's doorway.

The man was tall but his rod-straight posture did not betray his age. Only after Ian had gotten close enough to see the man's long-receded hairline and the drooping flesh of his face did he realize that the farmer was old. An antique two-pronged hay fork was clutched in one hand. He was dressed in corduroy trousers and a pale chambray shirt, both of which looked uncharacteristically clean.

Ian couldn't be sure, but he thought that the sight of his own lame step brought a twinkle of delight to the old farmer's grey eyes.

"Sorry to bother you," called Ian. He shuffled forward to narrow the gap between himself and the farmer.

"Looks like you could use some help," the old man replied. His Welsh accent lent his voice a melodic lilt, not unlike birdsong.

"Yes, I could."

Ian noted, with curious relief, that the man's face was rather benign. He was looking closely at Ian.

"That accent, lad; are you an American?"

Ian shook his head, "Canadian." He slightly lifted his injured leg. "I twisted my ankle running on the road there. I was hoping you might be able to drive me back to my hotel."

The man raised a hand, flexed it in a strange and seemingly noncommittal gesture. "That's a problem."

"I'm staying at the hotel just on the high street back there. And I'll gladly give you some money for gas."

"Begging your pardon, lad," the man returned, "but the problem is that I haven't anything for you to put petrol in. These old legs o' mine are the only carriage I have!"

"Oh."

"I can offer you a rest though. And a spot of food if'n you're peckish."

As though on cue, Ian's stomach gurgled noisily, reminding him of the many hours he'd gone without nourishment.

"Uh...okay."

The farmer moved his skullish head in a nod and began toward the wooden house, which Ian only then spotted. He was grateful that his host's pace was geriatric, for he was able to keep in step with his injured leg.

"Mind the railing, it's in need of a good sanding," the man advised once they reached the porch.

Within, the farmhouse's walls did little to fend off the heat. If anything, their purpose was reversed. Ian leaned against the doorframe long enough for his eyes to grow accustomed to the dim interior. The living room to his right was framed in wooden shelves that bowed under the burden of seeming junk. The room was made impassable by four bulky picnic tables, the tops of which were also smothered under bric-a-brac: costume jewellery, lanterns, books, and plastic dolls with grubby faces. Ian recalled a so-called 'reality' television show Cari had loved to watch that dealt with compulsive hoarders. He also recalled, much to his dismay, the infamous crime scene photos from the home of Ed Gein.

"This way," the farmer advised. Ian followed with boyish obedience. Once inside the kitchen, he accepted his host's offer of a wobbly wooden chair.

It felt as though he had entered a brick oven. Everything Ian touched seemed ember-warmed. The kitchen was another over-packed nook, with a chunky refrigerator that looked only faintly newer than the woodstove that squatted in one corner. The windows were all fully ajar, but their lack of screens gave the bluebottles freedom to crawl in and buzz about the room. It also allowed the hot winds to deliver blasts of fine field grit.

There came an unpleasant creak as the farmer pulled the doors of the Victorian pot dresser open. From this he extracted an iron saucepan. He tugged hard on the oversized chrome handle of the fridge, which clunked as it gave. From the sour-smelling icebox the old man produced a large mason jar filled with brackish liquid. Ian felt his stomach flip.

Wordlessly and with an ease that comes with habitual actions, the man fired up the woodstove and began to heat the green-brown liquid inside the iron skillet. Either he knew exactly how much wood was required to cook this dish or Ian was too overheated to notice any further increase in the room's temperature. Either way the fire from the black iron hull was hardly noticeable.

Ian was about to lie to his host about lacking an appetite when the aroma of the warmed dish reached him. It made his stomach rumble eagerly.

"Barley soup," the man announced as he set a steaming wooden bowl before Ian, "made it myself."

Ian smiled crookedly and took up his spoon. His initial sip was done purely for etiquette's sake. The broth was the finest thing Ian had ever tasted.

He ate greedily and when his dish was emptied he felt sated, almost dozy.

"How's that ankle?" his host asked.

"It feels a little better. I must not have actually sprained it. You know, I just realized that I didn't even introduce myself. My name is Ian."

The man slid his fingers around Ian's offered hand. "A pleasure." Ian waited for the old man to reciprocate, but it was not to be.

"Tell me, Ian, what brings you to Palemarsh? Not many folks venture this far from Cardiff."

The room's tightness and sweltering temperature hit Ian afresh. He was so reluctant to answer his host's question that he very nearly rose and exited the house.

"Holiday," he uttered at last.

"Alone?"

Did the old man know something? Was he related to Cari? What if he and the woman in the hatchback had conspired to bring Ian here in order to mete out some familial punishment?

Ludicrous...

"I was originally supposed to be here with someone. It didn't work out."

Who was he to pry into Ian's affairs? A bit of hospitality did not render him Ian's Father Confessor.

"Did she stand you up at the altar?"

He did know. Ian was certain.

"I'm not...Look, I don't want to go into this. And I'm sorry; I didn't catch your name..."

The old man rose with a grunt. "If you're able to walk, why don't I show you a shortcut back to the high street?"

"Um, sure, okay."

The sun practically blinded Ian as he trailed across the yard behind his aged host.

Precisely where the field merged with the forest stood a pair of lean stones. They were, by Ian's estimation, roughly six feet in height and were set slightly askew, one planted just ahead of the other. This gave the impression not of a barrier but a passage.

"You see that squeeze-stile there?" The man's pointing finger tapered toward an unpleasantly overgrown fingernail, scuffed and ragged and yellow.

"I see the stones. Is that what you mean?"

"Aye, that's a squeeze-stile. They were used to mark the boundaries between one man's land and another's. You slip between those stones and you'll find yourself on the path. It's a fine walk. Eventually you'll come to a wooden step-stile at the far end of the trail.

Climb that and you'll set down at the head of Wheat Sheaf Lane, right at the high street."

"Sounds straightforward. Thanks for everything."

"Remember," he advised, raising higher his finger with its unsightly nail, "you always want to keep the sun on your left shoulder when you're passing through that glen, lad."

Ian nodded, despite not caring to understand the wives' tale advice of rural folk.

He crossed the last of the field. Perspiration was already beginning to dampen his underarms and back. The tree-shaded glen would be a welcome relief.

The stones of the squeeze-stile seemed to radiate coolness, as though they were righted ice floes instead of granite slabs. Vein-like ribbons of moss suggested the stones' age as well as lending their appearance a strange texture, like a relief map of some remote land.

'Squeeze' was an apt name, for, as Ian soon discovered, the gap between the off-set rocks was claustrophobic, and their uneven faces were made almost hazardous by jutting keen ridges. When he was pressed between the two standing stones, desperation flushed hotly through Ian, followed instantly by a tarry sense of despair. Childishly, he shut his eyes and held his breath before pushing through to the other side of the stile.

The grove expanded all around him. The velvet leaves of the oaks pulsated and the insects offered up a subtle fanfare. While he knew that his passage through the squeeze-stile had not been anywhere near as dramatic or traumatic as he'd imagined, Ian was nonetheless grateful for the verdant expanse at his elbows, the soft trail under his soles. This new environ seemed to lessen the dull ache in his ankle. He was already fantasizing about lying on that King-size bed, his bad leg propped, the air conditioner blasting at full power and the television playing loudly.

In what seemed to be no time at all, Ian spotted the wooden step-stile that marked the trail's end.

Age and the elements had smoothed the wood steps to such a degree that they felt ice-slick beneath him. Ian scaled and descended the inverted-V carefully, experiencing an unwarranted sense of achievement when his feet struck Wheat Sheaf Lane.

But this spike of exuberance became lost in a sudden blast of terror; a terror that was as inexplicable as it was unbearable. About him, the midday sun shone warmly through the screens of healthy leaves. Swallows trilled and a temperate breeze pressed the entire scene as rhythmically as the evening tide. There was nothing that should have upset him. Ian scanned his surroundings more closely, hoping yet at the same time *not* hoping that he might glimpse whatever obscured threat had aroused in him this pulsing dread. But there was no danger to be seen, not even the potential for danger. All was thoroughly pastoral. Ian could even see the rooftops of the high street; a reminder that civilization was but a few steps away.

But it was all still somehow unbearable. The openness of the lane, the visibility of the cloudless sky was too immense, too open. Rather than providing airiness and relief, the space aroused a reverse claustrophobic response in Ian, who began to view himself as exposed; a speck of tender prey standing unprotected and wholly visible.

This, Ian realized, was true panic.

Instinct urged him backward, until he was up against the wood stile. Turning about, he clamoured up the rungs and down again, sighing with unalloyed joy at being concealed once more.

The forest, or rather some unseen aspect of the forest, enveloped Ian, wrapping itself around him, sealing him protectively, as a wolf-mother would her cub.

The woods had changed. Ian was aware of it the instant he turned to walk back along the trail. Both light and temperature had noticeably diminished during his brief stint on the lane. He assumed that the density of the trees was capable of shielding the sun's rays and its heat to such a degree, but the further he walked the less likely this reasoning seemed, for there was an undeniable chill to the air, a crispness that was indigenous to October. Halting, Ian craned his head back, shielding his eyes with his meshed fingers.

A thunderstorm; yes, this was the obvious explanation for the sudden and drastic change to both temperature and light. It must have been rolling in swiftly, for the sky was now deeply leaden.

Reasoning that he should rush to shelter before the storm hit, Ian prepared to run when a detail of the woods froze him in place and forced him to look up again, and then, doubting his senses, a third time.

Why should there be so much more of the sky visible now than only a few moments ago?

Because the trees that lined the path were now leafless.

Ian stared dumbly at the naked branches that domed him like skeletal wings. He looked down the path, at the fire-vivid hue of those leaves that still clung to a few of the trees, at the brown carpet of fallen foliage. Mist swayed lazily above the slumbering soil, obscuring the further bends in the trail.

The words of the old farmer coursed through Ian's mind, about the need to keep the sun on his left shoulder. Had the farmer somehow entranced him? Possibly drugged his food?

The wooden stile exit was only a few feet behind him. Perhaps the panic he'd experienced on the open lane had also been part of the old man's spell. But now Ian knew better. He needed to get back to the high street. He turned about and ran toward Wheat Sheaf Lane.

After several minutes his predicament became clear to him, for the trail wended and curved in bewildering ways, stretching to an impossible length. The lane beyond the woods was nowhere to be seen.

He turned back around and retraced his steps, still running as hard as his aching legs and burning lungs would allow. The air was perfumed with smoke and damp earth. Perspiration cooled rapidly on his flesh, chilling him. To his right Ian spotted blotches of colour that brightened the otherwise uniform grey. An apple tree was flaunting red fruit. The apples dangled from its misshapen limbs like gaudy costume jewelry.

As he rounded the next in a seemingly endless array of twists in the path, Ian caught sight of movement.

The carpet of leaves rustled as something rose up from the ground.

Ian nearly tripped, so startled was he by the sight of the richly coloured moth that was hovering above the leaf-laden ground. The pattern on its wings was unsightly—a blotchy mess of purples and blacks and greenish-yellow. The moth had perched itself upon a chalky-looking stone. It was a hideously large bug.

Only it was not a bug at all, and the pale slab that supported it was not old stone. It was old flesh. Ian could now distinguish the head and the arms that were but skin-draped bones. The dark blotches were not moth wings, but the ugly patches where the figure's un-circulated fluids had pooled. Gripping branches for support, the shape pulled itself upright, turned, and made its way onto the path.

At fist Ian thought the figure hermaphroditic, for breasts sagged above the distended belly and the genitals were almost comically small. But then Ian could see the drooping testicles, the stubby penis. It was a young man, or had once been.

Its jaw was slack. The eyes were closed and sunken. Ian could distinctly see the manner in which the eyelids seemed to be drawing into the sockets, as though the jelly they guarded had deteriorated.

Within the gape of the mouth: leaves, a tangle of sharp October hues. The thing's head was like an overstuffed yard-waste sack. Excess leaves were tugged free by the damp breeze and went flitting off like startled birds.

It raised one of its rope-thin arms.

Ian ran.

Slowly, as though time did not matter in the slightest, the pale thing began to follow him.

The pain in Ian's ankle flared, wordlessly pleading for him to cease. But terror was his prime mover and it refused to let him yield.

Finally Ian found his way to the opposite end of the grove, near the farm with its standing stones. The squeeze-stile was visible, jutting up from the damp October mud like granite fangs. Well beyond it was the wall of the old host's barn. Ian shouted something, waved his arms, all on the thin hope that the aged farmer would step out from that crumbling structure.

Ian glanced backward. What he witnessed caused him to stumble, to fall and get partially subsumed by the cold, sucking clay of the path.

There were three of them now, a colourless trio shambling awkwardly along the path. One of them, the woman, was the latest to join. She stood up from her shallow resting place between two yews, then cut a wide and manic stride onto the path. Like the first boyish revenant, these others also stalked the trail with their eyes unblinkingly shut.

Ian unleashed a wordless cry then lunged toward the squeeze-stile. He could see the hay field basking under the summer sun whose heat he now yearned for. Here, the October chill seeped in deeper and deeper, causing him to shudder and curse his light attire.

From the still woods Ian now heard a low gassy noise. It was emotionless, meaningless; stray air passing through grave-withered throats. The sound encouraged him to press frantically between the squeeze-stile.

The righted stones were so deceptively keen that Ian didn't realize he was cut until he saw the fresh red stippling upon the sun-bleached granite. 'Are the stones weeping blood?' he wondered. Then he felt the stinging in his forearms and his wrists and upon the back of his neck.

"Jesus," he cried, staring in disbelief at his wounds. He was queerly offended by the very idea that he could be harmed in such a way. He pressed deeper into the gap in the stiles and was stricken with the cold and shrivelling realization that he was now stuck between the stones.

His attempt to call for help resulted in a stifled grunt as his lungs struggled for air. The further Ian tried to press, the tighter the stones' grip became. Every jerk of one of his bleeding limbs tightened the crag-vice. He shrieked and wriggled and, unexpectedly, began to sob.

He looked down to see his own tears and blood falling onto the tops of his runners.

Under his muddy soles lay an array of objects. There was an envelope whose inscription had been smudged to the point of being illegible. There was a thimble and a man's wallet and a St. Christopher's medallion.

There was also a ring.

As to the how and the why, Ian was at a loss, but as to what, he was certain. There was no mistaking it, not after he'd studied it so long in the jeweller's in the Mervish Village. Cari had adored it, worn it proudly. And finally, on that final ugly night, had twirled it around and around as she sobbed and kept repeating "Please, Ian. Please..."

But he'd fled. Whether or not it had simply been a case of the proverbial cold feet, Ian couldn't say, but just nine days before their wedding, every one of Cari's needs, her afflictions, became inflated in his mind, until they were as smothering as this squeeze-stile.

So he'd left. He'd shattered her world and then left her there among the shards. Could he have endured such a blow, even with his supposedly healthy psychology?

He hearkened back to the flurry of 3 a.m. voicemails, the mountain of emails (most of which were scarcely more than a sentence). She had begged him. This was, Ian now realized with an awful lacerating clarity, much more than obsessive attachment. Cari had been desperate. Her pleas were just that; not for Ian's hand in marriage, but for his help. She'd been slipping. She'd known it. And on some level Ian knew it. His reneging of his proposal had blasted the scaffolding out from under Cari. Now she was clinging to the ledge, feeling the winds sucking her toward an endless freefall, all the way down into the abyss that was her own fractured soul.

He likely couldn't have cured her, but at the very least he could have been there for her. Perhaps something as minute as replying to an email or making a phone call to Cari's sister, advising her of what had happened, perhaps these measures could have kept Cari from falling.

Instead he'd run. He'd raced out of his apartment at the time when he and Cari had supposed to be catching their honeymoon flight. Instead it was just him and a stubborn childish impulse. His landline had rung. He'd known it was Cari, known it. But he let the phone ring lonely and raced out the door.

His last sight of Cari had been of her curled foetal-like in her apartment hall, wheezing out a pathetic "Please" while she spun the ring on her finger. This ring.

Now he was racing still, running for his sanity if not his life.

Unable to press through, Ian resorted to pulling himself backward.

When the stile birthed him, he laughed with relief, an elation that was ruptured by the sight of the shut-eyed creatures shambling down the path. There had been three a moment ago (Or had he been ensnared for much longer? What else could explain the harvest moon gleaming blue and cool above the trees?); now they were too numerous to count. The figures moved in a great horde.

Ian then heard the low, thick awful growling of hounds. Their barking startled him, made him cry out.

His voice drew the attention of the sightless things.

Instinct caused Ian to reach back between the stile stones. He tried in vain to retrieve Cari's engagement band. His mind spun back to the image of the old farmer's house and he imagined Cari's ring soon being stored with the rest of the clutter.

He rose and he ran, this time back toward the step-stile at the head of Wheat Sheaf Lane. He argued with himself, first positing how futile his attempt to escape was, then reasoning that he had to try. There was no other option.

He ran off the lane, weaving and ducking between the old growth trees. A rumble of thunder shook the forest and when the storm clouds began to knit across the moon's face, Ian pined for its cold light.

Assuming he was hearing correctly, Ian swore that the throng of revenants were racing to one dead end of the path, then coming about and retracing their steps, again and again and again. Was this wild hunt for him, he wondered?

Exhausted, he wrapped his arm weakly around an old oak. He bent over and breathed deeply. His jaw was chattering from the frigid night air.

A figure bolted up opposite him. The leaves which had concealed it fell from the luminous body like wide black snowflakes.

The woman, whom Ian could only see from behind, stood.

Her body was familiar enough for Ian to shut his eyes in order to shut it out.

He ran madly, not daring to turn back. The hunt, he heard, had reached the far end of the path and was now circling back toward him. The woman from the forest, however, was much nearer. Ian knew he was within her reach, or would be soon.

He opened his eyes and saw the wooden step-stile once again. It was forty, perhaps fifty yards ahead.

The cabal of rasping creatures rounded the bend. He could see them, and though their thick eyelids remained closed, Ian was sure they were seeing him.

He slid down the decline and landed back on the footpath. He flung himself at the step-stile and scrabbled up its smooth beams. Reaching its topmost rung, Ian dove headlong into a blinding light.

The first clue he had regarding his safety was a blazing heat against his face. His eyes fluttered opened. The sight of the cloudless summer sky was too bright. Ian sat up.

He purposely avoided looking back into the woods. Even the peripheral image of the tapered hand slinking back between the slats of the wooden stile could not tempt him to peek. His eyes remained locked on the high street that was only paces away.

Crossing under the sign for Wheat Sheaf Lane, Ian examined his bloodied hands. His wounds required care but were nothing he couldn't treat himself.

The window for the druggist's shop hurled a shocking self-reflection. Ian took a moment to wipe the blood from his still-weeping cheeks and to pull the leaves and twigs from his hair. He tugged his torn T-shirt down and hobbled back to the hotel.

The same concierge was on duty. At first he looked relieved to see Ian coming through the entrance, until he spotted his guest's condition.

"Mother Mary!" he called.

"I'm okay, I'm okay," Ian muttered, barely loud enough for him to hear himself.

The concierge moved out from behind the counter.

"I'm pleased you're back, sir," he said. A fan of pink paper slips was held in one fist. "There've been several messages for you, from back in Canada."

Ian glimpsed the names and numbers that had been scribbled on the Message slips; one was from Cari's father, three from her sister, and one from a mutual friend of his and Cari's.

"Not bad news, I hope," the concierge said, though his tone seemed to convey just the opposite.

"Yes," Ian said, his voice scarcely slipping past the fresh lump in his throat, "yes, I'm afraid it is."

Mare's Nest

I.

THEIR INGRESS INTO the corridor is retarded by a leaden energy; the heavy aura of apprehension, perhaps even of fate. The purpose of this visit is undoubtedly the factor that taints their passage.

As he walks with his beloved, his hand clasped around hers, the man can't help but note the subtle changes in the faculty's glamour as their heels drum against the floor. For instance, the faux Grecian columns of cheap plaster that distinguish this ward from the others suggest that this is a place of passage, perhaps into an ancient world, a more rarefied plane.

The ivory walls with their moulding of black rubber grow up from a floor whose linoleum is the red of psoriatic flesh. Both the man and the woman are versed enough in topics soft and secretive to note that this trio of colours—the moon-pale, the menstrual red, the vertigo black—is alchemical in nature, and this knowledge manages to shift the meaning of this place. To her it is now less a clinic as a Lodge. For him the whole colour scheme sweats fatality.

They slip through the appropriate sliding glass doors. At his insistence she nestles into the waiting room's only available chair. They silently study the other patients, most of whom are either pretending to read magazines or are muttering distractive conversations between themselves or into slender mobile phones.

When her name is finally called the pair moves solemnly into the specialist's narrow office, their every step akin to those being marched to the scaffold.

The tests had been a frightening, draining affair, but jokes had been mumbled between them. On that day there had been humour, been hope. This morning's meeting hosts neither.

Results are given. Never has the word 'positive' sounded so vile, so toxic, so methodically cruel.

A treatment regimen is explained in detail, but with the grim caveat that it is at best a stalling tactic against an inevitable end. Though the prognosis is hers, she sheds no tears. He weeps enough for them both.

2.

A mute journey from clinic to homestead. He goes straight into the kitchen and begins preparing their supper, numbly, mechanically.

He ladles out two bowls of stew from the stove and joins her at the table of walnut. Its natural dark hue and sheen bring to his mind the image of a polished casket lid. The thought robs him of his appetite, which was only slight to begin with.

They poke at their meal with their spoons. He studies her and although she senses his scrutiny, she pretends not to notice and makes an effort to avoid eye contact.

Her hair sits bound in a sloppy ponytail. Most of the wisps were resistant to her comb and now halo her head like some loose and delicate nest. Has her face changed or is it his knowledge of her condition that makes it seem so drawn and sallow? The mouth that he'd kissed on their wedding day is visibly thinner and the eyes seem to hold the ghost of the woman he'd married.

"Well?" she asks at last.

He is nonplussed and his face advertises as much.

"Don't you think now would be a good time to talk about it?"

"About what?"

"My idea. The idea."

He sets down his spoon, tents his hands before his tired face.

She delicately closes her hands over his. "Please," she says, "please."

He shakes his head. His eyes begin to leak fresh tears and he feels foolish and fatigued by this new demonstration of sorrow. "There's nothing to discuss."

"But there is," she replies. "There's a lot to discuss."

He rises from the table, moves with heavy footfalls to the living room fireplace. He grips the mantle of stained yew and, though he tries to resist doing so, he feels his eyes scanning the meticulously carved chimney stones. They'd selected each stone from quarries, beaches, and burying grounds. Once chosen, every stone was engraved with images and glyphs of painstaking precision. From the earliest phase of their courtship the pair had enjoyed a rare mode of intimacy.

She enters the room and goes to her desk. The cedar of its drawers perfumes the still air, suggesting lush renewal. The desk was a gift from the man who now sits broken at the far end of the living room. He had carved it for her with his own hands, decorating it with the most delicate of filigrees, of phantasmal forms. Standing in the nook of the living room, the desk has been her tiny sanctuary, the place where she would add patiently-forged stanzas into one of the leather-bound notebooks that stand side by side on the desk's upper shelf, surely and reliably as soldiers.

Her poems are Classical, though less so in structure as in intent. She writes of that which cannot be captured but merely conveyed, the things that are most ancient and yet so hotly present at all times in all the Earth's corners. Her words are as signal fires in the night that lies between poet and audience: they illuminate that which exists independently of both. Her stanzas point toward the unseen.

Some, though not many, of her poems were inspired by her dreams. Ironically, these are the poems with which she feels the least resonance, often dismissing them as either forcefully wish-like or too opulent in their imagery.

'Mare's Nest' is the lone powerful exception. Penned in a white heat some three years prior, this poem is one that she considers her finest. He had encouraged her to submit it for publication, but she, taking for good or ill after Dickinson, her favourite poet, stashed the poem in her desk along with all her others. Her poetry, she believes, is hers alone and therefore she would be the one to choose who could read it.

He has read every one of her poems more than once.

She selects the appropriate journal from the shelf. It falls open to the proper page as if by fate, but it is undoubtedly due to her obsessive re-reading of 'Mare's Nest.'

She begins to read aloud,

'The egrigore, the effigy,
such as my spirit longs to be.
Blacker than the starless climes,
Adorned with bones and hellish slime,
a fount of foreign ecstasies.
Grotesque upon a crypt wall, creeping,
Night-Ride that frees the Dream from sleeping.'

Like a child in tantrum, he stomps toward their bedroom.

He is lying on his back, staring up at the evening shadows of the leafless tree branches that pulse upon the ceiling. A new shadow joins the pattern; hers. She is stationed in the doorway, the poetry book held to her breast. Wordlessly she advances and sits upon the foot of the bed.

"Can you hear me out at least?" she asks.

His hands are folded upon his chest as if to convey relaxation, yet she can see his heart pressing against his chest in a rapid rhythm. She touches his leg.

"I can't do it," he admits at last, "I'm sorry. I just can't. I couldn't bear it. As it is I can't even bear the thought of it."

"I know it's asking a lot, probably too much..."

"Stop," he tells her. "Please don't apologize to me. I feel low enough as it is. Knowing that I'm putting you in the position of having to explain yourself makes me feel...I don't know, sadistic."

"You're not."

"If you say so."

"I do. But I still need you to hear me out on this."

He sits up. "I did, remember? We went over this whole thing weeks ago when you first learned about having to go for tests."

"And back then you said yes, you'd do it."

His hands lift to hide his face, which now glows with shame. "I know. I know I did. But you have to understand that this...none of this seemed real then. I'd have said anything to keep your spirits up because I honestly thought that everything would turn out alright. Now I'm lying here and wondering how I could have been so naïve, so fucking stupid."

"You're not stupid," she says firmly. "Don't even think that. You were keeping things positive, like you've always done, and that helped me to feel more positive about everything. But that was then and here we are and everything is different now."

He looks at her. "I'll just come out and say it: you're going to go for treatments."

"No, I'm not. You know my thoughts on this. I told you that even a positive diagnosis wasn't going to change my mind. I'm not going to let modern medicine kill me. I'm going out my way. You've never witnessed this process before. I have. Twice."

"Your mom and then your sister, I know."

"Right. And after seeing my sister basically Xerox the process that our mom went through I became more determined than ever to shun that poison if my fate turned out to be the same as theirs.

And it has."

"But there's a chance!"

She shakes her head. "I don't buy it, I'm sorry. It's a factory mentality in those places. They'll just pump me full of toxic chemicals and irradiate me and leave me feeble and vomiting and unable to even lift my head off the pillow. And if they stall the growths a bit, they consider themselves heroes. If I die in the meantime, well, then it was bound to happen either way is probably what they'd tell you. Forget it. I'm going out as I will."

He rubs his face. "This is just *crazy*. Nobody does this!"

"So what?"

He feels evil for saying so, but: "Have you given any thought as to what this is going to do to me?"

"Yes," she calmly returns, "I have."

"Don't get me wrong, I know how all this sounds and I know how what you're going through is far, far worse than anything I'm feeling, but I can't help but wonder what it's going to be like for me once...after it's all over. You'll be gone and I'm going to have to live with what I've done."

"What you will have done is grant me my final wish, the thing I've wanted more than anything else in my entire life."

He sits up. "All this because of a dream? Scratch that. All this because of a *nightmare*?"

"Yes." Her tone is so certain that he knows any further discussion would be redundant; merely the two of them spiralling around the same issues again and again.

3.

That the task would require supplies is a given, but the fact that the character and quantity of these supplies required great sacrifice elevated them to a more meaningful level; perhaps not quite sacraments but certainly a fledgling gestalt, the seeds for an object that would be greater than the sum of its parts. Of course his skill and their mutual resolve would have to be stretched to new and terrible lengths, but it could be accomplished. Her wish could be made flesh.

The first needed criterion is scale. She spends the better part of an afternoon standing naked within his workshop while he presses a tailor's measuring tape against or around every part of her.

When she stands on the bathroom scale to be weighed he gives her gentle jibes about too much mocha ice cream. She laughs and swats his shoulder.

The details recorded, they begin researching which substance would be the optimal choice. He suggests onyx for its lustrous beauty, its durability, and for the fact that it is her favourite. But she argues him down, making solid points about the value of black gemstone and how using it could make the final product alluring to thieves. This is a fact he has not considered and it shoots a chill through him.

Ultimately they decide on black granite. It will still be costly given the quantity needed, but it is still far cheaper than any precious stone of the same midnight shade.

His initial sketches are rudimentary, a means of engineering the basic structure of the piece. Boring will be required in order to hollow out the main segments. Strategic holes would have to be drilled and fit with iron rods that would support the various segments in their place. Load bearing would be crucial, particularly for the more ornamental bits. The careful use of mortar and black lacquer would likely camouflage the seams.

As to the actual design, he requests as much instruction as she could provide.

4.

Like celestial guests, the leaden clouds squeeze into the sky above their meagre home the morning of his first sketching session. He has stationed himself at the kitchen table. The kitchen lights glow against a gloom as though still fending off the night. He optimistically, foolishly, scrambles her two eggs in addition to her customary mug of boiled rose tea. He places the meal on the little teak tray which has lately doubled as both her eating table and her writing desk. He watches the tea wobble in the cup as he carts the tray down the hall.

The tea she accepts, but her aversion to the food is visible. He feels low for even placing it before her.

She expresses a sense of guilt for "all the trouble" to which he'd gone through in order to prepare her food. This makes him feel lower still.

He watches her sip at her tea. He takes the tray back to the kitchen.

Even before he is able to set the untouched plate on the counter, he can feel it; the spate of emotion rising from the lowest chamber of his heart. He had fashioned this chamber into a dungeon, one that he hoped might keep his sorrows imprisoned. But the feeling has grown darker and wiser and more powerful. It breaks free.

He fumbles to turn on the kitchen faucet in order to drown out the sound of his weeping. The sobs are so deep they cause his entire frame to jut. He cries until his throat feels shredded and his sides throb. He then fills the chrome basin with cold water and presses his face into the pool. The liquid cools his burning flesh, and for a moment the man allows himself to be carted off by the fantasy of the water rushing through his pores and gushing through him, cleansing him of all his unnumbered ugly sorrows. The reverie is a balm, but like all balms, its relief is fleeting.

He rights himself, pops the plug from bottom of the sink, pats his dripping face with a dish towel. Shuffling once more to her room, he checks on her and finds her adrift in a shallow slumber. He kisses her brow before collecting his jacket. He is hoping for a more lasting balm.

5.

The garage had been converted into a workspace back when money was less rare than it has been in recent years. He is now inexpressibly grateful for his tool-littered sanctuary.

He shuffles to the centre of the room, tugs the power chain for the hanging fluorescent work light. Its clinical glare falls upon the workbench that squats beneath it, and upon the metal shelves that line the walls. Some of these shelves are burdened with the raw materials he employs in his art: large blocks of granite, smaller chunks of volcanic glass, veined marble, jet stone. Other shelves display the finished products of his labours; statuary in forms hideous and pacific, fantastic and banal.

Bags of unmixed plaster are piled in one corner like the beginnings of a floodwall. Saws, sanders, chisels, and files hang from racks according to size. The centre of the room is a cluster of electrical tools.

His soles make raspy scuffling sounds with each step he takes, for the un-swept floor is carpeted in granite dust and the shards of material that have been chiselled from their source. Often throughout the years he would hearken back to the legend of Michelangelo studying a block of marble for weeks on end, claiming that he was "working," scouting for the figure that was occulted inside the stone, awaiting the liberation of his creator's hand. He'd always regarded such apocryphal tales as dubious at best, but perhaps this was because he himself could not relate to a flow of creative genius. He regards himself as a craftsman, plain and simple. A journeyman of sculpting for whom creation is driven only by the tranquil sense of satisfaction it affords him on weekend afternoons.

He moves to the workbench and fingers one of the chisels. Its wooden handle was once painted orange but is now pale and worn from so many hours in his fist. Today the tool feels foreign against his fingers, a curious relic, crude and remote. He cannot recall the last time he sculpted in this room.

He goes to the storage rack and tugs the sketchpad free from a pile of yellowing papers. Its cover is gritty with the same fine granite dust that enshrouds everything in here. He finds the box of pastels in the red plastic milk crate at the foot of his workbench. He takes the pastels and the pad under one arm and uses his free hand to switch off the overhead lamp. He crosses the driveway, pausing momentarily to watch an eel of fallen leaves lunge and rise in a wind-wrought vertigo. The pinwheel pattern is like some ruddy effigy of a spiral galaxy, with dead and curling foliage in place of blazing stars. He inhales and his breath lines his nostrils with wood-smoke. The wind is cold, not wintry, but it carries the fat dampness of autumn proper.

Entering the kitchen he finds her at the stove. She is heating milk in a saucepan whose bottom has been scorched cauldron-black. A shapeless brown sweater hangs from her torso. Threadbare black leggings run down and are tucked into heavy wool socks. She smiles. Her eyes are red, as though infected. But he knows it is her sadness, her terror, her rage that has been passing through her in the form of tears. He does not question her. He goes to her and kisses her brow before stationing himself at the kitchen table.

"I'm glad to see you drawing," she tells him.

"I'm glad to see you resting."

"I think I'm going to take this back to bed with me."

"That sounds like a good plan. Sleep some more."

She nods faintly. "I think I will."

He spends a few moments in thoughtless silence then he flicks the black pastel across the page, forging nothing in particular. This meandering continues to the point of irritation

Frustrated, he turns the sheet aggressively, refusing to stain the fresh leaf with any strokes born of listlessness. He inhales until his lungs reach capacity. He exhales slowly, centering his psyche to his own inmost night, wreathed as it is in a fiery ring of secrecy from the outer world. This darksome stratum has always been his true north.

Suddenly, as though spat out from this inner night itself, a series of black crosshatches and strokes begin to darken the milk-bright parchment. The patterns seem to deepen the page into a great white chasm. What is forming there is still vague but nevertheless seems to be drawing itself into a discernable form. Like a distant figure approaching through a frantic blizzard, the shape comes, comes...

What he first assumes to be two tunnels transmute into great nostrils that flare above a snout containing misshapen teeth. The head is elongated and the mane that lines the neck in profile is haggard, tangled. As the torso is sketched the figure loses its equestrian form in favour of an emaciated human one. The breasts are large and rest upon a belly that is distended, from illness? Gestation?

A sludgy milk drips blackly from the Mare's nipples. The muscular ropes of her arms taper down into appendages that are neither hooves nor hands, but instead what look to be splayed fans of malnourished root matter.

The hind legs are folded, which lends the Mare a sagacious air.

He takes up a stub of charcoal and smudges the Mare black.

"Hi," she says. Her voice is creaky from her nap and it startles him. He eyes the clock and is startled by the amount of time he has unconsciously poured into his task.

"Hey, sleeping beauty. Feel better?"

She shrugs then raises her eyebrows; a means to express her interest in the pad that he holds out of her sight.

He turns the drawing toward her and for a moment there is no response whatsoever. His heart sinks.

But the sight of her clasping her hand across her mouth then lifts his heart.

"It's perfect," she manages to utter.

"Really?"

"It's just as I dreamt it."

"Well it's only a sketch."

"I know. But do you think you can build that?"

He sets the pad down, examines the drawing further. "Yes, I think so. But before I do I want to build a working model, just something out of balsa wood or wire. And then there's another obstacle."

"Which is?"

"The location."

6.

She enters his workshop and her entire presence echoes the numberless depictions of The Needy, The Afflicted. Wrapped in a periwinkle blanket, her face is slack and drawn; crescents of deep grey darken the bottoms of her eyes. She offers him a fleeting feeble smile as she shuffles toward an upturned milk crate. Getting off her feet brings a wave of relief to her aching joints. She stares at him as he manipulates a large roll of chicken-wire, snapping patches of its mesh in two with a pair of cutters.

"What are you doing?" she rasps.

He points to a wall with his wire-cutters and immediately resumes his work. She looks to the indicated space and sees the sketch of the Mare hanging there by bits of masking tape.

"This is going to be a working model," he explains. "Once I get the skeletal shape right I'm going to cover this with papier-mâché, then paint it black. It shouldn't take me long. I want..."

"You want what?"

It is a sentence he regrets having started. He stalls by pretending that he didn't hear her.

"You want what?" she repeats.

He wipes his sticky brow with the back of his gloved hand. "I want you to see what you'll look like."

The words are so final. They make the end feel that much more imminent, that much more inexorable. Death is charging toward her like a manic, fuming train. She is lashed to the tracks like a silent movie damsel.

And he stands helpless on the platform, unable to do anything but watch and wait for the inevitable horror.

Her reply catches him off-guard: "Thank you," she says. He goes cold and loses his ability to even hold a thought in his head, let alone focus on the task at hand. A few inept cuts frustrate him enough to pick up the bale of chicken-wire and hurl it across the garage.

She does not even flinch. He removes his work gloves and apologies to her.

"I really do want to see it," she tells him.

He nods once. "Then I better get back to it."

She watches as he labours, heartened at the fact that, once his wave of frustration ebbs, he is lost in the process. It is the kind of focus she has seen many times before, though with increasing rarity in recent years. It makes watching him a pleasure.

When the skeleton is complete she is able to spot certain features, most notably the elongated head and the swollen globes that will serve as the breasts. The hind legs are hunched, suggesting that the subject had been captured immediately before a leap. The forelegs are strategically raised menacingly, threatening an impending trample or perhaps showing a state of terror. The ears jut up sharply. He explains that the tail will be fashioned from actual horsehair.

He moves to the workbench, retrieves a white plastic pail and a large bag of flour.

Seeing him mixing the paste rejuvenates her enough to take one of the bundles of newspaper from the lopsided stack and begin to reduce them to long strips.

"You don't have to do that," he tells her.

"I want to."

"Okay."

7.

It is the mummification of a beast that never was, the enfleshing of a dream. The man and woman pace the fledgling idol, wrapping it in lengths of dripping paper. An unspoken sensuality charges both the couple and the grotesque they are fashioning. Each layer of papier-mâché reifies the nightmare that much more, draws her outré aspiration that much nearer to material existence, to reality undeniable.

They sit and wait for it to dry. They share a can of soda and reminisce about old television shows.

He pries off the lid from the can of black lacquer and offers her a brush. They stain the effigy lampblack.

On the final pass of the brush her hand slips across his. Their fingers are slathered in the paste that is the life's blood of their effigy. He hooks his forefinger around her pinky and tugs her nearer. The look in his eyes is well known to her. Today it is especially welcome, for she feels so vulnerable, so diseased.

Reflexively she lifts her other hand to fix her unkempt hair, realizing too late that her palm is smeared with glue. He aids her in the untangling, in the plucking free of the few stray hairs that come off with her hand.

Wordlessly, her face emanating no readable emotion, she takes his hand and guides it to her right breast. He cups it, noting how it has reduced in size as she herself has grown thinner, more wane. He begins to massage it, then the left with his other hand. She stops him just long enough to disrobe.

Their coupling is frantic, bordering on aggressive. Manipulat-

ing her the way she demands in guttural mutterings makes him feel
uneasy. Her body has grown delicate, or at least that is how he per-
ceives her. Though it shames him to acknowledge it, even in this,
a rare throe of passion, he regards her as merely a vessel for the
illness. She is a fleeting thing, a flesh-ghost fading like an antique
photo in a neglected album.

8.

He awakens to the sound of her hacking. The workshop is cold and
it is late and he feels a certain shame over having allowed his lust to
overpower him and leave his wife here in such dingy quarters when
a warm bed is waiting for her inside.

Sitting up he feels the ache in his reasonably healthy limbs and
he wonders how poorly she must be feeling.

He enters the house through the side door that connects the garage to the cluttered mudroom. His new proximity to her makes the
coughing sound chillingly severe. He draws in a bolstering breath
and follows the hacking sound to the bathroom.

She is hunched over the open toilet. A russet-tinted strand
stretches from her petite lower lip to the bowl. He tugs a tissue free
from the box on the basin and wipes her mouth. Tears dampen her
face. She tries to smile but succeeds only in conveying her exhaustion. He helps her to their bed.

She curls up beneath the duvet like a contented kitten. He runs
the back of his hand down her cheek, which while drawn, has lost
none of its architectural beauty.

"I was thinking," he begins, "that I'd take the day off tomorrow."
She nods. "...nice..."

"I thought, if you're feeling up to it of course, that we could go
for a drive."

"...where to..."

"Up past the city limits," he says. "We can go scouting."

She smiles as if this news is soothing her, nourishing her. "Good
idea."

He believes she has dozed off and is exiting the room when he
hears her add softly "We don't have much time."

9.

They drive until buildings, including farmhouses, are scarce. Every turn is instinctually guided. They are as creatures of the sea en-

tranced by the fisherman's lure. This journey is a pulling, a luring by something meek but nonetheless irresistible.

When the collapsed barn comes into view they slow and veer onto the lane's stony shoulder. She rolls down the window with the old creaking hand lever. The dampness and the cold waste no time taking advantage of the breach she provides. The clouded plastic of the speedometer and broken AM/FM radio are soon coated in a pattern of minute water beads. He wipes the moisture away with his hand and suggests that they walk over for a closer look.

The field has been neglected long enough to grow knee-high. The blades poke and press stiffly against the couple as they make their way toward the ruin. Mud clings to their hiking boots, weighing them down like cement.

They reach the clearing. He immediately makes his way to a large rock and begins scraping the clay from his footwear. She advances slowly, studying the caved-in barn as though it was an equation to be solved. He smiles when he sees her nodding absently; her wont when lost in thought.

He goes the opposite way toward what had once been the rear of the barn. Looking over the ruin, he wonders how it is that this sizeable structure could succumb in such a way. The barn looks less to have collapsed and more to have been crushed from above. The centre of its roof is bowed and broken. Beams jut up through the cracked thatch like the fractured bones.

Perhaps the barn has been bearing some invisible weight, its pitch burdened with it as Atlas was with the globe itself. It must have buckled under the sadistic strain and collapsed into splintery shards.

Adjacent to these leavings sits something sizeable enough to catch his eye. It is a stout configuration of thick wood, sturdy and cube-shaped. It has been built at the edge of the clearing, just where the mud yard touch the unkempt field.

The man moves to it, runs his hand across the object's surface. The rain-soaked wood feels deceptively soft, as though this mere graze of his hand could topple the edifice like the greater barn behind him.

She appears in his periphery. He calls out "Come see this!"

She heeds and asks him what it is.

"Could have been a butcher's block," he suggests. "Or an altar."

"Or both," she returns.

He raps on the top. "It feels solid enough. It could work for us. What do you think?"

"Is it large enough?"

Moving back three paces, he assesses it and then nods. "I think so, yes."

She looks over the surrounding area and she winces faintly. "It's not quite right. It's too near the road for one thing."

"Well," he offers, "we could always transplant this block. Move it to wherever we finally decide upon."

"Yes I suppose we could."

They begin the dirty trudge back to their car, which the man secretly worries may not start again, when she suddenly points to something across the field. The man doesn't see it at first and so she leads him to it. They have to wade deep into the grasses to reach it.

The object that had caught her eye turns out to be a balloon, as she had guessed; pale and half-deflated, like a white pear left to wither on a bough of pink silk ribbon. This ribbon has been tied to something that she believes to be a crooked stick until she notes that it has teeth.

"Sheep's jaw, it looks like," the man says, kneeling to better scrutinize the bone. The pink ribbon is knotted around the groove of the chin. The balloon lolls weakly, for it no longer hosts enough helium to properly fight its losing war against gravity.

A gift; an artefact that weds joy with morbidity. Any other couple would likely have been more stunned by this discovery, would have wracked their minds over the why and wherefore of its creation, but the man and woman are as two seeds sown in the acre of the unworldly, thus to them this was but another signpost.

They return to their car and after a few attempts to make the aged engine turn over, they drive on.

10.

The journey becomes, seemingly of its own accord, circuitous. Like ploughs sliding into existing ruts in a field, the couple take familiar turns and find themselves faced with familiar sights. Nearly two hours are spent on this shallow exploration, at which point she tells the man to stop it.

"Stop what?" he asks, opening his hands to demonstrate his ignorance, his innocence.

"Stop keeping us on these dull side roads. If you don't want to help me find a place, please just say so. But deliberately keeping me on these safe roads isn't going to deter me. I'll just find some way to explore on my own if I have to."

For the first time in ages the man experiences a flare of anger toward his partner. He grips the wheel and holds back the tide of righteous indignation. If he was keeping them on the more occupied 'safe places,' he certainly wasn't doing so consciously.

"All right then," he begins, easing the car to a creaky halt, "tell me which way feels right to you?"

She points to a narrow lane that feeds off the side road and says "There."

He heeds. Thus begins the weaving of the raw, odd pattern. They go wending past abandoned cottages and patches of tightly huddled old growths. They risk lanes that are perilously narrow. Here the sycamores stand like skeletal mammoths in a museum; remnants of some impossibly remote species. Their limbs fan toward the car like the skinless wings of a vast bat. They scrape the paint and tap the windows as though beseeching entry.

"Park here," she instructs, "we'll have to walk the rest of the way."

He is about to ask her how she knows this, but realizes on his inmost level that she has dreamt of this place, or an approximation of this place. She knows its character and trusts the version from her slumber enough to use it as a guide.

They hike deep into the woods, weaving through trees. He winces as the black mud sucks on his boots with each step. The scent of clay and fallen leaves is redolent. As the sky's light passes through the filter of the trees it assumes an almost ultraviolet hue, prismatic and vivid. It washes over all things spectrally.

She is marching ahead of him, purposefully, excitedly. He can see the plumes of her anxious breathing and can hear her panting in a way that he had only ever heard when the two of them were entangled and enflamed.

"Slow down," he urges. He is gripping various trunks and branches like towlines in order to stay aright. The damp air feels as though it is raking the insides of his lungs.

Abruptly she stops. She is standing between two crooked trees of a species the man cannot identify. When he staggers up to stand next to her she tells him "This is it. This is where it's to be."

The land beyond the forest dips into a valley. This earthen bowl is lined with long grasses that seem unseasonably verdant. A few bulrushes sprout up here and there in bunches. The woods stand dense around the entire parameter as if protecting the valley, keeping it secret and secure, just for them.

On the far rim there stands an oblong box, the half-rotted remnants of a standing shed. She points toward it and says, "I can hide in there."

The location is so apt that it causes the man to doubt for the first time the notion that this entire endeavour was simply a figment of his lover's dream-life.

Departing, they fashion a makeshift map like children playing treasure hunt. They return to the car and drive back, stopping once at the barn where they struggle to load the butcher block/altar into the trunk. It weighs the car down as surely as a millstone.

II.

It isn't until they are home and he places the wire-mesh model upon the absconded wood block that the imminence of the deed hits him. She is in the kitchen boiling pasta after insisting that she is well enough to cook.

He approaches the kitchen with a forced smile upon his face.

She doles out the pasta and the cream sauce and they settle into the tiny nook that still bears the teacups and cereal bowls from breakfast. The man pushes these remnants aside and marvels at how long ago this morning seems. Their discovery of the sacred site seems as though it happened years ago.

"So I've crunched the final numbers," she says, sliding a sheet of foolscap across the table. "This is how much we'll need to pay for the granite and other supplies."

He eyes it and cannot mask his shock. "Wow. But there's something else to be added to it as well."

"Oh?"

"I'll need a handheld jackhammer."

"That sounds expensive."

"They are. But unfortunately there's no other way I can see being able to make some of the cuts I need to make in the granite without one."

"All right, no problem, we can just add that to the total cost."

He shovels in a forkful of pasta. It seems flavourless to him. "I did some checking online to find out about the car's value. It's not good."

"Well we both figured as much."

"I know. Still, it means we're going to have to pawn a lot more of our furniture and books than we'd planned."

She looks at him very directly, unblinkingly. "Are you going to be okay with that?"

"Sure," he says with a shrug. "Are you?"

"It's not going to affect me, remember?"

He lowers his head and pushes the noodles around his dish. He has to choke down the food in order to bypass the growing lump in his throat.

12.

She is demonstratively amorous. The uncovered skin of his body is made livid by the slab of moonlight that illumines it. She is doing her utmost to awaken his muscle. He is doing his utmost to wilfully control his response. He does this not to inflict hurt or humiliation, but rather because he feels himself shrinking, coiling up like a spring, turning cold and barren and untouchable. Is it an impulse to prepare himself for his solitude, which is now so imminent, so inexorable?

Jilted, she eventually halts and slithers back to her side of the bed, rolls on her side, lies silently.

When the thin rasp of her breathing suggests slumber, he slips out from beneath the covers and shuffles toward his workshop.

The night air chills his naked flesh. Stationed in the doorway, he leaves the workshop unlit and unvisited. Spillage from the hall light lends just enough illumination to contrast the Grotesque from the clutter that surrounds it.

Unsure just how long or how briefly he spends meditating upon the figure, he closes the door and returns to bed. His initial aim of studying the Mare in order to fully envision his beloved in the Grotesque, as the Grotesque, is unsuccessful...at least until sleep lays a track upon which the black Mare thunders from Her outer pasture and into his dream.

It begins wildly, with a sensation of thrashing. His dream-self is flung to and fro. All is perceived as whorls, as smears of dull light and thick bands of blackness. The motions are so violent they snatch the air from his lungs. He attempts to cry out but something cold and unyielding is wedged between his jaws. A reflexive graze of the tongue reveals something smooth, something that tastes putridly metallic.

He juts his head upward and winces as the gag of steel pulls hard against the corners of his mouth. He emits a noise that is akin to whinnying. He falls onto all fours.

Pain ceases, tension eases, and vision is restored all in one swift instant of relief. He stares down to see his arms elbow-deep in brackish water. Squinting, he hopes to discern his own reflection but the sludge is nearer to a cluster of thunderheads than to a mirror.

Bringing up his hand, he wriggles the cumbersome object from his mouth. Clinking as it falls away, the gag is revealed to be a heavy-gauge chain of steel. It had been strung between his jaws like a bit, but now it sinks beneath the surface.

By blind feel he grips both hands around the chunky links and drags the chain above the surface.

The chain seems to distinguish the ambit of a great marsh; a magic circle of corroding iron. Dangling from the links are objects startling and dreadful. They hang like charms on this vast bracelet.

When he spots the first object the start it gives him causes him to drop the chain in order to confirm that his dreaming self is indeed still in possession of both hands. Relieved to see himself intact, he finds and hoists the chain once again, this time studying the severed hand that dangles from the dripping steel. The snapped wrist bone is wedged firm into the loop of one of the links and the fingers are flexed in the fashion of a Hand of Glory. Skin the colour of curdled milk clings to the bone for as long as its waterlogged sinews can mange. Finally the loose flesh slips free. Chunks plop down into the dark water and squiggle away like logy oysters shucked from their shells. He watches them sink until they disappear. He imagines them settling into the sediment, wonders about what strange flora might bloom from the swamp bed thanks to this morbid fertilizer.

Further down the chain, a gunmetal canister, the design of which is not unlike a cocktail shaker, or an urn of unsentimental design. He wrestles off the lid and peers into the open vessel. Within, the effigy of an ongon reposes. The shape of its body is dizzyingly complex.

Working his way along the steel garland, he trawls up further canisters and struggles to correlate their contents, which consist of desiccated willow leaves, feathers of birds which he finds impossible to identify, and a stew of half-clotted blood.

His investigation is obscured by a swiftly-moving shadow that stretches across the marsh, dimming the reeds.

A great vine rises from somewhere deep in the swamp's heart. It ascends and grows instantly firm, aroused like a phallus poised to seed. Its summit is crooked. It gradually morphs to form an equestrian skull.

This skinless head bends nearer and nearer to him. The man begins to scream.

The agrarian Mare parts its jaws and unleashes a thunder that shocks the man into wakefulness.

Oxygen feels almost intoxicating as he gasps and gulps. He rouses her.

"Oh my god," she murmurs, "breathe, babe, breathe."

He laces his fingers between hers and says, "Don't do this. Please, I'm begging you. I can't go through with it. I can't be without you."

She embraced him. "But you will be without me. At least with my way, there's a chance we'll be together again."

13.

The ensuing days are laden with activity but bereft of conversation. They give their notice to their landlord and pawn those possessions that are saleable. He finds an apartment in his price range and submits his application. It is in a low-rise building with a lobby that stinks of laundry exhaust and cat urine.

He calculates the final measurements and maxes out their only credit card purchasing the required black granite and necessary tools, which are delivered to the garage-cum-workshop; the last room in the house to still be filled with furniture, debris.

Re-entering the house he finds her crumpled on the kitchen floor. A faint stream of blood runs from her nostrils to the floor tiles. A shattered milk glass glints by her limp hand.

"No," he whimpers, "no..."

He has to consciously muster the courage required to place his ear against her chest. He finds a heartbeat, strong and regular.

With a cloth soaked in cold water he rouses her. All told, her blackout lasts less than five minutes. But it is time enough for her to tell him, "Tomorrow night. I want it to happen tomorrow night."

14.

He manages to postpone the process, but only by a day. He busies himself beginning the rudimentary cuts. The slabs are hollowed, are hewn into haunches and a torso. It is a monstrous shell that awaits its soul; a golem of shining black rock.

Taxed to where he is practically sleepwalking, he enters the house.

Excitedly, she sits him down at the breakfast nook and presents notes that detail how her vanishing can be explained. The pair has no friends to speak of and their relations consist only of his sister, from whom he is all but estranged.

Her cover story consists of their moving away to a distant province, and something about her landing a new job. He pays no attention to the details, despite her urgings, her persistent reminders of how crucial a consistent story would be. He merely humours her, for he knows that not long after her assumption into the black graven vessel he will take his own life. Whether this self-annihilation will be born of unsupportable guilt or inconsolable grief he cannot say at this point, but he understands himself well enough to accept that the end result will be the same.

15.

Illumined by a quartet of white tapers, the workshop thrums with the unsullied solemnity of a temple. She is stationed between the Stonehenge of granite slabs. Her body is unclothed. Her face is free of makeup. Never has he seen her look more radiant; a fact that sticks uncomfortably in his psyche.

He opens his mouth to speak despite having nothing to say. What emerges is a squeal, a blubbering wordless expression of his horror and his pain.

She moves to him and embraces him. Her flesh is surprisingly warm, supple. "You're doing this for me," she reminds him. "Never forget that. Never forget that I'm telling you this right here and now, telling you how grateful I am. You're doing this for me."

They part.

He reaches for his chisel.

He labours through the night. The project remains an abstraction, one that consumes him with its scope, its precise aesthetics, its sheer labour-intensiveness. When it comes time for her to enter the Mare, the endeavour instantly blazes with finality.

With great care she enters the cold unyielding shell.

The equestrian legs are ropy, muscular, and thus accommodate her spindly ones with room to spare. She is unsure if the design is deliberate, but the interior of the grotesque is akin to a chair. She is able to sit, to watch as he slathers the frontal plate with creamy white mortar. The trowel wobbles in his unsteady hand. His back is to her but she can clearly hear his whimpers.

"Look at me," she urges.

He turns and locks his red-rimmed eyes with hers.

"Kiss me," she whispers.

He presses his face to hers. Their flowing tears merge. His fear and grief and declarations of love undying gush out in one breathless spiel. She mutters confirmations, consolatory phrases.

She touches his face and, after an extended exchange of love that runs deeper and broader than any language can reach, she withdraws her hand and says, "I'm ready."

He shuts his eyes. His breath degenerates into a panicked huffing. Finally he clutches the torso shell and presses it against the base, shrieking as the mortar oozes out from the seam. It hardens at a pace that feels both excruciating and far too fast.

He scrapes off the excess cement and then backs away.

In its completed phase her tomb is of black granite, contoured by his masterful hands. From the looming blocks of midnight marble he has hewn an isolated figure. The statue's legs, hooved and thick, are arched in a kneeling position. Balanced upon this was a vaguely human torso with swollen breasts from which droplets of black milk poured. The head was a leering Mare, its eyes without pupils.

Utterly unsure what he is to do with himself now that the deed is done, he makes his way inside the house and stands before the kitchen window.

The sun is beginning its ascent.

16.

It is her crossing of the abyss, the sojourn that leads one from the mother's milk of the known to the electric uncertainty of the Other, the Beyond.

A vision quest to be certain, for no studying eye can perceive the journey, which occurs beyond the plateau of flesh and stone. Her shell of sculpted black rock is static only to those without it. Within? Within, the grotesque is as a chariot, a forward-going force of boggling velocity and astonishing grace.

A Mare. It is a Mare. It is The Mare. Black as the hours over which She presides, vivid and vast as the dreams that bear Her name.

The woman is riding the Night-Mare. The woman is the Night-Mare's living host. She is a ligature, a tenuous bridge of flesh-rope, a suspension track of latticed bones riding the black that goes on forever.

Rushing wakeful through a realm she had only ever glimpsed in slumber is intoxicating, ecstatic. Hunched within the unyielding shell, she finds limitlessness. She hopes that he can hear her noises of delight on the opposite side of the stone.

She is crossing the Abyss.

She reaches the hideous midpoint.

The exciting vista is now half behind her, and what lies ahead is a journey equal in size but one that must be made using her rapidly depleting life.

It strikes at her lungs first. She attempts to draw in a patient breath in order to re-align herself with the quest. Instead she begins to cough. The deflating air sacs are awakening to their crisis. They are resisting. They are sending out wordless alarms to the rest of her body.

Each gasp serves only to spend what little oxygen there is left between her body and her tomb. The rough granite interior of the Mare's snout is soaked with the condensation of her exhausted breaths. It is an unpleasant feeling, one that reminds her of trick-or-treating too long in her Halloween mask; the cold foul moisture against her lips.

Her arm flinches but finds it has no leverage. Her bent legs have grown useless from poor circulation.

Somewhere in the most deeply humanistic nook of her heart she sees the path not taken; spies herself in a bed with crisp white linens and an intravenous tube that whisks her into painless death with its drip of sparkling poison.

The path not taken first saddens, but quickly infuriates, her. She begins to scream. She hates the way the granite stifles her cries, as though she is under leagues of black water.

The Mare, she notices, seems to have halted.

17.

He stands in a house now wholly depleted of its soul. The loss runs beyond the furnishings which have been carted off or sold, stretches past the silence and unsentimental barrenness of plain white walls that echo every noise. The house is manifest loneliness. He is the last man on Earth.

Within he feels the push-pull of his desire to be near the Mare and an overwhelming repulsion. Part of him wishes he could tear himself to pieces, to rend flesh from bone. Part of him yearns to coil up right here on the tile floor and mewl like an infant. Whatever fears he harboured over not being able to live with himself, the reality is exponentially worse. That he will end his own life is now a certainty, one that he looks forward to eagerly.

But before he can think about ending his pain he knows he must complete the process, since it cannot be undone. He must fulfill her wish.

A reservation slip hangs from the refrigerator door by a magnet. He is to pick up the moving van at eight o'clock tomorrow morning. There is but one item to be transported.

He steals a mouthful of water from the faucet then shuffles into the living room where he lies on the carpeted floor. His muscles are screaming from strain and his head it throbbing. He shuts his eyes under the foolish notion that he may sleep.

Though he cannot recall drifting off, something hurls him into panicked alertness. Moving faster than thought, he races through the cavernous house and tears into the workshop. Grabbing the first blunt object he can find, in this case a length of pipe left over from a failed sculpture, he steps toward the black granite Mare and swings, hacks, jabs.

He is crying out her name. He is trying to turn back the clock's hands. He is striving for life.

What slumps forward from the splintered shell is almost unrecognizable to him. It is a limp, cold, bloodless thing; the husk of someone he loves...or rather loved. Her teeth are broken and ruined from the reflexive bites against her prison. Her flesh is very, very cold.

His attempts to reverse his blasphemy are too late, and this is a revelation that brings him to his knees.

The sole consolation left is to realize her wishes. Then and only then can he seek an escape route for himself.

He works. His belly is empty and his throat is parched. He has not known sleep for days. He works. Attempting to restore life to the dead may lie well beyond his ken, but repairing broken stone is a task for which he has a special gift.

He takes up each shard and chunk, working them together with mortar like a great jigsaw puzzle until at last the Mare is whole again. Once more he smoothes the caking mortar, once more he lacquers Her façade lampblack.

Finally he lays himself at her pedestal and he sleeps.

18.

The morning sun is punitively bright when he begins to back the moving van toward the garage door. The elderly woman from four houses down interrupts her morning constitutional in order to mull over the meaning of the van's presence. She smiles widely before walking on.

They never had any use for their neighbours and he does not expect either of them to be missed after today.

He waits until the street is vacated before retrieving the Mare.

It is mummified in dirty grey moving blankets that are held together by bungee cords. The weight of the structure overwhelms him. He is able to push it along on the flatbed cart that came with the van rental. The question of how he might get the Mare across the overgrown field to its shed distresses him. It is all he can think about as he drives out of the city.

19.

Her map is surprisingly effective. He finds the proper lane with the narrow inlet where he parked just days ago with her.

Absolute solitude is required for the task ahead. And while he is grateful for it, it nonetheless causes him anguish.

Pulling himself together, he exits the van. He is intensely alert as he creeps through the trees to confirm the presence of the oblong box. The breeze bullies the boughs and the nearby grasses, filling the area with a seashell susurrus.

The shed stands in perfect isolation. There isn't as much as a bird in sight. The man stretches his arms, puts a mental stopper against the terror that is climbing up from the base of his spine. He makes his way to the van in order to begin.

He sets the cart upon the lane, cautiously pulls the Mare near. He mistakenly bumps it more than once and each time he winces and curses his carelessness.

Laying the statue horizontally across the carpeted board, he resecures it with the bungee cords and begins to push.

The chore is arduous. Each painful shove serves to nudge the Mare only incrementally closer to Her destination. He is pleased when the forest envelops him because it fortifies him against any potential passers-by. He now acts in rustic secrecy.

Reaching the hem of the woods refreshes his anxiety. As he fumblingly pulls the wheeled cart into the clearing with its long tangles of standing grass he feels as scrutinized as a stage actor. The sun radiating from an unclouded sky only increases this sensation, acting as a vast limelight whose gaze upon him is unwavering.

At the journey's midpoint he collapses. Sweat streams down his flushed face. His palms are worn raw. Exhaustion peaks in the form of a nausea so potent he doubles over to vomit. Lack of sustenance means he can but heave and wretch. He wants nothing more than to rest but doesn't dare; not until his beloved is secure. Not until her last wish is fulfilled.

Like a tired pack-mule, he hitches the pull-rope over his shoulder and presses onward.

A faint, bone-low creak insinuates itself into the wind-wrought hush of the valley. He quickly detects it as the shed's ill-fitting door grinding against its jamb; a sound that is foreboding and beckoning at once. He reaches to pull the door open but finds it still out of reach.

Howling, grunting, he tugs the Mare nearer to its ultimate perch. Then nearer still.

His fingers worry in the crack that separates sagging door from crooked structure. He draws it back, leery about what he may expose.

Inside is nothing, not even a dappling of sunlight. It is as if the shelter's interior has been hermetically sealed. He looks over his shoulder and wonders if she, or She, is responsible for this quirk in nature.

He removes the cords from the butcher block-cum-altar and positions it on the shed's earthen floor. Then, with religious care and attention, he unfetters and rights the Mare. She fits with enough room to spare for him in his future observances.

Though he wants nothing more than to stay with her, he begrudgingly accepts that he has miles to go before he's through.

Her wishes contained a specificity that, now, too late, he understands, not only fulfill her dream but also keep him safe.

He must return the rental van. Tomorrow he can return, but on bicycle; the sole means of transportation he has left.

He mutters his goodbyes and secures the shed as best he can. Taking up the wheeled platform under one arm, he runs.

The lane is customarily vacant. He feels marooned out here.

Driving back he turns the radio volume up to where the music is compressed into a wall of noise. Periodically he screams along with it. These are measures to stave off the realization of what he has done and exactly how irreversible it all is.

20.

It is the first time he has entered the tiny apartment without her. Futon, bookcases, coffee table; all are as they'd placed them.

Late afternoon light filters through the window, struggling against its inevitable demise to the night. He lies down on the mattress. His body screams for sleep yet his conscience does what it can to punish him by resisting it.

Ultimately the flesh won out, as it inevitably must. He opens his eyes to a dark apartment. It takes him some time to recall where he is, who he is. There are vague memories of a dream in which she was sleeping beside him.

He turns the digital clock toward him. Dawn is not far off.

Rising, he dresses in fresh clothes and prepares for the long journey.

The day is uncharacteristically arid for late autumn. A few stubborn leaves of yellow and amber still cling to the trees that he pedals past on his way out of town. Though his periphery is studded with occasional movement, from joggers, from early-bird geriatrics, from a newsstand proprietor, his world feels colourless, lifeless. The buildings and their occupants go past like so much set dressing.

He eases onto the shoulder of the rural road to rest. The bottled water tastes metallic. It stirs memories of his nightmare involving the chain-bit in his mouth and the invisible rider mounting his back. He caps the bottle and chews the humble food he's brought.

A quick reference of her hand-drawn map restores the Mare in his mind and heart. He mounts the bicycle and pushes on.

He is relieved when his amateur sleuthing determines, such as it can, that the only tire tracks on the appropriate lane are those of his moving van. He pauses to listen and finds the area retains its ghostly stillness.

Inching down between two old growths, he secures his bicycle with a chain lock and takes the added precaution of obscuring its vibrant frame with some old brush.

Setting his foot onto the valley's base is unpleasant. His boots leech cold water from the grassy soil. His confusion halts him. He reaches down to graze the blades, which are dripping. His only explanation is dew, for there has been no rain for days and even the dirt lane beyond was parched.

He continues to the shed, breathing a sigh a relief when he sees its door is still secure. His plan to quickly release the door's makeshift latch and slip within the concealing shadows shrivels the instant he spots the change.

The sanctuary of the Mare has been breached.

Heaped around Her butcher's block perch is an array of what he can only call offerings; dolls of twigs, root vegetable heads festooned with numberless nails, a braid of hair (human or horse, he cannot tell).

The terror that bolts through him is unlike any he has ever known. The partitions of his mind are obliterated as a vortex of possibilities, theories, worst case scenarios swirl wildly inside his skull. Has someone been watching him? Who has fashioned these items? Why?

His paranoia peaks as panic. He slumps down beside the granite Mare, unable and unwilling to step outside. He will stay here, all day and night if need be.

21.

He is sitting with his back against the shed's splintery wall. His head is inclined in order to keep his red and weary eyes with Hers; uncanny, pupil-less, gleaming dark.

Fear of discovery prevents fatigue from truly taking hold, but he is drifting nevertheless. His eyelids flutter as though weighted. It is not sleep that both body and mind beg for, it is a lowering of the veil, some means of casting away all the clutter and din of the world that presses in from outside, some means of drawing him elsewhere.

The sound of his breathing fills the angled room; a sibilant rhythm that recalls the sound of the wind pressing through the long grasses outside. The noise calms him, dims his frantic imagination.

He is drifting.

She is drifting.

Somewhere in the unfathomable dark of their internal nights, these lovers reach a point of convergence.

He finds Her, but not as he had known her. She radiates with the essence that, while incarnate, had merely glowed like a red coil of want somewhere deep inside her. However, no matter how much his beloved had tried to express this fire, this force, in poetry or on a canvas smeared with oils ghoulish or incendiary, the result was inevitably lukewarm.

But now, here, in this new form, She is no longer separate from the heat source. She is no longer his beloved, but is Love entire. She no longer triangulates the poem's inspiration with words on paper, She is the living language of the Poem.

Images roil about him as an immaterial core of his being hovers near Her. She is the Mare; night-spirit that charges from Beyond, tramples through the endless acres of dreaming, leaving Her Mark that queers the sensitive away from the waking life and toward an unspeakable secondary realm.

He wonders if She is asking him to ride.

Without, in the nocturnal woods, he feels something stalking nearby, watching them.

He accepts the offer, and as his pulse quickens with terror, love, lust, and then ultimately seizes, he is no longer saddled.

They ride...

Ω

Like a black discordant key in the chorus of progress, the oblong box lingers in its sylvan sanctuary, protecting and obscuring its progeny inside its stilted womb. Winds press through matchstick-thin cracks. They blow temperate, cold, scorching, then temperate once more. This cycle repeats, and again.

Season by season, the water pools in the valley; melted snow, fresh summer rains, seepage from occulted springs well below the soil crust; all of them commingle and conspire to obscure these secret gift. They fill the grassy valley like libation in the beggar's bowl.

Grasses become firm reeds that gradually lilt and become weeds that sway lazily at the bottom of the stagnant marsh.

The butcher's block pedestal falls loose, lodges askew in the gorgeous black sludge. Persistent leakage causes the wooden walls to crumble, to float upon the pond's murky surface as though a shipwreck has occurred.

But this is of little consequence, for the secret these broken walls once held have long sunken. They sit at the base of the swamp like a pre-arranged shrine. The Mare reposes regally. And at Her feet are lodged the bones of the Artist. He has given himself, both flesh and soul, to his Muse. She has accepted his offering and, with a love so great it cuts the tongue to speak of it, maims the brain to ponder it, has pulled these skeletal leavings about Her. They form a Mare's nest; a homestead, a throne, a mute testimony to the great transcendence known only to those who make the ultimate sacrifice of self to Other.

ACKNOWLEDGEMENTS

"Primeval Wood" first published as a chapbook (Burning Effigy
Press, 2009) and first collected in *The Darkly Splendid Realm* (Dark
Regions Press, 2009).

"A Cavern of Redbrick" first published in *Shadows & Tall Trees* Issue
5 (2013).

"Fume" first published as a limited-edition chapbook. (Dunhams
Manor Press, 2016).

"Goatsbride" first published in *Fungi*, edited by Orrin Grey and
Silvia Moreno-Garcia (Innsmouth Free Press, 2012).

"Weaned on Blood" first published in *Monk Punk*, edited by Aaron
J. French (Hazardous Press, 2015).

"Tinder Row" first published in *Shadows Edge*, edited by Simon
Strantzas (Gray Friar Press, 2013).

"Wormwood Votaries" first published in *Penumbrae: An Occult Fiction
Anthology*, edited by Richard Gavin, Patricia Cram and Daniel A.
Schulke (Three Hands Press, 2015).

"The Old Pageant" first published in *Children of Old Leech*, edited by
Ross E. Lockhart & Justin Steele (Worde Horde, 2014).

"The Stiles of Palemarsh" also published in *Autumn Cthulhu*, edited
by Mike Davis, (Lovecraft eZine, 2016).

All other works in this collection are previously unpublished.

The author wishes to express his heartfelt gratitude to his wife
Lora for her undying love and support. Also, to Daniel A. Schulke
and James Dunk, for the vision and energy they both lent to this
project.

This first edition of Sylvan Dread was published Spring 2016 by
Three Hands Press in trade paper, limited hardcover, and special
full leather editions. The hardcover edition was limited to a total
of one thousand copies. The special edition was limited to 37
hand-numbered copies in full burnt umber deerskin with marbled
endpapers and slipcase, handbound by Pettingell Bookbindery,
Berkeley, California.

SCRIBÆ QUO MYSTERIUM FAMULATUR